DIRTY KINGDOM

COVINGTON HIGH BOOK 1

AMELIA WINTERS

Copyright © 2021 Dirty Kingdom Covington High Book 1, Amelia Winters

ISBN: 9798455763397

Imprint: Independently published

All rights reserved. No portion of this book may be reproduced in any form without permission from the publisher, except as permitted by U.S. copyright law. For permissions contact: Amelia Winters, author. amelia.winters@protonmail.com

AMELIA WINTERS

Sign up for my newsletter to keep in touch. Find out about beta or ARC opportunities, get sneak peeks at new books, and have access to giveaways!

http://eepurl.com/hBcvpr

Covington High Series

- Dirty Kingdom, book 1
- Dirty King, book 2
- Dirty Queen, book 3
- Dirty Court, book 4

The Family Series (Covington Continuation)

- Dirty Reign, book 1

The Savage Dark

- Lords of Darkness

CONTENTS

Chapter 1	1
Chapter 2	7
Chapter 3	13
Chapter 4	21
Chapter 5	27
Chapter 6	33
Chapter 7	39
Chapter 8	45
Chapter 9	51
Chapter 10	61
Chapter 11	73
Chapter 12	81
Chapter 13	91
Chapter 14	99
Chapter 15	107
Chapter 16	115
Chapter 17	127
Chapter 18	137
Chapter 19	147
Chapter 20	157
Chapter 21	169
Chapter 22	179
Chapter 23	187
Chapter 24	197
Chapter 25	207
Chapter 26	215
Chapter 27	225
Chapter 28	235
Chapter 29	245
Chapter 30	251
Chapter 31	259
Chapter 32	271

Also by Amelia Winters	285
About the Author	287

1

"P*issy pants, pissy pants! Ev-er-ly has pissy pants!*"

A group of kids gathered around me on the playground, laughing and pointing at the mud that had splattered on the brand new pair of tights Mom had picked out that morning.

It was the first day of second grade at a new school and things were going miserably for me.

"I do not!" I wailed and backed away from them. There were older kids. One boy who was probably in fifth grade was the leader of the group. Another girl with bright blonde curls and piercing blue eyes followed me, pointing and taunting menacingly.

"Do too!" she giggled. "Ain't that right, Jimmy?"

"Looks like it to me," the older boy snickered.

They were the source of the mud. I'd been playing with two girls from my class when the blonde had decided to toss a handful on me. I hadn't cried, though. Mom had told me no good could come from crying at school. I had to save my tears for home, where it was safe.

We had just moved to town to move in with her new husband, my new stepdad. He was a nice guy, and my grandparents even liked him, and he was the real dad to my little sister, who was just a baby.

I was sad to move away from my friends in the trailer park. We all went to the same little school across the dusty dirt road. But now we lived in a house that looked like a mansion. It had an upstairs and a basement and even had a special room just for eating fancy dinners. I couldn't remember what it was called, but the smooth wooden table and chairs in there were so beautiful. I loved running my hands over them when I walked past.

We had three bedrooms, too, and grandma and grandpa had promised they'd come visit soon.

But at school, things fell apart. Nobody liked me much. My clothes were different and my hair was short, while all the girls had let theirs grow. And I carried a SpongeBob backpack, but he wasn't popular anymore around here. Everybody liked a Japanese cartoon girl instead.

"Pissy pants!" the kids shrieked and laughed, and I felt the pinprick of tears on the backs of my eyes. But Mom said don't cry, don't let them see you cry. "You have pissy pants!"

"She does not!"

A loud voice broke through the group of kids, and a little boy from my class pushed his way to the front of the group. He was tall and skinny, like a bean pole, my Mom would say, but I didn't even know what that was. He had thick glasses that made his eyes bulge when he stared at you, and his hair was black like mine, a curly mop.

"What did you say to me, Kingston Taylor?" the older boy, Jimmy, said. He walked over to Kingston and shoved him in the chest.

To my surprised, Kingston didn't budge. He stayed put and looked up at Jimmy, set his jaw in this crazy stubborn way, and swung up with his fist.

He connected, and Jimmy cried out. Blood started pouring out of his mouth, and he tried to speak.

"I bit ma tung," he gibbered and started to cry. More blood poured forth, and he babbled some more. Blood dripped down the front of his cartoon tee shirt, and the blonde girl comforted him.

"You'd better go to the office," Kingston said, and turned to look at me. He pushed his glasses up his nose, squinted, and added, "I'm Kingston. Who are you, new girl?"

"Ev-Ev-Everly Hayes," I stammered and sucked in my breath to hold back my tears. He smiled at me, and everything bad ran away from inside my head, leaving it filled with bright colors and happy things.

And that's how I became best friends with the coolest kid in school, Kingston Taylor, who was also my next-door neighbor. He had those thick glasses to fix his lazy eye, was as skinny as a rail, and had a mop of black hair that was never brushed properly, but he was so much fun that everybody loved him.

And from that moment on, my elementary school years were filled with adventure and laughter. And I was ever present by Kingston's side.

We became inseparable from that day forward. We spent every lunch hour sitting on the swings at the edge of the playground, eating our sandwiches and getting braver with our jumps to the ground.

I somehow always managed to jump higher and farther than Kingston, yet he was never angry about it. My success seemed to excite him as much as his own.

The rest of elementary school was much the same. We would have sleepovers at each other's houses and camped out in our backyard. We did swim lessons together, learned to play the piano at old Mrs. Weston's across the street, and even wore the same costumes for Halloween all the way through our school years.

Our childhoods were mirrored perfectly, and each night after our parents had tucked us into bed, we would wait until they left so we could say goodnight. Our windows looked into each other's rooms, and we would sneak to open our curtains, wave at each other, go back to bed, and sleep like that for the entire night.

It always brought me comfort knowing that if I was scared in the dark, I could sit up and see his bedroom there, his Toy Story nightlight illuminating the inside just enough for me to see a rectangular glow coming from his window.

Sometimes he was even awake and we would just sit and look at each other in the night, not moving and not talking until it was time to go back to sleep.

I was sure Kingston was going to be my one and only true love, and so were our parents. They would talk about it openly, about how adorable we were together and how they'd all be related one day.

But ours wasn't meant to be a love story from point A to B with nothing in between. Just before we went into eight grade, he came to me to tell me something that would break my heart.

"My parents are splitting up," he said, his voice cracking. Normally I would laugh at it, but not today. Today, it hurt too much to mock him for his voice changes.

Kingston was hitting puberty, and puberty was hitting back twice as hard. He was normally a super skinny, really tall kid with that mop of hair and those piercing blue eyes—he'd outgrown his bubble glasses a couple of years before—but with puberty he'd gotten really awkward, his Adam's apple was starting to bulge in his throat, and acne peppered his cheeks.

I still loved him, though. He wasn't about looks for me; he was just Kingston, my spirit and soul mate.

"How can they do that?" I asked, and I'd been serious. It felt back then like they'd been married forever, and I didn't think people could just casually break up like that. Especially with kids around.

"My mom met some guy online," he said miserably. "We're moving to New York."

"What?!" I exclaimed, a sob choking my throat. I wasn't an attractive kid back then, either. I had a frizzy mess of thick black hair, braces, and was knock-kneed and scarred from being a tomboy. "You can't leave!"

"I know," he said and sighed. We were sitting under the big tree in my backyard and he put his arm around me for a little hug. Just to comfort me, I knew, but I wasn't going to let the moment slip away.

I turned my head, and I did the boldest thing I'd ever done. I kissed Kingston Taylor.

Our first awful kiss. Our teeth clacked together, and it felt weird to have my mouth touch his like that, but it lit something inside of me. Something in my preteen brain caught fire, and I knew I was in love. I would never love another like I loved him then.

After the shock was over, he lifted his hands to my shoulders and pulled me closer. He kissed me back that day, and it became magical. It was tender and exciting and filled with the future we could have together someday.

"I don't want to leave you, Evie," he moaned when we were finished. He still held my hand in his, and I thought I saw his breath hitch in his chest.

"I don't want you to go," I said, my voice quivering. I could feel tears prickling my eyelids, and my cheeks were flushed from the kiss and the stress of losing him.

"Promise you'll write to me every day," he said intently. "Promise you won't forget me."

"I promise," I whispered, and I meant it with every fiber of my being. I didn't want to live in a world where Kingston Taylor and I didn't talk to each other every night before bed.

When the day came for them to leave at last, I ran alongside their car until his mother turned left at the end of our street and I watched them disappear. The last thing I saw was the look of sorrow on his face as he looked at me through the back window, his hand held up against the glass.

I didn't think I'd ever get over losing him, and I didn't think I'd ever stop pining for him. I tried to keep in touch, but something happened, and I never heard from him again.

I wrote his mother's email daily for the first month and then every few days for at least a year after that until my emails started bouncing back. We even got his address from his dad next door, and I sent him cards for his birthday and holidays but never heard a single thing from him.

It hurt when he rejected me, and it left an aching need in my soul that I wasn't able to fill. I became even more of a hermit and hid away from the popular crowd.

I didn't know what had happened to Kingston Taylor, but I managed to put him out of my mind.

Every once in a while, I would sleep with my curtains open just in case I woke up and saw his night light on, but I never did.

He was gone. My young love had disappeared, and life moved on.

2

Penny was waiting for me by the library entrance when I showed up ten minutes late.

"I'm sorry, uh, I got caught up watching the brat," I apologized with a stutter. "You know what it's like."

The brat was my little sister, my half-sister Natalie. I'd been hanging out with her and was annoyed that it had made me late. Even though there were still four weeks before the start of school, Penny and I were meeting for our weekly science roundup.

I was earning a little extra allowance by babysitting the brat while my mom and stepdad were at work, but mom had been late coming home again. She only worked part time as a personal assistant to some CEO, but she loved going for drinks with her friends afterwards.

My stepfather, Reg, wasn't around much either. I actually preferred it that way. It wasn't that we didn't get along; we just had an uncomfortable relationship. It was strained, and he gave me the creeps at times. Nothing had ever happened. It was just a feeling.

"I know what she's like." She laughed. "No biggie, though. There were some guys here skateboarding earlier, and I didn't mind the view."

My best friend Penny Pascale was endlessly patient and almost always waiting for me. She was a really pretty blonde, smart as a whip, and boy crazy like nobody's business. She didn't have to get the kind of grades that I did since her grandpa had left her enough money in a trust fund to cover all her college tuition, but she liked getting away from her strict family any chance she got. They were really religious and watched her like a hawk, and if she even hinted at straying off their chosen path all that college money would disappear in a heartbeat. She was the youngest in a family of all boys and was the only one left at home. They had some weird purity ideas, believing that Penny must be protected or she would lose her standing in the church, or some anti-feminist bullshit.

"Was it anyone we knew?" I asked, knowing she was boy crazy enough for me distract her by using her horniness against her.

"Mostly rich douche bags from Covington," she said with a curl of her lip and a snort of disgust.

Covington High was in the wealthy section of town, far from us. We went to a local public high school, Oakville High, in a poorer area of town, but we lived kind of in the middle between the two. I'd always envied Covington's money, the science lab, and their theatre program, as well as their pilot training program at the local flight school.

It would be so much easier to get into a decent college coming from Covington. I'd already be part of the assembly line leading directly from their doors to the best schools. I would already be considered one of them instead of having to prove myself like I did coming from Oakville.

"But they were cute?" I asked.

"Oh, hell yeah," she said, laughing. "There was this one... He took his shirt off, right?"

I nodded, and we walked up the front steps of the Oakville Civic Library. She continued to gush over the skateboarder. "He had these abs that were so bumpy, like more than a six-pack. An eight pack!"

She continued singing his praises all the way through the library, even though we got dirty looks from a few of the patrons.

We found our way to the back and were pleased when our usual table was empty.

We set our books out on the table and sat across from each other. She chatted on about the boy on the skateboard with the washboard abs, and I got my notepad out, ready to take notes on the latest research in cellular gene therapy.

My mom didn't have college money, my stepdad made it known he was giving me nothing, and I didn't have grandparents leaving me a big inheritance, so I was relying on scholarships to get me through.

I had already been in contact with a few different schools, and my prospects were looking good. One place in particular was probably my best chance. They had already put me on the short list for a full ride based on my academic excellence in this final year.

Penny finally ran out of breath and looked across the table at me. She took a deep breath and said, "Oh my god, I can't believe I didn't tell you. Or do you know?

Of course you don't know or you would already be talking about it!"

"What?" I asked. "What's wrong?"

"Nothing's *wrong*," she exclaimed and clapped her hands together. "I can't believe you don't know about this!"

"Just tell me!" I laughed. "This is going to kill me!"

"Oh, should I make you wait?" she giggled. "Am I that evil?"

"You know you are not an evil girl," I replied. I was nervous about whatever it was she was about to tell me. I hated surprises anyway, preferring routine to anything out of the ordinary. Even if it turned out to be good.

"Okay, I'll tell you," she said with a wide smile. "Guess who's coming back?"

"Uh, like from the dead?" I asked.

"No, silly. Like from the past," she replied, and her face lit up with secret glee. "Think... You've got this."

And then it hit me like a ton of bricks.

I knew exactly who she meant.

And I felt sick to my stomach with fear and excitement in equal parts.

"Kingston Taylor?" I asked, and my eyes widened. I fought the urge to put my hand over my mouth and squeal like one of those girls in the old Beatles movies. I felt like it, though. My stomach was flipping and turning over on itself so hard that I felt like I couldn't catch my breath.

"The one and only," she replied with a triumphant wave of her hands. "I heard from my mom. You know her friend's husband works with Kingston's dad in the city works yard. His dad has been talking about it for days now, he's so excited."

"But why?" I asked, my mouth bobbing open and shut like one of those novelty singing fish you hang on the wall to annoy your friends and family. "He's in New York. Why would he leave the city for Oakville?"

"Maybe he's coming back because he loooooooves you," she said with giddy delight. "Maybe he misses you like you miss him."

"I don't miss him. I've barely thought about him for years!"

And that would be a damned dirty lie. Just two nights ago I looked across at his window, hoping to catch a glimpse of him. I wondered what he looked like now, how his tall, lean body had developed. Was he still super skinny? Would he be even taller? What would he think of me?---,

"Nice try," Penny giggled. "But seriously, I can't wait to see what happens when you two meet up again. It's going to be like fireworks crossed with cupid's arrow."

I nodded and smiled but had my doubts. Penny was the eternal, daydreaming optimist. She could envision a situation where Kingston came home and fell in love with me.

I could not.

He'd been gone for years, and not once in all that time had he reached out. We'd vowed to keep in touch, and that kiss had been heart achingly sweet and tender, but it had meant nothing to him.

He'd ignored me from the moment he left, even though I'd tried to maintain contact, so I doubted there was going to be a fairytale happy ending for my neighborhood crush.

But a girl would always hope. And I did hope it

worked out and that my cynical view of things was proven wrong.

I did hope that I would get my ungainly, tall, skinny boy back in my arms and we could carry on falling in love and getting our lives going from where they'd left off.

But my negative outlook and low expectations had been proven correct far too many times. My mom called me morose; I called myself realistic.

I suspected I'd be one of those thirty-year-old virgins and wind up living to an old age as an old maid with a house full of cats. And honestly? I'd be okay with that. There weren't that many guys around who caught my eye, and even though Penny tried by pointing out cute ones everywhere we went, none had actually given me the zap I'd known with Kingston.

My brain was more science than sex, anyway. I'd be fine if he didn't want to pick up where we'd left off. As long as I had him as a friend, I'd be okay.

I smiled and nodded again as Penny began to wax poetic about the Covington skater boy's broad chest and bulging arms, and for a moment, I forgot that the boy I used to love would be returning.

And for the last time in a very long time, I was truly happy.

3

"Ooh, looks like quite a commotion at Rick's place," Mom said, peering through the slats of the blinds in our front room. "There's a big black pickup truck, one of those obnoxious lifted ones you hate. The 'little dick dude planet killers,' you call them, remember?"

She let the slat fall and looked over at me. I nodded halfheartedly while I underlined notes in the book I was reading. It was an autobiography of the first female astronaut, and her outlook on love and marriage was enlightening.

She said never fall in love and never get married, and I was inclined to agree with her.

"Somebody's getting out and they have a lot of luggage. Was Rick expecting company?" she asked to nobody in particular. I was only half listening to her as she rambled on about the neighborhood comings and goings.

It was one of her favorite hobbies while we waited for my stepfather, Reg, to come home for dinner. He was out doing one of his favorite hobbies—not golf, for once, but shooting. He went to the gun range once a week with his buddies, and we were expected to wait for him before we sat down to eat.

The brat, my little sister Natalie, was sitting across the table from me and gasped. "*Oh Em Gee!* Is it Kingston coming home? He wasn't supposed to be here until next week. Did he come home early?"

She practically squealed as she pushed away from the table and ran to the window. She lacked Mom's subtle stalking skills and yanked the entire blind up with a *zip* sound. She pressed her face against the window and craned her neck to see next door.

My heart basically threw itself off a cliff at the mention of his name, and it took a moment for my brain to catch up.

First, Kingston was seriously home for good?

And second, how did the brat know about it, and why did she care?

I wanted to stand up and join her, but my dignity demanded that I didn't squeal, and I didn't run across the room despite my legs twitching and my heart doing ridiculous little fluttering motions that made me feel seasick.

"Is it him? It will be nice to see him again," Mom said and turned back to look at me. "Did you know he was coming home, honey?"

"I might have heard the rumors," I replied and pretended to study my book. "You know, gossip about it and such, but I didn't know what to believe."

Natalie pushed back from the window and cocked her head. "You're kidding, right? Of course you must have heard. I mean, he was your one and only crush, and from what I've heard now, he's really filled out."

"I don't know, I haven't talked to him in years," I replied and looked up at her.

She was everything I was not. Even though she was only eleven, she was already modelesque, with big, bright blue eyes and a head of thick luxurious honey blonde hair that tumbled down her back.

She was outgoing and athletic, and I had to admit it... She was already more popular than I was. The only reason I had to babysit her when our parents were at work was because she was a typical youngest child, headstrong and prone to getting into trouble. Only in her case, she acted more like a single child with a father who spoiled her rotten and gave her anything she ever wanted.

I hated it. She should be old enough to be left alone, but she wasn't. She was a pain in my side and a constant reminder that I wasn't popular and I wasn't beautiful, and I would never fit in with kids in this town like she did. And she was a constant reminder that although I was my mother's biological child, I would never truly fit in with this family.

"Darn it, I didn't see anything," Natalie pouted and yanked the string on the blinds, letting them drop with a dramatic flair. "I hope he's back. He's been playing football, you know."

"Yeah, I heard," I replied, fighting to keep myself nonchalant.

Still, it was irritating that she was that many years younger than me and yet she apparently knew more about the goings on of the senior class than I did.

And I couldn't blame her. I would do the same if I had the chance or if my father's family had money. She would have her college paid for completely by her grandparents— the grandparents I'd always tried to bond with as a kid, but the same ones who hadn't ever sent me a birthday card or a Christmas gift. They let me know where I stood, and that was far from Natalie's guaranteed easy life.

I thought about getting up and taking a peek through the blinds myself, but my stepdad came home and we had to clear the table and sit down for dinner. He opened the cabinet behind him, put his two guns away, a rifle and a handgun, and closed it up. There was a constant battle in our house because Reg didn't lock his cabinet, but he always said if we were stupid enough to touch his things, then we were stupid enough to deal with the consequences.

Neither one of us was that stupid, though, so we never touched his gun cabinet. Not the one here or the one in the garage. We also never touched his tools, his toys, or the collection of alcohol he kept in a cabinet near the front window.

Once we started serving ourselves, Reg remained quiet. This was our signal that he wasn't ready to hear us talk and we should wait until he started before we did. We understood this, so there was silence at the dinner table. I mean, other than the clanking of serving spoons hitting plates, of course.

"I hear there's extra pressure for scholarship students this year," Reg, said after asking me to pass him the side dish. It was Thursday—meatloaf and green beans night for dinner. "You might want to consider taking on an extra AP course, you know, just to beef it up a little."

"She's already got a full schedule plus piano practice, plus helping us out with our willful, rebellious youngest daughter," Mom replied. "One more course might be the thing that breaks the camel's back."

"Did you just call Everly a camel?" Natalie snorted and made a face at me across the table.

"I'm going to get a hump if I keep hunched over reading all these books." I grinned and made a face back. Sometimes she wasn't that bad, and we got along. She was simply clueless about how her life affected mine.

"Maybe you will get more than one hump now that Kingston is back." She giggled and raised her eyebrows.

"Girls!" Mom exclaimed.

"That's disgusting table talk, young ladies," Reg said in a low, warning tone. "You should be more careful with your language, Everly Rebecca Hayes."

"Me?! Natalie was the one who said it," I wailed.

And there we were, back to the brat ruining my life. This kind of thing happened all the time, with Reg taking her side and my mom stuck in the middle trying to make peace with everyone.

"Reg, that isn't fair," Mom said, then she looked at me with a pleading expression on her face. "But maybe you shouldn't have said the word hump, dear. Natalie looks up to you and is easily influenced."

I hated this family, and I hated this house sometimes. That was my dirty little secret. On the outside, I was boring old Everly Hayes, sister to the stunningly beautiful Natalie Robertson. I was an ugly duckling without the big reveal at the end. Eternally trapped in oversized hoodies and my Mom's hand-me-down yoga pants and jeans, with no makeup and my hair yanked into a messy braid because I couldn't be bothered with a proper cut.

I was dull, focused, never caused a fuss, and was polite to a fault. I was like a little mouse scratching through the background of life, nobody ever noticing me until I was already gone.

But sometimes on the inside, I raged. I burned with anger and hatred at the way my life was going, and I sizzled with dreams of a life I could have without this town and this family. I hated that I was a stranger in my own home, that my biological father had abandoned us, and that nobody gave a shit whether I lived or died.

I wanted more than this, and sometimes it all came spilling out at once.

I stood up, my chair scraping on the newly finished hardwood floors as I pushed it back. "This is so unfair, Mom, and you know it. You always take his side, and he always takes hers!"

"It's not that big of a deal," Natalie said, trying to sooth her father's growing anger and make me feel better. That was the worst thing about the brat. She was annoying and a lot of work, but in the end, she was the only one who tried to make things nice for me around here. She wasn't that bad to me, and she never made fun of me outside the home.

But I still hated her, so there was something desperately wrong with me. There was a darkness that I didn't know what to do with, that simmered under the surface and threatened to spill over if I didn't keep control of it and let it all out.

I turned and ran out of the dining room, leaving them sitting in stunned silence as I pulled on my shoes and ran into the street and down to the park where I could go for a walk in the woods and clear my head.

I liked to climb a certain tree, the one that Kingston

and I used to climb, and I would sit up there and think about things until I calmed down. There was something about being immersed in nature that made me feel happier about the world.

I scrambled to the top of it, knowing it like the back of my hand, I'd climbed it so many times. Once there, I swung my legs over the massive limb near the top and rested there, thinking about things until I realized I had acted like a freak. I hated it as much as I hated my life sometimes. I couldn't control when I felt like that, and through the years, I'd had a few meltdowns—in school even—and it had earned me a bad rep.

The freak. The spazz. Even 'pissy pants' from kids who'd been around since the old days. I'd heard them all and worse. But I couldn't help it when things built up inside me. I could keep them bottled up for months or even years at a time, but when they needed to come out, they burst out of me without any regard to who was around.

I carried darkness in me, and sometimes it terrified me. Other times, it made me feel so damned powerful. And that was the part that scared me.

The light dimmed all around me. It was one of those late summer evenings where it felt like the horizon stayed lit up long after the sun was gone, but that also meant it was really late.

Now that I had cooled off, it was time to go back. I shimmied down the tree and headed back home through the treed pathway. I had my head down, looking at the trail, hoping maybe I'd stumble across a geode or something interesting on the path.

I was humming a tune to myself and not paying

attention to my surroundings when I ran smack into something hard—a wall of muscle.

Panic lit my nerves on fire, and adrenaline flared inside of me. I'd heard stories about bad men here in the park, and I freaked out inside. What if I had just run into somebody dangerous? "I'm sorry," I stammered as I looked up. "I was just—"

I didn't have time to finish my sentence because Kingston Taylor looked down at me, and in a slightly amused tone, he said, "Hello, Evie."

And just like that, Kingston Taylor returned to my life. And while he was still tall, he was no longer gangly. My jaw almost dropped when I looked into his eyes and realized my childhood friend was now the most gorgeous man I'd ever seen.

And suddenly, I found myself unable to speak.

4

"What the fuck are you staring at, spazz?"

I turned to find the source of the mocking female voice, and of course it belonged to the most beautiful girl I'd ever seen in person.

She had tawny tanned skin, dirty blonde hair with rose gold highlights, and light blue eyes that seemed to pierce my very soul. Her makeup was done to perfection. She was wearing a cheerleader's uniform that hugged her curvy body and had her hand around Kingston's arm, clinging to him like she owned him.

I looked back up at Kingston for a sign that I was hallucinating the most perfect girl in the world, or that I was imagining he was like a tall, chiseled Greek god himself. I needed support from my old friend, but he only looked down at me with a cold, impassive face.

"Babe, what's her problem? Is she, like, *special*?" the girl hissed under her breath to my dream guy.

"She's my neighbor," he said with a sneer. "And no, there's nothing special about her."

Kingston's voice was so rich and deep that I swore I

felt it vibrate in my chest. But it was also so cold and distant that he wasn't like my childhood friend at all anymore.

"I, um," I stammered and finally managed to close my mouth like a normal person. "I'm Everly. Who are you?"

I stuck out my hand, and she looked down at it like it was dirty.

"This is Sofia. She's a friend of mine," Kingston said without emotion.

"A *friend*?" Sofia exclaimed and elbowed Kingston so hard he winced. "Come on, babe, tell her the truth."

She then turned, locked her eyes on me, and said, "I'm King's *girlfriend*, spazz. Don't fucking forget it."

King. She called him King. He hated that nickname growing up and had always insisted on Kingston. He wasn't my old friend at all; he didn't even look like him. He didn't have glasses or acne or crooked teeth.

I felt disoriented, so I mumbled something about not caring if she was or not, and I took off like a streak back through the park. I reached my house and snuck inside, closing the door carefully and creeping up the stairs so I could process my emotions alone in my room.

Everybody was in their rooms. I could hear the murmur of the TV from Mom and Reg's and the sound of music and Natalie singing along from hers.

I locked my door and finally exhaled, releasing the pent up adrenaline that I had been keeping inside since seeing Kingston again for the first time in years.

I flopped onto my bed on my back and drew my hand up to my forehead. I sighed and replayed the event from the park over and over in my head.

That gorgeous girl, Sofie... Her cruel, sneering face

Dirty Kingdom 23

and her mocking laughter when she called me *spazz* and *special*.

I didn't even know her. I'd never seen her at my school, but maybe she was from Covington. I could at least rely on that. I had access to Kingston that she wouldn't have; I was his neighbor, and she wasn't going to the same school. Maybe, just maybe, I could talk to him and find out why he seemed so different. Why he was so cold.

But then again, she had on that cheerleader's outfit. Ugh, she looked incredible. There was no way I could pull off something like that. I didn't have a body that I could show off like she did. And if I tried to do any cheerleading flips or jumps, I'd probably break my own neck.

No wonder Kingston was dating her. She was perfect. She was everything I wasn't.

I decided to give my mind a rest and go to bed. This kind of circular spinning of my thoughts wasn't going to do me any good.

I stood up, stripped down, and crossed my room to my dresser. A nice fuzzy onesie was on my mind, something for comfort, to ease my spinning mind.

I paused midway through and turned my head. The light from a single lamp lit my room, giving it a golden glow. I looked across the yard to Kingston's house, mostly by habit at this point.

I turned to face his place straight on and lifted my hands to run my fingers through my hair.

And found Kingston staring from his window directly into mine.

My first instinct was to cover my nude form, to leap out of view and hide from him in shame, knowing my body would never compare to his girlfriend's.

But something came over me, as if I were possessed. The moment I'd been waiting for over the past few years was suddenly laid out right in front of me, and something took hold.

I stared back at him, and I lifted my hand to draw my finger across my chest. I slid it up my neck and into my mouth, where I sucked it slowly and then trailed it back down.

I could see him there in the dark of his room, his silhouette outlined in shadow. The glow of their yard light brightened his features just enough for me to see the intensity as he stared.

I lowered my finger along my quivering abdomen and rested it there, feeling how much he affected me.

And all at once, I snapped out of it. I opened my eyes and gasped, rushed to the window, and yanked my curtains shut.

I didn't know what had come over me; it had been like a fever dream. I shook my head and pulled on my unicorn onesie and dove into bed to forget everything from the day.

I could start fresh in the morning and pray that nothing out of the ordinary happened again.

* * *

I SLEPT IN, which was wildly unusual for me. I guess

the day before had been more emotional than I'd suspected.

I slunk down for breakfast and wondered if I was too late, or if anyone wanted to see me at all after my outburst.

Mom was already cleaning the kitchen table, so I joined her and helped her in silence.

It didn't last long, though. She stopped, took a breath, and looked at me.

"What the hell was that last night?" she asked.

"I don't know. I'm sorry," I replied. But I did know what it was. I was so tired of feeling like I was less than anybody else in this house. I couldn't tell her that, though. She would overreact and start crying, wail about what a horrible mother she was, and then I'd feel guilty as fuck. I'd done that dance before.

"You know Reg is so pissed off," she hissed. "He was ready to kick you out of the house today, I can promise you that."

"I'm sorry," I repeated. "I'll apologize to him too if it will help."

"I don't know if it will help at this point," she said. "I don't know what got into you, but Reg works hard to provide a home for us, and you need to show more gratitude."

I bit my whole tongue at that and simply nodded in agreement.

"I know you're under a lot of pressure to get a scholarship, but Reg might be right. Adding an extra AP class will keep you out of trouble and give you that slight lead ahead of other students."

"I'm already so exhausted," I complained. "And I

have zero social life. I do nothing but meet Penny at the library."

"I know it sucks, but it's the only chance you've got to have a good life," Mom said, shrugging her shoulders. "Besides, what on earth would you do with a social life?"

She laughed at the last part and shook her head as in disbelief.

I felt humiliation flood over me, but as always, I sucked back my tears and kept them in check while I was the obedient daughter and continued to help her.

Sometimes I felt like my life was one big joke, and I would do almost anything to shake it up, to give it a kick and take it up a few notches so it was more exciting.

If only I'd known just what kind of trouble I was inviting into my life with my wish,

I might have done things differently. But I didn't, so I plunged headlong into it all.

5

I DIDN'T SEE Kingston again after that time in the window after the park. I kept my curtains closed every night just to be certain I didn't repeat anything like that again. I wasn't sure if I couldn't trust him—or myself.

About a week before school started, I walked into the house after a library date with Penny and heard the brat squealing with joy.

I rushed into the kitchen and found Mom, Reg, and Natalie there. Natalie had a paper in her hand and was jumping all over, yelling about her life being complete now.

"What's going on?" I asked. Reg didn't look at me or respond. Things had been very strained between us since the night of the park.

Mom did, however.

"You're going to Covington!" she exclaimed. "Oh Everly, this will get you into the college of your dreams."

"Covington? But I didn't even apply. And we live way too far away."

"They're letting our street join their catchment

area!" Natalie shrieked. "I'm going to be a Covington cheerleader when I'm old enough!"

"We're way too far out of their area. How is this even possible?" I asked. Horror slowly took hold over me when I realized that I might be going to a school filled with strangers. Rich, beautiful, snobby strangers.

"They want Kingston," Mom said with a grin. "He's apparently such a good football player that they want him on their team and will go out of their way to make sure they have him. Legally, he has to be in their zone for him to qualify."

"Oh god," I groaned. "This is a disaster."

"Why can't you take anything with good will?" Reg grumbled. "Why are you always looking for the rain cloud? Huh? Don't you ever appreciate a goddamned thing?"

My heart skipped a beat in fear, and I stammered, "I'm sorry, Reg. This is good news. Really good news."

I never wanted to attract his attention, especially when it was negative like this. His voice made me curl up inside myself like a little rabbit in the dark.

"It will help you find some money for college and finally get you out of our hair," he griped, mostly under his breath, because even he was tired of the same fight he had with Mom over and over again. He wanted me gone, and Mom tried to soften his negativity towards me. She was always stuck in the middle of it.

I made an excuse about studying and went upstairs straight away. I had to talk to Penny about it. She could help calm me down.

It turned out she was no help at all.

"You are so lucky!" she texted. "I wish!"

And then I felt like an ungrateful asshole all over again.

I couldn't catch a break, so I changed into some loose clothes and went for a run to clear my head.

I made my way through the park like I always did, headed towards the lake, and decided to challenge myself by going around it.

I had dark thoughts slipping through my brain, rippling in time with the beating of my heart, so I tried to outrun them.

Why was I never satisfied with anything I was given? How did I always manage to find the bad in everything?

Reg was right. I was such a downer in the household, they'd all be happier without me.

As I rounded the last corner of the lake, the sun was dropping behind the trees. I hadn't realized how long I'd been out, and the park was emptying of people with each yard of the path that I covered.

I glanced over at the lake and had a brief moment of urgency to run towards the water and dive in.

Not to swim but to drown. To end my suffering and stop the thoughts that kept circling through my mind.

I was such a loser, the world would be better off without me. I didn't bring anything good to the table, and nobody would miss me if I was gone. Mom and Reg would be fine, the brat would be fine, Penny would have other friends.

And that was it. That was the extent of my influence on the world.

And then I scuffed my foot on a crack in the paved pathway and came back to my senses. Sometimes I experienced suicidal ideation, but I wasn't serious about it. At least that's what I told myself. I wasn't serious.

I kept running, and by the time I hit the pathway back through the forest, it was much darker. I was nervous about going through but laughed at myself.

You were just going to throw yourself into the lake, I thought. Now you're worried about your safety?

I was almost at the spot where I'd run into Kingston and the beautiful Sofia, when I heard somebody call my name.

"Everly! Hey!"

I skidded to a stop, pulled the one earbud from my ear so they were both uncovered, and looked around.

"Wait up," he said, and Kingston came jogging slowly towards me.

"What do *you* want?" I asked, standing with my hand on my hip to convey my annoyance. In reality, I could feel my heart speed up, and my throat went dry. His mere presence affected me physically, on a chemical, hormonal level.

"You should be more careful out here," he said and stopped in front of me. He looked down and narrowed his eyes, studying me. "You could get hurt."

"Like anybody's going to jump *me*," I scoffed. "Besides, what do you care?"

He shook his head and really looked at me. It was as if a switch was flipped, as if he remembered I wasn't his friend any longer, because his expression changed from concern to hard granite.

"Call me crazy, but I care because I don't want to see *anyone* get dragged into the bush and raped," he replied in a cold tone again.

"So you're just worried about anyone? Not me in particular?"

"You got it," he said as he exhaled a sigh of irritation. "Not you in particular."

"Then why did you stop me? You should have just let me keep going," I replied.

"I should've," he said and started to walk away. I couldn't help myself. I scrambled to walk alongside him.

"So, why didn't you?" I prodded.

"I'm always saving your ass," he replied and didn't look down at me. I felt like a bratty little sidekick, like I was his little sister instead of his equal. Always the annoying side character instead of starring in my own life.

And, possibly irrationally, it fucking pissed me off.

Sure, I was fucked up and kind of a loser and even thought about stupid shit like running myself into the fucking lake from time to time, but that didn't mean he got to shit on me like this.

"What the fuck is your problem, Kingston?" I blurted and immediately regretted it when I saw him tense up and ball his fists.

We were leaving the protection of the trees and hitting the edge of the park and the sidewalk back to our street.

"I don't have a fucking problem, Evie," he replied, again without looking at me. He called me by his special name, the old name he used to use. I hated that I loved hearing it.

He kept walking and staring straight ahead, clenching and unclenching those hands of his.

"Then why are you being such a cunt to me ever since you got back? I haven't seen you in years. Why the fuck are you being like this now?"

"I'm sure if you searched that empty head of yours, you'd find the reason rattling around in there," he growled and stopped abruptly. He grabbed my shoulder and his fingers gripped it so hard that it hurt. His eyes locked on mine, and I wished he'd look away like before. All I saw in them was a simmering hate. "You know exactly why we aren't friends anymore, *Everly*. You know."

I scanned my memories for anything that could explain his behavior but found nothing. I opened my mouth to protest his accusation when he made a noise of disgust, released my arm, and turned to walk away.

This time he was too fast for me to catch up to him, and I walked home, staring at his back, wondering what the hell I'd ever done to him.

And if I'd ever find out.

6

The first day of school rushed over me like a wave in the ocean. I had to bus it to Covington on one of the crosstown city buses, and by the time I got there, my clothes were hot and sticking to my sweaty body, and my hair was a mess of tangled curls and knots.

I had a Covington hoodie now. The school had sent it over, and I had stretched it long enough to cover my ass. I liked swimming in my hoodies; I wanted to obscure anything that even resembled a curve on my body. I wanted to blend into the background and suffer through this last year unnoticed.

I got through the first day, though, and I even talked to a couple people. I saw Kingston a couple times, once with Sofia on his arm and once surrounded by a group of other guys—all of them tall, hot, and probably rich as hell.

Everybody there was rich as hell, and I stood out like the proverbial sore thumb. Even more reason to crawl into a hoodie and hide for the year. Even though

Kingston was from my neighborhood, they accepted him as one of their own. I wasn't so lucky.

The second day blended into the rest of the week, and I was able to get through unscathed.

When Mom asked me for an update during Friday's dinner, I was happy to tell her, "It's actually way better than I thought. Did you know they have a riding club? I can take lessons on one of the school horses since we don't have one. I've always wanted to learn how to ride."

"See? You had nothing to worry about," Reg said, and he gifted me with one of his rare smiles. It was ridiculous how much I loved his approval when I got it. I suspected I'd have to hit therapy about my daddy issues at some point, even though there was always an unsettled feeling in the pit of my stomach around him. A gut instinct that he didn't have my best interests at heart.

"You were right, dear," Mom smiled at Reg. "Now, Natalie, how were your classes?"

"I have that stupid jerk face Miles Nelson in my group again," she moaned and went off on how much of a stupid jerk face Miles actually was.

I smiled and listened, and for the first time in a long time, I felt like everything might work out for me.

Penny grilled me at Saturday's library meet up, and I tried to remember as many details about as many of the cutest guys I'd seen just to appease her boy crazy side. She was dying to see that guy with the skateboard and the abs from in front of the building that one day.

The second week, however, shattered my illusions and left shards of them around me on the ground like broken glass.

Monday morning wasn't so awful. The city bus was

late, so I slipped into my chemistry class ten minutes after the bell rang. The teacher stopped speaking and stared at me, leading the entire class to follow her. I had eighteen sets of eyes on me when I found an empty chair at a table in the back.

"How lovely of you to join us, Miss Hayes," she said in a tense tone. "Now, if you don't mind, I will continue going over today's experiment."

I looked at the whiteboard behind her and desperately hoped for notes, but it was empty. I leaned over and tried to sneak a look at the girl next to me, but she glared and moved her MacBook away so I couldn't read the screen.

I tried to pick up what was going on from what the teacher was saying, but it was hopeless. The ten minutes I'd missed had been critical, and there was no way for me to catch up now. I was going to fail my first assignment.

As soon as the teacher stopped talking, everybody paired off and began to work. I was left alone and desperate again but refused to cry. I could make up for this failed experiment with extra credit. I could catch up.

"Are you having trouble?"

I heard a familiar voice and turned to find Sofia behind me. She smiled at me, a warm and inviting smile that threw me off for a moment.

"Uh, um, yeah," I said. "The bus was late, I missed so much I have no idea what we're doing."

"Listen, we got off on the wrong foot. I'll help you with this to prove to you that I'm sorry," she said, her warm smile broadening. "Can you forgive me?"

She extended her delicate hand with its perfectly

manicured nails in pink sparkles and Swarovski crystals. I shook it, aware of how big and sweaty and utilitarian my hand was in hers and smiled back.

"Oh thank god," I said. "I don't know if you thought I was after Kingston or anything, but no. God, no, we don't even talk to each other anymore."

Her smile froze on her face, and she widened her eyes in surprise. "No, I don't think that," she laughed. "I know you wouldn't have a chance with him. I was just in a mood that night, that's all."

"Okay," I replied. The massive insult was so obvious that I could barely ignore it. But I did. "So now what do we do?"

She opened her laptop and started reading the notes in order while I went through the motions.

It was a simple chemical experiment, an equation followed by the mixing of two different ones and then adding a third. Sofia emphasized that you had to do them in the correct order or it was going to be a disaster.

I worked carefully. Chemistry was an easy subject for me, but I wasn't familiar with this experiment or the chemicals involved. I got ready to add the last element when Sofia said, "Wait. I want to record this to upload. It will add to our overall mark if we have a digital example as well as our notes."

I nodded and waited for her to pull out her phone. I leaned close, adjusted my safety goggles, and squeezed the eyedropper. It was supposed to turn the solution bright pink mixed with little clouds, and from the sounds of excitement all around us, it was beautiful.

Sofia held her phone close to me, and I added one more drop. I wrinkled my nose at the acrid scent and puzzled over the thin strange plume of smoke floating up from the flask.

"I don't think it's supposed to do—"

A loud clapping sound popped out of the flask, and I felt hot liquid smatter against my face and front.

"I think we did it wrong! That's the acid!" Sofia yelled. "Get it off before it hits your skin! Oh my god, I used the wrong chemical. It's going to burn you!"

"What the hell did you do?" I screamed and began to beat at my hoodie, terrified that the acid would melt through to my skin. "You did this on purpose, you fucking bitch!"

I was horrified that it would scar my face or chest. I panicked, blind, thoughtless panic. I tore the hoodie off, dragging my tee shirt with it. I stood in the middle of the classroom in my bra, still screaming, as I feared acid eating away at my flesh. I could feel pinpricks of pain on my face where it had splashed and tears began to stream.

"Oh my god, did you get that, you guys?" Sofia laughed and turned the phone towards her as she continued to talk. "Live from chemistry class, spazz on display. She tore her own clothes off. What a fucking loser."

She had been live streaming the whole thing on her social media account for everybody to see. I hoped there weren't that many people watching, but I knew she must be a huge influencer with her perfect body and her awful personality to go along with it.

"What is going on over here?" the teacher exclaimed as she rushed across the room. "Why are you getting naked in my classroom?"

I explained what had happened, and the teacher

laughed. "She pranked you, plain and simple," she said. "You were feeling extreme cold, not acid. Look, your skin is fine."

I pulled off the safety goggles and touched my face with my hand. There was nothing wrong with my skin, and I no longer felt pain.

I looked at the clothing in my hand, and it had wet spots on it but no melted areas. I didn't know what had happened, but Sofia had tricked me somehow, and now I was shirtless in front of my classmates.

They had the good manners to not burst into laughter, but as I pulled my clothes back on over my head, I noticed several phones out as they recorded me.

The teacher waited until I was dressed again then said, "I did hear what you called her. That kind of language might be acceptable in Oakville High, but it is not acceptable here at Covington. You have earned one demerit, and as you know, after three demerits you will face permanent expulsion."

She said the name of my former school like she was talking about a garbage dump. Her disgust was noticeable, and she walked away before I could protest or defend myself. Not that it would do any good. Sofia was clearly the little darling here, and I was the trashy interloper.

I fought back tears and looked over at Sofia. She was now sitting back with her friends and they were whispering together, shooting me nasty looks, complete with even nastier giggles.

I was miserable, and I knew it was only going to get worse.

7

I AVOIDED Sofia and her friends and Kingston and his friends for the next couple of days. I brought a sandwich for lunch, and I ate it in the girl's change room, tucked behind the basketball storage cart. I texted Penny and tried not to spill over all my misery into her life. She was having a good year at school so far. I couldn't ruin it for her.

I even lied to her about my life at Covington. I began to fake scenarios where I was making friends and having lunch with them. I was hiding my true feelings, and the depression that kept creeping up on me was again threatening to take over. I'd lived with depression and emotional problems on and off for years. Sometimes, it would come out of nowhere and I would wake up with a crushing weight on my chest, like a massive beast sitting there, squeezing the breath out of me.

Other times, I would lose entire days and nights of my life. Usually on the weekends, which Google told me was a time that my brain felt safe to let go. This is why sometimes I would go to sleep Friday night and not wake up until Saturday afternoon or evening. My brain was cocooning, taking time to heal itself.

I always felt worse after these episodes, though, which didn't make sense to me. I'd spent a Saturday night and all day Sunday feeling groggy and out of sorts. Like I was slipping out of sync with the rest of reality. Like when you're streaming a show and the words are a second ahead of the video. Nothing lined up properly.

I felt like that now somewhat. Everything in my world was discombobulated, as my grandpa would say.

Hiding out worked for only a short time. I flew under the radar, and nobody noticed the spazz from Oakville High.

But on Thursday, I was eating my PB&J sandwich behind the basketball cart while scrolling TikTok when I heard voices. I quickly shut my phone off and wrapped my sandwich up. I crouched in the small space between the cart and the wall and hoped they'd go away quickly.

"Come on, babe," a girl said in a singsong tone. "I don't have time for this."

"You got me hard with that little crop top, you have to do something about it," a guy replied with aggression.

He had a deep, demanding voice. The kind you don't easily say no to, the kind that was used to being obeyed. I felt a little tweak in my belly as he continued and the rich bass vibrated my eardrums.

"You know you get me hot when you look like that. You know what you do to me. You owe me," he insisted.

"Babe, come on. You know I have cheer practice," the girl said, pleading with him.

"I know you have dick practice, so drop to your

knees," he said with a laugh. That seemed to do the trick.

"Ugh, bad joke, but okay. Just make it quick," she agreed.

I heard the muffled sounds of two people moving, but no more words. I was dying to know who was in here sneaking sex during the school lunch, so I peered out around the edge of the basketballs.

One of Kingston's friends, Valen, was standing there with his jeans down and his cock out. He was facing me and had his huge hands cupping a girl's head.

She was a cheerleader. She was wearing the Covington uniform, but I didn't know exactly which one she was. They were all interchangeable drones for queen bee Sofia. The girl was on her knees in front of him, as if in worship, and her hands were gripping his muscled thighs.

He was looking down, and I was fascinated. The tweak in my gut had spread to warmth and moved lower, and I wanted to watch despite it making me also feel like a gigantic pervert.

It was hot seeing him get his dick sucked like that. I wondered what it would be like to be with somebody. To kiss them, suck them... have them suck me, my clit.

I slipped and fell forward, moving the cart about an inch. Valen's gaze moved from watching the girl working on his dick to where I was hiding, and he caught me.

I blushed a furious red and nearly choked, but I didn't move. I couldn't move. It would be so obvious if I moved.

So I stayed there, huddled and frozen, knowing he was staring at me while he was getting a blow job. It was the most awkward thing I'd ever gone through.

"Oh my god," the girl's muffled voice sounded out. "Stop it! You're gagging me!"

"Come on, I know you can do better than that," Valen chuckled.

I heard a wet plop as the girl pulled back, and I took a peek as she sat on her haunches looking up at him. I finally recognized one of Sofia's meanest sidekicks, Cassie Reynolds.

"You know what? Fuck you! You won't even call me your girlfriend, and I'm sick of this. You only use me when you want your dick wet and then you kick me out like I'm trash. Fuck you and fuck all of you Kings! I never wanted to be the Tribute anyway. It's a bullshit game for virginal losers!"

She jumped to her feet, pulled the back of her hand across her mouth, and stood staring up at him. He looked down with his mouth curled in amusement.

"What? Don't you have anything to say?" she exclaimed.

"I dunno." He shrugged his shoulders and grinned. "Is your friend Daphne free right now?"

She shrieked at that and stomped out, leaving him alone.

I took the chance to slide back behind the cart so he couldn't see any part of me, and I hunched over, squeezing my eyes shut.

I expected him to shove his dick back in his pants and leave, but he didn't. He stayed there motionless for a moment or two.

And then he spoke.

"I saw you back there, spazz," he said with humor. "You might as well creep out here and finish me off."

I froze and didn't reply.

"Listen, I can stand here all day with my cock out, but it's not going to suck itself," he said. "Either you get out here, or I'm coming over there. One way or the other, this is gonna happen."

I knew I could run past him if I could just pretend I was coming out to give him head. I would walk towards him and then make my move to the door.

I stood slowly, pulled my hoodie as low as it would go, and hunched my shoulders as I stepped out and walked a couple feet towards him.

"I was just, uh, I didn't see anything," I said, refusing to let myself look down at his monster dick.

"You mean you didn't even notice this?" he asked, grasping it in his hands, shaking it at me. "It's still rock hard and needing some relief before math class. We're in that one together, aren't we? Mr. Baker's math class? Fuck, it's boring. Maybe we could have something to think about together when we're sitting there this afternoon."

I hated how warm and friendly his words sounded, half convincing me that this was normal. That we were just two friends hanging out and one friend should suck the other friend off.

It was hypnotizing and so alluring. And I almost fell for it.

Almost.

I looked him in the eye and gave him a lazy smile. And when he relaxed and smiled back, I turned and bolted for the door.

Right into the hard, muscled arms of Kingston Taylor.

8

"Whoa, where are you going so fast, Everly?" he asked and held me by my shoulders. He looked down and said, "Did something happen?"

"Your friend tried to force me..."

My voice trailed off as I lost my train of thought. And then I began stammering to try to explain myself, but I was babbling too hard to get the words out. "He tried to... He wanted to force me... A blow job—"

"I wasn't trying anything. She was into it." Valen interrupted me with a scoffing laugh. "Come on, spazz, I won't tell if you don't."

"Is that true? Were you about to leave my friend hanging?" Kingston asked. Again, he was using a confusing, friendly tone, but I could sense the cold steel under his words. "Now that's not nice. Do you know what blue balls can do to a young man's developing brain? You're causing him damage and real pain. I suggest you finish what you started."

That command left no room for interpretation. He wasn't going to take no for an answer.

I couldn't, though. Even if it was my first love telling me to get on my knees in front of his friend. Even then, I would be giving into their demands. That stubborn streak reared up in my head, and I refused to give in. They were using me for their own sick pleasure, and they would go right back to thinking of me as trash when they were done. I would get nothing out of it at all.

So I grabbed onto my grim resolve, stared him down in defiance, thrust out my lower jaw, and said, "No."

"Wrong answer." Kingston laughed. He reached up and grabbed hold of my thick, dark braids in his clenched fist. He narrowed his eyes and dragged me down. I struggled against him, but he was too strong, and the pain in my scalp was too much. I sunk slowly to my knees as he said, "We don't enjoy hearing that word around here, do we, Vale?"

"Not at all," Valen replied and sauntered towards me, his dick still out and even harder now, if that was even possible. "It's probably because nobody ever says it."

"That's *exactly* why. Especially not trashy little whores like Everly here," Kingston said, giving my braids a jerk with each word for emphasis.

Tears ran down my face at the pain from my hair being yanked, but more so at his words. Was that really what he thought of me? What had I done to earn his disgust?

"You know," Kingston continued, with me trapped on my knees before him. "Her mother was fucking my neighbor even when he was married. I remember my parents talking about it. I made friends with her back then because I had no idea what trailer trash was, and I

Dirty Kingdom 47

was dying to know if there was anything special about them."

"So what did you find out?" Valen asked and stood in front of me. Kingston held my head tightly in place, and tears streamed faster now as the pain increased and Valen's cock head touched my tightly pressed lips.

"I found out there's *nothing*," Kingston said, jerking my head. "There's literally nothing special about them. So, you hear that, Everly? There's *nothing* special about you, so there's no reason you can't join the ranks of eager young women willing to take one for the team, drain our balls, and help us perfect those football plays our coach wants us to run later. Won't you think of the Covington Kings?"

The name of the football team, the heroes the entire school worshipped. I hated them all now even more, hated every last one of them for doing this, but also for seeing me as nothing.

"Fuck you," I hissed with my as lips close together as I could, hanging onto my defiance. "This is assault. I'm going to the principal the minute I'm out of here, and I'm filing charges."

"Go right ahead. Do you think anyone is going to believe you?" Kingston scoffed. "How do you think future colleges are going to take that when you're sniffing around their doors begging for scholarship money? Nobody wants an uptight little bitch on their campus. Nobody."

He was right. That was the worst part of it. He was *right*. He knew the system from the inside, and he knew how it was weighted against girls like me. Sad girls with sad eyes, with no futures and no worth to future senators, governors, CEOs, and all the other places these Covington boys were heading.

He was right. I was nothing. I was a loser. I was useless. I was all the things he thought about me, even worse if he knew how much anger simmered just below the surface. If he knew the secret world contained inside my head, where I locked myself away and sacrificed my true feelings in order to maintain my outer image as the good girl, he would be even more disgusted.

But I couldn't give in just yet. That oppositional stripe inside of me always managed to get me into trouble. It was like a stubborn rage that threatened to spill over at times, and sometimes it actually did. I was afraid of it, though. Afraid that if I gave into the feelings that stirred inside me, I'd lose control. I'd become a violent woman full of anger and indignation.

I held back, but still I struggled against his hand in my hair, and I flailed my fists, trying to strike out at them. Both boys started to laugh at me, and a third joined in behind me, adding to my humiliation.

"Is this where you assholes have been this whole time?"

Kingston's other best friend, Archer, came into view. He was equally tall, muscled, and powerful in the hierarchy of the school. I was fucked. They were going to have their way with me no matter what I did.

Archer got behind me and held my arms. Kingston kept my braids wrapped in his fist so I couldn't move my head, and Valen pushed the head of his cock through my tight lips and into my mouth at last.

The tweak in my guts bloomed into a full, hot blossom of curiosity that settled in my core. It felt good.

I felt good. As much as I hated them and hated this, it felt natural for me somehow.

And yet, Valen didn't press farther. He didn't choke me like he'd choked Cassie. He didn't force his entire massive dick into my throat like he'd done with her.

Like I wanted him to.

He looked down at me with a cruel twist to his lips, petted the top of my head like I was a dog, and said, "Good girl. Now we know what we can get you to do."

And with that, he pulled back and shoved his cock back into his jeans, where it looked painful because it bulged so big.

After that, the three of them let me go. I was left panting on my knees with my hands at my sides and my scalp aching from the strain.

"Now you'll really have something to think about during math class." Valen chuckled as they left me alone in the locker room. "The fact that you wanted it *so bad*. From all three of us."

"She's a whore like her mother," Kingston said with disgust. "Not that I needed any more proof of that."

"She's hot, though," Archer said, looking back at me. "Under those clothes, I mean. I'll bet she's got a tight little body and nice big tits."

The three of them laughed as they walked out, their voices carrying along as they hit the busy hallway outside. The door creaked and slowly shut on its pneumatic hinge, leaving me still kneeling on the floor in the middle of the change room, my head whirling. The only sound I heard after it clicked shut was my own beating heart. The only thing I felt was the pain in my body and the humiliation of the experience filling my head.

But again, they were right, and that was the worst part of how I was feeling. I would have sucked them all off just now. I would have done it even though the mere thought of it filled me with anger and shock. They knew it, and I knew it.

Maybe I was exactly who they said I was after all, a white trash whore. Whispers in my head told me this is how the world would see me, but again, my own stubborn core refused to back down and give in.

I rose up on shaking legs, brushed my knees off, and exhaled a long, quivering breath.

And for the first time in a long time, I felt alive. I had purpose. I had a reason to live.

I wasn't entirely sure what it was, though. Not just yet. I existed somewhere in the middle between fucking Kingston and his three friends or turning them all in for sexual assault.

Only time would tell which side of the fence I'd come down on. Until then, I would continue to avoid them and live under the radar with a new fire in my belly and purpose in my heart.

9

"Okay, you might not like this, *but I'm not taking no for an answer*," Penny said on Friday afternoon. I'd survived my first week with only those two incidents, one in the lab and one in the change room, and now I just wanted to lie low for the weekend. "I was invited to a party, and you're coming with me. It will be good for you to get out of the house! We need to try new things. It's our last year in high school and we've never done anything."

I turned her down at first. I tried more than a few excuses from me maybe being sick to me having homework. Penny wasn't having it. This was a party at her new friend's house and she insisted that I had to join her. Her words echoed Kingston and Valen's, though, and I felt sick when she spoke them.

"What's wrong?" she asked when I didn't respond. "Was it that bad over at Covington?"

"Nothing's wrong. I think I had a bad salad at lunch," I lied. Truth was, I'd had another PB and J while hidden in the change room. Part of me had hoped they'd come back, but mostly I knew I'd be safe. There was a big game tonight and the football players and cheerleaders were off doing whatever it was that they did.

"Aww, I hope you feel better now," she said over the phone. "Because you're coming with me! I told my mom we're studying and I might spend the night. Dad's out of town, so she's lending me the minivan to drive. This is one chance we can't miss, and if you don't do it with me, then I'll never get invited again."

I was lying on my back on my bed, and her voice was so filled with pleading that I smiled. "Fine," I sighed. "But don't say I never did anything for you."

I hadn't told her about the chemistry prank or what had happened in the change room. Both were too humiliating for me to share, and I was at that point where I wanted to put them behind me.

"*Thankyouthankyouthankyouthankyouthankyou!*" she exhaled in one long continuous jumble of words.

I laughed and felt lighter already. Penny was right. It would be good to get out of the house and try something new. And going to a party for Oakville High kids might be good for me. A palate cleanse to get the foul taste of Covington off my tongue.

I went downstairs and found Mom and Reg watching TV. Nat the brat was at her friend's house for a sleepover, and it was their night to chill out and ignore the fact that they had kids, so they'd be more inclined to give me a wide berth.

"Can I go study with Penny tonight?" I asked. I was immediately sure they'd see through everything. I felt like I was wearing what happened in the change room on my skin like an announcement and my humiliation painted on my face like a scarlet A.

Dirty Kingdom 53

Reg looked me up and down, and I felt even more exposed. I'd never liked the way he looked at me when my mom wasn't paying attention. As if he knew what I looked like without any clothes. As if he'd seen me like that.

"Where are you going?" he asked. Mom was cuddled under his arm and barely looked away from the show they were watching. Something about living in the bush in Alaska or whatever boring married people watched on their nights in. The TV was much too big for our cramped living room, and Reg had bought this ridiculous leather recliner couch that made the space even more claustrophobic.

I never hung out in there anymore, not that I'd felt welcome in the first place, but now there was nowhere for me to sit with them. It was for the best for all of us. I preferred to keep my family interactions to a minimum these days.

"The library. They are open late tonight. And then maybe we'll grab a pizza after that," I said. It sounded so lame there was no way they were going to let me go.

"Be careful. Don't want to get fat," Reg said and raised his eyebrow. "Although a little meat in the right spots might be good for you."

I shuddered in disgust and noticed the drink in his hand. Whiskey on the rocks. Just how he liked it. I looked at my mom for her response. She also had a drink, something hard and fruity, and she waved her free hand and said, "Sure. Just don't be out all night."

"Thanks," I replied and bolted out of there before Reg had a chance to keep grilling me for information or creep me out even more. It fucking sucked sometimes that he was a creep right under Mom's nose, and she was either too wrapped up in herself or too hammered on fruity booze to care. I couldn't wait to get out of there. I couldn't wait for college to start. Just a few more months... I could make it if I kept my head down and controlled the anxious anger that flowed through my veins.

Penny pulled up shortly after I got dressed. I had decided to go all out and show my old high school classmates that maybe Covington had done something to change me. I watched a makeup tutorial and did dark cat eyes with liner and glittery shadow. I wore my hair loose and flowing in curls down my back.

I borrowed one of the brat's little tee shirts that was obviously too small but made my breasts look way bigger than they actually were. It had some anime girl on the front and was super cute in pink. I pulled on a pair of black jeans, black runners, and I was done. I looked better than I normally did. I even felt great, and that was unusual.

I ran downstairs, said goodbye before Mom and Reg noticed what I was wearing, and climbed into the passenger seat of the minivan. Penny was hyped up and looked dangerously sexy in a little black dress and tall boots. We turned up the music, and we were soon singing at the top of our lungs to Olivia Rodrigo.

"Like a damn sociopath!" we yelled to the lyrics and burst into laughter as she sped through the streets of our small town. The sun had gone down and the streetlights and buildings along the way lit up our journey, flashing and brightening the inside of the minivan, giving me hope that my life could be good. That my future was going to be okay. I would survive this last year at school and come out stronger for it.

If only I'd known that I would survive and would be stronger in the end, but not in the way I ever expected. Not in any way anybody would have expected.

$$* * *$$

When we walked up to the front of the house, there was a security guard waiting at the front door.

"Are you sure this is an Oakville kid's place?" I asked Penny. "It feels too rich, don't you think?"

"Her mother is an actress in town working on a project. She wanted to live in a smaller place and mingle with the locals to get into the role."

"This is their idea of a smaller place?" I asked and felt like a hillbilly with my jaw hanging open as I looked up at the massive house. It was three stories high and probably four times as long as our place, at least. It was done in modern, sleek architecture and had glossy, glowing windows from floor to ceiling everywhere I looked. Metal and cable verandas were in front of every room above, and the front doors looked like some exotic, expensive wood.

"Phones, please," the guard said and held out a container. "We'll hold them for you, and you can pick them up on your way out."

"What for?" I asked. "What if there's an emergency?"

"No photographs allowed inside the home. My client has a reputation to protect."

"I guess that's the price you pay for fame." Penny shrugged and dropped her phone in. I followed her and heard mine land with a clunk on the pile already there.

We were allowed inside, and it was packed wall to wall with every single kid I knew from Oakville and hundreds more I didn't know but recognized.

"Hey, check it out," Penny said when we found a free spot near the kitchen. This was her new friend's house, and the girl's mother, the actress, was out of town for the weekend. I still felt like a slack jawed yokel standing in there because the house was so nice. It felt like I was in the middle of an Architectural Digest photoshoot.

"What is it?" I asked, and Penny opened her cross-shoulder bag, showing me a little bottle of vodka. "I took this from my brother's stash. He'll never notice, and even if he does, he can't say a word about it."

"Genius," I laughed. "Pure evil genius."

Her older brother was in some Christian college down south and was the shining beacon of her family. If the parents knew he'd been drinking, he'd be in massive shit, so even if he did notice it was gone, it wasn't like he'd tell on her or anything.

"We need to find some mix," she said, and I followed her to the kitchen for some soda or something to add to our drinks.

The room was packed with kids talking, drinking, and dancing to the music blasting from the living room. It was heavy on bass and featured pretty dirty lyrics, but I liked it. As Penny poured juice in two red Solo cups, I sang along and swayed to the rhythm.

"Fuck you like an animal... feel you from the inside..."

I already felt fantastic before she handed me my first drink, and after I downed it in one gulp, I felt even better. I could physically feel the vodka spreading warmth from my stomach out to my limbs as I loosened up and let myself go.

"Another," I said and held out my cup.

"Are you sure? We should pace ourselves," she replied.

"Hit me." I grinned. "I need it to relax."

"And man, you *need* to relax, sweetheart," I heard from behind me. When I turned around, I found my former lab partner from biology standing there with a big grin.

"Stewie," I yelled and threw my arms around him. "How the hell are you?"

"Better now that you're here." He smiled and held up his beer in salute.

Penny handed me another drink and joined in with her second. She had always had a crush on Stewart, and I stepped back so she could get closer to him. We chatted for a bit when he asked the both of us to dance.

I followed him and Penny into the living room, but not before she and I downed our third and fourth drinks and the last of the vodka.

We swayed and danced with him until a slow song came on. I pushed them together where they were obviously interested in each other, and I really should have gone to find a seat. Maybe a quiet corner where I could stop my head from spinning.

But I didn't. I kept dancing to the slow music. I closed my eyes and imagined it flowing through my limbs, letting it carry my hands across the front of me like little birds, fluttering and tracing trails over my body.

I was so into it that I didn't even open my eyes when I felt somebody bump up against my back. I didn't open them when somebody else bumped into me from the front.

But I did open them when I heard Archer say, "I knew you had a tight body and nice perky tits. You look good, even for a white trash whore."

The thing was, he didn't sound mean when he said it. Not like Kingston, who called me white trash whore like a weapon. From Archer it felt like a compliment, a confusing, fucked up compliment.

I turned around and scanned upwards to find him towering over me. He was tall, almost six and a half feet. Ten inches taller than me, maybe even a foot.

His shoulders were broad and imposing, and he knew it. He was wearing a tight black tee shirt that emphasized the bulges of his biceps and clung to his chest, showing off his pecs.

His hair was dirty blonde and shaggy, like he'd be better suited on a beach in California riding the surf. His eyes were blue, almost violet, and had an intense piercing quality that belied his easy going persona.

I couldn't help myself. The way he was looking down at my chest left me feeling exposed and vulnerable, so I drew my arms across it and looked back at him.

"Don't be shy about your beautiful breasts, Ev," he chuckled. He reached down and took me by the wrists, spread my arms wide, and looked me up and down. "Besides, I've already seen you in a bra."

I couldn't figure out what he was talking about until I remembered Sofia. Of course, she'd shared the video. Her or any one of the other kids in the class.

I blushed and tried to pull away from him so I could

hunch over and disappear. I longed for the protection of my oversized hoodie.

Archer laughed, and I finally jerked my hands free to bring them back in front of me.

"I can't believe you saw that," I wailed to Archer. "Sofia is such a fucking bitch."

He wasn't even supposed to be here. Covington kids never made it to Oakville High parties. I didn't know how he was even allowed through the doors.

"Don't be embarrassed, pussycat," Valen said from behind me. "Your body is gorgeous. You should show it off. That's why Sofia is a bitch. It's because she knows you're hotter than she ever could be, even with all her cosmetic enhancements and designer clothing."

He reached around and gently pried my hands apart. I hadn't even realized I had them clenched together so tightly in my attempt to shield myself from Archer's heated gaze.

Archer stepped forward and stroked my cheek with the back of his fingers, and his smile was so warm that I felt calmer. More relaxed. He ran his fingertip along my jawline and down the curve of my neck and settled on my shoulder.

Valen pressed closer behind me, and I felt his body, hard and hot against my back.

It must have been the vodka doing the deed, but the moment I felt his lips on the nape of my neck when he brushed my hair to the side, I fell into the sensation and let it happen.

We all began to sway together, slowly and sensually, until I forgot where I was or that I shouldn't be doing that kind of thing. The anxious darkness that resided in my deepest heart was brought out by their double touch, and I couldn't help myself. I had to give in just that one time. I had to loosen my control and let myself go.

Maybe I was a whore after all, because dancing with the two of them was like dancing on the clouds in heaven. I never wanted to come down.

10

"You're so sexy and so fucking sweet," Valen murmured against my neck from behind, and I shivered. He was tall, as tall as Archer. He had the slightest trace of a British accent, and I remembered somebody telling me he'd moved here when he was ten. "Like a little deer coming out of the woods on shaky legs. Doesn't she make you feel like a wolf, Archer? Like we're going to devour her in one big bite?"

Valen was leanly muscled and had tanned skin, thick black hair like mine, and brilliant green eyes that sparked brightly when he was teasing me.

He was stunning, a gorgeous guy who looked like he could be a runway model or a dancer instead of a football player.

"She does," Archer replied and cupped my face in his hands. "She has this innocence about her that makes me feel like I want to tear into her. To ruin her. To rip her to shreds and make her scream my name."

I wasn't sure if they were threatening me with torture or pleasure, but either way, it did something to awaken the dark torment inside of me. I purred and let them rock against my body, envelope me with their desire.

"Hey, what's going on?" Penny asked, ripping me out of my reverie as she touched my arm. "Are you okay over here?"

"I'm sure she's fine. She looks happy," Stewart said and nodded towards the guys from Covington. He put his arm around Penny's shoulder and pulled her away from me. "Why don't we go get another drink and then I'll bring you right back to your friend?"

"She's driving," I protested, but Penny went with him and left me alone with the guys. "She shouldn't be drinking now. She's driving."

"She'll be okay," Archer said. "We'll make sure she gets home safe."

"She's staying at my place," I said, my brain slowing down as the alcohol and their hot bodies distracted me from what I was protesting.

"Don't worry about it. We'll handle it," Archer assured me. "You just need to relax, Ev. Just lean into it and have fun."

For once, I was a good girl and didn't fight his suggestion. I got back into the beat and the feel of the two of them against me, one in front and one in back. They weren't touching me everywhere, but their fingers were skating lightly along my skin wherever it was exposed, and it was so thrilling.

I felt sexy and powerful, beautiful and desired. These were all such strange states of mind for me, and I didn't quite know how to process them.

So I let my inhibitions take over and sunk into the

sensation. I allowed myself to feel it, to feel good, for the time being at least.

And then I remembered Penny. I didn't know how long it had been since I'd seen her. Enough time that the living room had cleared out somewhat, and the music had gotten louder in the back of the house.

I should check on her, I thought. I tried halfheartedly to pull away, but Archer switched it up, and the two of them switched places. Once more, I let myself sink into the feeling of being the center of their attention. Even if just for the night.

As the alcohol began to wear off, a growing sense of alarm took over. Penny should have been by my side by now. She hadn't come back. It didn't feel right, knowing Penny was off drinking more on her own with Stewart.

"I need to find her," I said and pulled away from the two of them. "I need to get Penny."

"Get her and come right back," Valen said. "There are a lot of losers at this party, any of them will take advantage of you if they can."

"I have to protect Penny," I reiterated. Even in my tipsy state, I knew I had to care for my friend.

"And we want to protect you," Archer said as I left.

I headed off on my own and saw Archer and Valen head the other way, towards the backyard where there was a large deck and a pool. I heard Penny's laughter coming from down a hallway, so I walked down it, looking in the open doors of several rooms before finding a bathroom.

I had to pee, so I went inside, locked the door and sat down. I finished up and was washing my hands when somebody began banging on the door. I opened it because I was ready to leave, but somebody pushed inside. It was a guy from Oakville High, but a year younger than me, so I didn't know him that well.

"Hey, you're Penny Pascale's friend, the weird one," he said and drunkenly stumbled to the toilet. He pulled out his dick and peed in front of me, like it was the most normal thing in the world.

"Yeah, I am," I said. "Her friend, not weird." I rolled my eyes and turned to leave.

"She's putting on quite a show upstairs," he laughed. "Man, I didn't think a chick like her could take that much dick at once."

"What do you mean?" I yelled, sobering up quickly.

"Up the stairs. Go on, take a look and find out what a freak you're friends with."

I ran from the bathroom and into the living room with his mocking laughter ringing in my ears. All around me there were crowds of kids from my former high school and many I didn't recognize. The party seemed to have doubled in size, with people pushing against me as I shoved my way through.

I finally found the sleek modern metal and glass stairs to the upper floor and raced up, passing kids along the way, some talking, some making out, and one girl dancing sexily on the stairs with three guys below her, egging her on.

Everywhere I looked felt chaotic, and I realized I was in way over my head. The feelings I had when I was dancing with Archer and Valen were gone. I was powerless here, like a salmon trying to swim upstream, fighting the current. I was being swept by the energy and movement of the crowd, pulled away from who I once had been. After a struggle, lots of swearing, and a

Dirty Kingdom 65

couple guys grabbing my ass, I made it down the hallway at last.

I heard them chanting her name before I saw her. "Penny! Penny! Penny!"

There were so many guys in what appeared to be the master bedroom. It was huge, modern, and stylishly decorated, but it was packed with high schoolers.

Penny was on a king-sized bed in the centre of it all. Her top was off, and her skirt was pushed up over her hips. She seemed almost passed out, with her head lolling to one side, but she had the ghost of a smile on her face. Just by looking at her, I could tell she wasn't even fully aware of what was happening.

"Penny!" I screamed, and several guys turned towards me. "Get off her!" I started swatting at them randomly, and a few of them laughed at me or tried to push me onto the bed with her.

There were several guys already on the bed, kneeling around her with their pants down already. One of them was between her thighs and he was pumping furiously, fucking my barely conscious friend. His white ass cheeks bounced and divoted as he plowed into her virgin body.

Rage washed over me, and despite me being drunk, I wanted to hurt them all for what they were doing to her.

Another boy was at her head, intent on shoving his semi-flaccid cock into her mouth. His friends cheered him on and laughed loudly as he failed then tried again. Several other guys now had their dicks in their hands and were jerking them furiously in some group effort to assault my best friend.

The horror of it all settled in harder, and the more I

looked, the more disgusted I became. I could see cum from previous participants all over Penny's pretty clothes. The ones she'd been so proud of. The ones we'd picked out at the mall before school started. Tears streamed down my cheeks as my anger spilled over.

"Get off her!" I screamed and shoved a few of them to the side. I made it to the edge of the bed and tugged at her foot, desperate to get her attention or get her free. One boy grabbed at me, and I whirled, kneed him in the balls, and went back to Penny.

The boys pushed at me or shoved me hard, but I powered my way into the middle and tried to drag the guy from between her thighs. I clawed at him, but everybody just laughed. Their laughter was so loud and horrible in my ears. I felt too weak and ineffectual to help her. I was completely helpless in the face of their numbers and aggression. I frantically looked towards her, and she was choking on another boy's dick now. He was balls deep, mouth fucking her.

I didn't know what to do. I had never felt so powerless and inconsequential in my life, and it had been a life filled with feeling small and unimportant. But seeing her passed out with all the boys using her body like that triggered a primal rage inside of me. A flash of a memory—but nothing I could grasp—slithered through my head, and I hated every one of them for treating her like this. Like she was just a piece of meat. Like she was nothing. Not even human.

"Penny!" I yelled again and tried to climb onto the bed. All around me, boys laughed like howler monkeys, mocking me and cheering each other on. "Get the fuck off her!" I clawed at them, hit them with my balled-up fists, and spat in their faces, but they just laughed like I was part of some great cosmic joke at Penny's expense.

And then, all at once, they parted away from me and scrambled off the bed. The group split in half and cowered back in deference, their eyes locked down to the floor.

I turned around to see behind me and found the Kings, the three who had tormented me just days before in the change room, two of whom had just been making me feel so good. All of three of them came striding into the room with confidence and power rolling off them like thunder before a storm.

Archer, Valen, and now Kingston.

"They're hurting her," I cried and pointed at my friend as I fought off tears of rage. "You need to make them stop! She's not even awake!"

The boy between her legs didn't realize who had come into the room, so he was still going hard. The rest of them leaped off the bed like rats from a sinking ship.

Tears streamed faster down my cheeks, and the three Kings rushed past me. I saw all the other guys clear out, and I slapped and kicked at them as they passed me. I spotted one holding his phone out, recording the whole thing. He made a mad dash for the door, but Kingston's hand snaked out and caught him by the collar.

"Give me the fucking phone," he growled, and the boy blanched white under his bright red-dyed hair but shook his head. "I said fucking give it to me."

Kingston held out his other hand, and the guy went even whiter, if that was possible. He looked like he was going to shit himself right there and dropped the phone into Kingston's hand. Kingston dropped him, and the redhead scuttled away like a crab, desperate to escape before he was snapped in half.

Archer and Valen took the last one, the one between her legs, and lifted him unceremoniously from the bed. He was still half-drunkenly pumping the air with his dick out as they pulled him back.

"Hey, wait your turn! What the fuck are you—"

His voice cut off when he realized what was happening and who they were. Valen pulled his fist back and slammed it into the guy's face the moment they dropped him to the floor.

"That's for fucking a drunk chick. You never fuck a drunk chick!" he snarled. "Consent is key, you dumb fuck."

The irony of his statement wasn't lost on me, and I shot them all an acerbic look and raised my eyebrow. I couldn't help but notice how Valen called him out for fucking a drunk girl but not for fucking a girl with a bunch of other guys present. Their morals were so messed up, these Kings. But at least they were helping me save Penny.

The last I saw of the boy was him crawling miserably from the room, leaving a trail of blood along the pure white silk carpet. He was babbling the entire way, apologizing and begging them not to hurt him again. He slipped through the doorway, got to his feet, and stumbled out of sight.

I kept all of their faces burned into my head, though. I would never forget this night, even if I had given into pleasure and danced with Archer and Valen. Even if Kingston had saved my friend. It was still something I would remember so that I could get revenge on them all one day. If I ever had the chance...

While they sorted out the phone, I walked towards my friend, gingerly climbed crossed the bed, and helped Penny sit up. Her eyelids fluttered, and she said, "Hey, there you are. I was looking for you. My head hurts."

"I found you," I said. "Let's get you home."

I found a decorative blanket that had been knocked off the end of bed, so I grabbed it and wrapped it around my friend before I helped her to her feet.

"Let us get you home safely," Archer said, helping both of us out of the room. "This is the kind of bullshit you have to be careful of, Ev. You can't trust these kinds of guys, especially not looking like that."

He rubbed my back and put his arm around my shoulder gingerly, like I was made of spun glass.

"We'll make sure you're okay now," Valen added and rubbed my arm. "You and your friend. We'll take care of you."

"Why are you suddenly being so nice to me?" I asked and looked at each of them as Penny sagged against me. "What's going on? Did you have anything to do with this? Was this your plan?"

Kingston let out a low, cruel chuckle. He looked me up and down, gave me a cold glare filled with disdain, and held up the phone. When he'd saved my friend and seemed to help by grabbing the one phone that had somehow been snuck into the house, it felt like he was mine again. My Kingston. It felt good, I desperately wanted the old Kingston back.

But he wasn't. He was ice cold and hated me still, and I still didn't know what the fuck I'd done to deserve it.

"We didn't plan this, but we can't pass up the

opportunity," Valen said, and he had the decency to look somewhat contrite. "Sorry, buttercup, it had to be done."

"What opportunity? What the hell are you talking about? Did you fucking set this up? Answer me!" I screamed, incredulous that they would betray me like that. "Why would you do such a thing? She never hurt you. She doesn't even go to Covington."

"We didn't do this," Archer said, gesturing to the bed. "We didn't arrange this fucking disgrace. But we're keeping the phone, and we're keeping you quiet."

"Why do you want the phone?" I asked, but it was starting to sink in what had happened. They saved Penny but saw the opportunity to trap me into submission. They weren't part of the crew from Oakville, but they were almost as bad if they kept the phone.

"Because we own you now, Everly Hayes," Kingston replied with a cruel curl of his lip. "If you want your friend's reputation to stay intact, you'll do what we say. If you want her kicked out of her crazy religious house, then feel free to tell me to fuck off."

Our eyes locked hard in a battle of wills as I processed what he'd said. They had the evidence of Penny's assault on that phone, and in a normal world, we could turn it in to the cops to prosecute all the boys involved.

But in Oakville, nothing would happen to them, and everything would happen to Penny. Her life would be ruined, her reputation destroyed, and her parents would disown her forever. She would be homeless, and I had nothing. There was no way I could help her.

I hated that this was the reality of our world, and I

hated that they knew it enough to exploit it, and I hated most of all that Kingston Taylor had me caught in his trap. They were offering me my friend up on a silver platter, and I was being forced to accept it on their terms alone.

We were both bullheaded to the max, and neither one of us would back down, so Archer finally said, "We'll give you the night to think on it. Let us know tomorrow. Until then, give me Penny's keys and we'll drive you back home safely."

Kingston's eyes flicked to Archer's, and I allowed myself a brief moment of smug victory that I at least had a night of reprieve. I'd won that small battle.

It was the last victory I'd feel for a long time; I was certain of it.

Everything had changed, and if I wanted to save my friend, then I belonged to the Kings.

I just hoped that I'd survive whatever they had in mind for me.

11

We snuck in late and Mom and Reg were already asleep, so they didn't even notice. One of the perks of being boring was being trusted. Neither one could imagine the kind of night we had, and we were able to use it to our advantage.

I encouraged Penny to have a shower and threw her clothes in the wash while she was in there. I had already changed into cozy pajamas, and on the way out I ran into Reg in the hallway.

"I thought I heard something," he said, watching me from the doorway to the kitchen. The laundry room was next to the garage, and although it wasn't a huge house, we were some distance from the bedrooms upstairs.

And for some reason I felt immediate panic. Like I had to get away from him. The hairs on the back of my neck stood up, and I froze in place.

"I had to wash Penny's clothes," I said. "Too much pizza, I guess. She got sick."

"Be careful," he told me as he stepped out in front of

me, his face unchanging in the dim light. "I wouldn't want you girls to get into trouble."

"We're always careful," I said and waited for him to move out of the way. He was blocking me in, and although he wasn't a tall man, he was wide. He'd also been a football player back in his day and still had the body for it. Not muscled but thick.

"That's good to know," he said and reached out to brush a strand of hair off my shoulder. I shuddered at his touch but somehow managed to suppress it. "You never know where danger is lurking, especially for a beautiful girl like you, Everly."

"Thanks for the reminder," I said and broke into nervous laughter. "Okay, Penny is waiting for me."

It was like he woke up suddenly. His eyes widened, and he shook his head. "Yeah, sure. Get back to bed, kid."

He stepped to the side and finally let me pass.

I went back upstairs and found Penny already drying off but still pretty wobbly on her feet. I lent her a pair of pajamas and she fell asleep immediately on the floor, curled up in the sleeping bag, looking like nothing had changed.

But everything had changed. She'd lost her virginity, and she'd gotten into massive trouble. I still couldn't believe what had happened, and I half convinced myself that it had been a nightmare hallucination.

I fell asleep at last, but my dreams were filled with boys laughing and holding me down until I screamed.

* * *

PENNY'S CRYING woke me up the next morning. It was later than usual, after ten, and she was sitting on the floor hugging her knees against her chest.

"Pen?" I asked. "Are you okay?"

She turned to me and her face was red and streaked with tears. "What happened last night?" she moaned. "I have some flashes of being kissed and a bunch of guys around me, but I can't remember anything else. My whole body aches."

I realized she was lucky and didn't remember the night before. I was stuck for a moment as I plotted the best course of action.

And call me a coward, but I made the decision to lie about it. I couldn't let her know what had happened. And as long as word got out that the Kings from Covington were protecting Penny, none of the guys were going to talk. None of them would risk having the shit beaten out of them.

There was just one last piece of the puzzle to fall into place. That was me accepting their offer. Letting them take my friend under their wing as long as I gave into their demands.

"I don't think anything happened," I said, rubbing her shoulder in comfort. "We drank way too much, danced way too hard, and had to get a ride home. That's all."

"A ride? Oh my god, where's the van?" she asked, drying her tears on the back of her hand.

"It's here. Kingston drove us home, and Archer drove the van. Everything is just fine. You're probably sore because we were being such idiots on the dance floor," I said in a calm voice to soothe her.

"Oh man," she said. "I can't believe I did that. But seriously, thank god that nothing happened. Seriously, thank god!"

"Yeah, thank god," I told her and we kept talking like nothing had happened. Like I hadn't just offered up my body to keep her safe.

She was my best friend, after all, and I would do anything to keep her safe and happy. She wasn't thick skinned like I was. Penny lived in a comfortable world with supportive but extremely narrow-minded parents.

If they knew what had happened last night, her parents would kick her out of the house and excommunicate her from the church. Her entire life and future would come to a smashing halt, and she wasn't the kind of girl who could bounce back from it.

Penny went home shortly after I gathered her clothes from the dryer, and I had a long shower to wash away all the tension and fear that coated me like a slick of oil.

I spent the rest of the day inside studying and planning my future and my great escape from this place, from my family and the Kings. It was the only thing that kept me going.

* * *

I WENT to Penny's on Sunday just to check on her, but she wasn't her usual bubbly self. She questioned me again, asked me about what had happened at the party, but I still couldn't tell her. It would break her heart and change who she thought she was. I just kept her company. The following week was terrifying. I kept waiting for one of the guys to jump out and force me to do weird shit for them at any time.

But they all ignored me like I didn't exist. Like I wasn't even on their radar.

By Thursday, I was relaxed enough to believe that I was going to be safe. That they'd forgotten all about me.

Sofia was still a complete bitch to me during chemistry class, but other than that... nothing. I could handle her dirty looks, nasty comments mumbled under her breath, and talking shit with her friends to the point that they'd burst into giggles. I just kept my head down and tried to ignore her, the Kings, and the giant axe hanging over my head in the form of them owning me.

Kingston did his best to pretend I didn't exist, but on Friday, I caught him looking at me down the hall when I was on my way to my AP extra credit course after school. He was standing and talking to Sofia and her friends. When I passed by, he gave me a heated look that took me unaware. I suppressed a gasp, but the heat reached my chest and coiled around my centre all the way to my toes.

When he saw me notice him, he looked away quickly, and that was it. Our one encounter that week. I still didn't know what any of them expected of me. I still hadn't fully decided if I would accept their offer, but every time I spoke to Penny, she sounded even worse.

Was I protecting her by hiding what had happened? I didn't know. But I did know that if I told her now, she would probably never speak to me again for hiding the truth from her at first.

On Friday evening, I was lying in bed after dinner, scrolling through TikTok with Netflix playing on my laptop. I was watching some teenage romance movie out of the corner of my eye and zoning out in general.

I heard voices downstairs, and after a few minutes, my mom knocked lightly at my door.

"Sweetie, Kingston is here to pick you up," she said.

I froze on the bed and imagined myself pulling my blankets up to my chin so I could hide under the covers and make him go away.

"Sweetie?" she asked. "Can I come in?"

Before I could reply, she opened my door and stepped inside. She was smiling and said, "Why didn't you tell me you had a date with Kingston Taylor? He's *soooooo* handsome now. He grew up so nicely. He even got rid of those glasses for his lazy eye. He's really good looking."

"You mean he's hot!" Nat said, sticking her head around the door as she pushed past Mom. She had a grin on her face and a knowing smile. "Like, super smoking hot. He's so dreamy, I can't believe you haven't been talking about your date nonstop. Why didn't you at least tell me?"

Her words tumbled out all at once and her excitement was palpable. I was sure she'd be taking it all in so she had something to impress her friends with when she told them how Kingston Taylor was at her house. Nat the brat loved earning social cred.

"I didn't know..." my voice trailed off lamely, and I

realized how stupid that made me sound. I also realized that I had no choice. If he was at my house, he wasn't going to take no for an answer. "I guess I should get dressed."

"God, yes! You can't go out like that. Why didn't you plan this a little better?" Mom complained.

"I don't know, maybe King likes it casual," Nat said with a grin. She wiggled her eyebrows at me when I shot her a look of annoyance, and it occurred to me that my little sister might know too much about the birds and the bees. I'd have to talk to her about it soon before she did something stupid.

I chose to ignore Nat and reply to Mom. "I don't know. I guess I'll work on my psychic abilities. I promise you, I had no idea he was coming over."

She didn't look like she believed me, but she left me alone to throw together an outfit. Nat followed her, but not before making a kissy face at me and giggling like crazy as she trailed Mom down the hall.

I stood in front of my closet and hated everything I owned. I could have gone with something like my usual giant hoody and loose yoga pants, but I suspected Kingston had higher standards for me tonight. I had to act fast, so I chose a pair of jeans that clung to my butt nicely and threw on an off-the-shoulder white sweater. I was annoyed about going out with him but understood he wouldn't enjoy the homeless cat lady esthetic.

I grabbed my phone and headed downstairs to find Kingston chatting it up with my mom and Reg. The two guys were talking football, and Mom looked bored. As soon as I arrived, Kingston stopped speaking in mid-sentence and looked over at me.

"Finally, there she is," he said in a friendly tone, but

I could see the icy cruelty under his smile. "You're late, silly goose. Everybody's waiting for us."

I tried to give him a 'what the fuck' look, but he stood up and looked past me.

"You kids have fun," Mom said and walked us to the door. It was all so fast and all so surreal that I thought about running back upstairs and hiding under the blankets to avoid whatever the Kings had planned for me, but there was no way out now.

They had me exactly where they wanted me—wiggling on a pin, stuck like a bug, and no way to escape.

12

"This is unexpected. Why didn't you tell me to get ready? I mean, I'm right next door," I said when I loaded up into Kingston's stupidly lifted black pickup truck. I hated these kinds of vehicles, monuments to insecure men and losers everywhere. Destroying the environment with one belch of black smoke at a time.

And yet, once I was sitting inside with him, I felt proud and powerful. Especially when he fired it up and the engine throbbed.

"If we'd warned you, you would have found a reason not to come out to play, Everly, dear," he said and smirked. "And that wouldn't be good for your little friend, Penny. Would it?"

"No," I agreed miserably. I glanced over at him when he was driving and sucked in a quiet breath when I really looked at him.

He had always been so tall and skinny but had always been handsome to me. It was always his eyes. They had always been a deep, gorgeous brown and filled with good humor and kindness.

Now, he had filled out incredibly well and barely resembled my old childhood crush. Especially in the eyes. They were still deep brown with flecks of gold when you looked close enough, but now they were flat and cold. They lacked humor and warmth, especially when directed at me.

His nose was strong and predominant, and his cheekbones were high. His chin was blunt with one of those little dimples in the end of it, making him seem even older and more masculine than most guys his age. His face was constantly screwed up in an intense frown that only served to make him even hotter somehow. And hair was black, thick, wavy, and messy all the time. Like he'd just been running his hand through it out of frustration. I wanted to run my hands through it.

But I think my favorite thing about Kingston, back then and now, was his mouth. His lips were full, and I still remembered kissing him, even after all this time. I still remembered how warm and insistent his kisses had become after the hesitation had passed. I could imagine they'd be the same way now with all the skill he'd picked up over the years.

"See something you like?" he asked, catching me staring at him.

"No," I replied and looked away. "I mean, yes. I mean, I like you. Or at least I used to."

I hated how he had me stammering with just a single sentence.

"Yeah, I was a real pussy when you knew me. You don't know me anymore, though. You know nothing about me."

"I know that. That's why I said I *used to*."

"So you don't like me now, Everly?" he asked, staring at the street in front of us.

Fuck, why did he do this? He sounded so much like my old Kingston sometimes that I wanted to ease his concerns and let him know how very much I liked him, even though he was a massive dickwad. The king of the dickwads.

But I fought it off and said, "I think you're a jerk. And I don't like jerks."

"Really? I would have guessed otherwise from what I've seen," he growled and gripped the wheel until his knuckles turned white.

"What the hell have you seen?" I scoffed. "*Nothing*, because I've done nothing."

He glanced at me again, shook his head as if he didn't believe me, then turned the truck down a side street in a really nice area of town. The houses got progressively larger and the yards more sprawling until the entrance we turned into led to a home that was set way back from the street behind tall hedges.

We pulled around a circular driveway and Valen was waiting for us in front of one of the largest houses I'd ever seen in real life.

It was two or three times the size of the house I'd been to the weekend before—the beautiful home that belonged to a movie star. Once again, I tried not to act like a dumb country hick by openly staring slack jawed at the beautiful estate, but it was hard not to.

Valen opened the door and grinned at me. "Hey, buttercup, slide over."

I unbuckled my seatbelt and did that, letting him climb in beside me. I was trapped in the middle between the two of them, and I didn't *entirely* hate it.

The two boys talked to each other as we drove, and I didn't pay much attention beyond the way it felt to be squished between two muscled, sexy bodies. They went on about football and girls and some fights they'd been to, until Valen said, "Did you tell her about tonight yet?"

"Not yet. I thought she could wait until we got to Sofia's. It is her plan, after all," Kingston replied with a laugh.

"Your chick is a bitch," Valen replied, then lifted his arm and put it around me. "Don't worry, buttercup, I won't let them hurt you."

"Hurt me? Them? What's going on here?" I asked, increasingly alarmed.

"You'll find out soon enough," Kingston replied, turning down another wide, fancy street to another beautiful neighborhood filled with homes ten times larger than mine.

We pulled up in front of one that rivaled Valen's, parked, and Kingston cut the engine. Luxurious, fancy cars of all kinds lined the entire place, and I could hear the sounds of a party coming from the house.

"Listen, I don't want you acting like a little bitch in there, okay? I've seen firsthand what you can take, and these girls aren't going to do anything to you that you can't deal with," Kingston said, staring at me. His eyes glittered black in the dark of the truck interior. For a moment, he sounded like he was on my side. Like his wall was dropping, and he was coming over to team Everly. But then he narrowed his eyes and they went stony flat again.

"Besides, I told you," Valen said, lifting my tousled, tangled hair to kiss my neck. "I've got your back."

Before I could protest, they opened the doors and Valen took my hand, pulling me out with him.

My knees were shaking as we walked up the wide marble front steps to the enormous double entrance doors. Kingston didn't even knock. He pushed one of them open, stepped inside, and called out, "Honey, I'm home!"

Inside was a huge foyer, all marble, glass, and expensive art, with a double curved staircase leading to the upper floor.

"There you are!" Sofia squealed and ran from one of the side doors. She leaped into Kingston's arms. He caught her, and they kissed in front of us. I could see their tongues entwine, and it made me sick to my stomach.

"We brought you a present," Valen said, holding my hand up. "Do you have her costume?"

"Oh yes, I found the perfect thing," Sofia said, dropped back to her feet. She looked me up and down with narrow eyes and said, "It might be too small for her because she's quite hefty, but I think we can squeeze the little piggy into it."

Humiliation flooded through me, overloading my senses and trapping any hint of a witty comeback deep in the recesses of my mind.

She motioned for me to follow her, and when I didn't, Kingston gave me a hard shove.

"She owns you tonight," he said as I walked away. "Obey her every command and we will uphold our end of the bargain."

"You didn't have to do that, dude," Valen said to Kingston, but we were out of earshot before I heard his response.

I supposed at least there was one person here who stood up for me.

"Okay, piggy, what size are you?" Sofia asked. "An XXXL? Do they even make clothes that big? You'd better smile once we get you dressed. You can't parade around for the Kings with a sour face like that."

I wasn't waif thin, but I wasn't as big as Sofia was making out. I had worried about my weight over the years, though, because my father's side of the family were all huge people. I didn't know them at all, but I'd heard rumors. I tried to stay under a decent weight, but I was muscular, and running gave me an athletic frame. I was curvy on top of it, but not stacked or anything.

I chose not to reply about my weight, but I did say, "The Kings? That's kind of a pathetic gang name when you think about it."

I wanted to convey how desperately ridiculous I thought they were and she was for clinging to their social standing like a little bitch monkey clinging to a tree branch.

She stopped, turned around, and slapped me across the face. I recoiled and raised my hand to slap her back.

"Go ahead and do it, bitch," she hissed and glared at me. "I fucking dare you. The Kings are run by Kingston this year. That's where he got his name in the first place, loser. He's Covington royalty. He might not have the money to back him, but he's got the breeding to give him a place in our school. Just because you live next to him doesn't mean you're worthy of them spitting on you. You're just the ride-along piggy who got into Covington for all the wrong reasons."

"I didn't want to come to your stupid fucking school, so back off, twat," I replied with my teeth clenched in anger. The dark wave inside me rose behind my eyes, and I envisioned myself punching her right in her perfect fucking face. I could imagine the orthodontic bill if I knocked out a couple teeth. At least her family could afford it.

"You are lucky we took your raggedy ass in, you stupid slut. Now shut the fuck up, dress up for the Kings, and play your part, or whatever they have on you will be exposed and your life will be over."

With that, she turned and flounced away, flipping her glossy, thick hair as she did. I wanted to scream at her or tell her they didn't have anything on me, but that would put Penny at risk if Sofia went digging.

So, I chose not to reply. It made me twitch with unspoken hatred for her, but Sofia didn't seem to notice. Everything she was doing was designed to make me feel like shit. I realized that the moment we were on our own. I just had to make sure she didn't get to me.

I followed her up a back staircase, and when she turned a corner at the top, we went through a door and were in what I assumed was Sofia's room right away. It was huge, as big as our top floor, and decorated in obnoxious, puke-inducing pink sparkles everywhere I looked.

We're talking pink, thick carpeting, pink furniture, a pink velvet bed with a pink comforter. And the cherry on top? Literal pink glitter sprayed all over her walls, like a unicorn bukkake party or some shit. God, I hated her so much just then.

"Okay, let's see what we can dig up," she said, and she walked into a closet bigger than my entire bedroom. She shuffled through a rack of clothes until she settled on something. She stepped back out and tossed it at me.

"Put it on, it's stretchy," she said and watched intently as I undressed.

I felt sick doing it in front of her, but I got down to my black bra and underwear and pulled on the little dress. It was skin tight and made of red leather. It had "whore" across the front of it in sparkling crystals and made me feel exactly like one in that moment.

"Ha-ha, perfect," Sofia laughed. "My sister wore it a few years ago to the pimps and hookers ball at her campus. The frat puts it on every year, and she got a lot of action in it."

"*Why* am I wearing it?" I asked in a shaky voice. I looked down and hated the way it pressed my C cup breasts out over the top to make them look double their size.

"You're our ring girl tonight," she said, surprised. "Did the Kings not tell you what's going on?"

I shook my head and fought tears. I wouldn't cry in front of this ghoul. I couldn't. I hated her too much to give into the pain that was breaking me up inside. I was made of tougher stuff.

"It's fight night! Where our guy beats the shit out of a fighter from Harrington Academy," she said.

When I squinted, not understanding, she sighed heavily and rolled her eyes.

"Fuck, you're stupid. This is about the Dirty Kingdom. You know, the underground fight club that basically the entire town—I mean, hell, the entire *state* —is involved in? You know, the last fight is at the end of the year. The fight that determines which school takes home the entire prize—for fighting, football, academics, you name it. If you win Dirty Kingdom, you sweep the state championship."

"I've never heard of it," I replied, confused by what she was saying. I'd heard rumors throughout town, but I'd always believed they were just that. Rumors. Reg and Mom had fought a couple times over Reg's gambling debts to do with fights, but I'd always assumed it was MMA or something else like that.

To find out the rumors were true all along and there was some kind of fight club being run right under my nose felt strange. Like I'd been sleepwalking through my own life. Or I was the victim of a colossal joke that I was just now finding out the punchline to.

I didn't like it.

"Of course, you haven't heard anything about it," she spat and grabbed my wrist, yanking me hard. "You're a nobody. I don't have time to spell it out for you. They're calling your name downstairs. Hurry up, piggy, your fans are waiting."

With that, she shoved me out of her room towards the stairs, and I had no other option than to go back down.

What I was moving towards, I had no idea.

But I did know I was terrified.

13

She was right about people waiting for me. I wouldn't call them my fans, per se, but the crowd was made up of hundreds of young people. Those from Covington were closest to the house, but I recognized some kids from Oakville High and others from surrounding towns. As we were descending to the first floor and out to the backyard, I heard them chanting, "Covington tribute, Covington tribute, Covington tribute," repeatedly. I didn't know what they meant by it, but I knew they were talking about me.

I even heard a few calls of 'whore' from the crowd, and a couple of people yelled, 'white trash' before I even got there. I felt sick to my stomach. I'd never had so many sets of eyes locked on me, expecting I would fail. I never knew so many people hated me.

"What am I supposed to do?" I asked Sofia, leaning towards her. She wasn't designed to be kind, and she hated me because of my tremulous connection with Kingston, but she was all I had to rely on at that moment.

She released my wrist and pushed me away from her with force. She sniffed sarcastically and said, "You're our tribute, of course. You just have to stay near the ring and try not to look too fucking stupid. Can you manage that, bitch?"

Before I could reply, she gave me one last hard shove, and I stumbled onto a wide marble patio overlooking an incredible estate. All I saw were lush flowerbeds, an expansive lawn, a pool, and an enormous crowd of teens and young people gathered around a central platform.

The platform itself was a temporary structure, a constructed black wooden stage with a large metal mesh circle, like a cage, in the middle of it. Inside the cage were two boys circling around each other. They were sizing one another up, dancing on the balls of their feet like prize fighters.

It still didn't sink in what was going on, and I stood there dumbfounded with my mouth hanging open. I'd never been this close to fighting, and I'd never been in such a bizarre position. I had no idea what was expected of me.

"Get up there," some girl, one of Sofia's bitches, hissed at me and pushed me towards the ring. More and more kids joined in and directed me through the mass of them, hurting me and jarring me along the way.

They were chanting for me, but this time it was, "whore, whore," again and again until I reached the edge of the platform. It was as tall as my chin, and there was no way I could climb up the sides. There were no visible stairs, and I didn't even know if I was supposed to be up there.

I searched the people above me, those standing on

the platform next to the fighting cage, and finally found a friendly face. Archer was smiling down at me with his hand extended to help me up.

"Get up here, Ev," he said. I reached out, and he pulled me to stand next to him. He looked me up and down, raised his eyebrow, and said, "God damn, now this dress looks good on you. You look so fucking hot. Exactly how I like to see you—ready to get on your knees for me."

I didn't bother to dignify his comment with a reply, so I gave him a snotty look and asked, "What the hell am I doing here? What do you want from me?"

"We're testing you out to see if you're worthy to be the Tribute," he said. "Do what you're told, and if the group likes you, then you'll qualify. Simple as that."

"I don't want to be the Tribute," I replied with force, and I didn't. All around me, kids were talking, cheering, and yelling while the throbbing bass of the music carried on. This kind of chaotic environment set my nerves on edge. I longed for the safety of my own bed, where I could hide under the covers and mindlessly scroll social media on a night like tonight. I wasn't the girl doing things; I was the girl watching from afar.

"You don't even know what the Tribute is, do you?" he asked with a lazy smile. And then it was as if he remembered who I was. "Shit, you don't know! You're new to Covington. I thought everyone in the entire town knew, but maybe you are naïve. I guess we get to break you in and break you down like you're a fresh little daisy virgin after all."

I glowered at him, then I noticed a guy motioning for Archer's attention behind him. "Yo! Arch, we doing this or what?"

Archer glanced back, shrugged, and said, "Calm your titties, Max, we're getting there."

He looked again at me, smiled, and then locked his huge hand around my wrist. I didn't resist much, but still, he dragged me with him around the platform to the entrance of the cage.

"Here is our second entrant," he called out and pulled me inside with several other people. "Let you all find her worthy or vote her out."

"What am I doing—"

I was cut off when the announcer at the center of the ring, some guy I'd never seen before, held up the microphone and yelled, "Shall the fight begin?"

I backed away and tugged at the hem of the dress. My heart was pounding so hard in my chest that it hurt, and I felt like I was going to stop breathing.

The crowd of hundreds of high schoolers cheered so loudly that it became a roar that filled my head, drowning out even my own thoughts of escape.

He edged me over to stand next to three other girls. Two of them I'd never seen before, but one girl looked vaguely familiar.

"I'm in your math class," the familiar-looking girl said, and she glanced nervously around. She was wearing sweatpants and a tank top. Her hair was loose and dark blonde, and her eyes were hidden behind thick glasses. She was beautiful, but not in the way that these cavemen would find attractive. "How did you get picked?"

"They bribed me," I replied. "I know Kingston."

"They forced me," she said with a trembling voice. "I thought that Francis liked me, but he was just using me to drag me here. I didn't know we were coming."

She nodded to the boy I didn't recognize.

"Who is he?" I asked. "I don't recognize him."

"Last year's winner. He graduated just last spring, and I was so fucking stupid. I thought he really liked me." Her eyes welled with tears, and I realized she wasn't handling this very well at all. She was emotionally fragile, like I was inside, but she lacked that dark edge I contained deep in my heart, the inner strength that fueled my stubborn streak and sparked my outbursts when it couldn't be contained.

I comforted her, but she just got worse. Tears flowed down her face, and she blew her nose on the edge of her tank top when it started to run. I made a choice right then and there, for her for and every other girl who was tricked by these fucking ghouls, by the guys who pretended to like them just to lure them into places like this.

I decided to take the heat off her once I figured out what everybody wanted from me. I'd been dealing with alienation from my peers and my family basically my entire life. So instead of cracking under the pressure of everything they'd done so far, I chose to lean into it. I would take on these assholes head to head. I wouldn't let them break me, and I wouldn't let them break anyone else.

"What's going on here?" I asked, as Francis rambled on a bunch of statistics and numbers about the fighters and about each school's previous fights. It was more organized into an actual league than I'd initially thought.

"This is one of the preliminary fights leading up to Dirty Kingdom," the girl from math class said. "They are held every week, but Covington only competes when we're up, depending on the category. At the end of the year, the two highest ranking schools send their best fighters for the final match."

When she saw my confusion, she went on. "It's not a Covington thing or a local thing. It involves all the best schools from this part of the state. Everybody thinks football determines the champions every year, but in secret, it's the Dirty Kingdom."

"But what is it?" I asked. "What do they do? Just fight?"

"Gambling for the adults, and fighting for us kids," she said. "These bored trust fund boys have nothing else to do but beat each other to a pulp every year. And every year, our Covington guys come out on top. That's why they brought Kingston into the fold. Like his father before him, he's the best of the best. The toughest fighter around."

"Are you serious?" I gasped and wondered when Kingston's dad had fought here, when had he gone to school for Covington.

I looked past her to the other two girls. Both of them were beautiful but also not in the way these Neandertals would find hot. They looked equally terrified to be here. "What are *we* doing here?"

"Oh god, that's the worst part," she groaned. "We have to hype up the crowd and help call the fight. We're the ring girls."

"I know nothing about fighting," I said, glancing over to the center of the cage where Francis was going over the rules with the two competitors. I could barely hear him, and none of what I did hear made sense.

And before I had time to ask another question, I was sent, along with the other three girls, through the entrance to stand on the outside platform. Archer was waiting for me with a proud grin on his face. He hooked his arm around my waist and pulled me to him.

He ran his finger along my collarbone and down my chest to my cleavage, where he slipped it between my breasts.

"I can't wait to fuck your tits, Ev," he said in my ear. "You're going to be so beautiful when I shoot my load on your face."

I grimaced and let him paw at me. I didn't think I had any choice in the matter. Not if I had agreed to be their property, if I was accepting their offer to keep Penny's reputation intact.

"I want you to win their love tonight," he said, and reached deeper inside, moving over to cup my breast in his hand. The dress offered no protection, so I was forced to stand there and take it. I was so tense as he touched me, I could barely breathe.

He squeezed my breast then pinched my nipple and rolled it between his thumb and forefinger. To my absolute horror, my body betrayed me, as a shockwave of pleasure rocked through me. It was like there was a direct line from my nipple to my clit, and I couldn't help myself. My eyes grew lidded, and I leaned into him.

"Mmmm, I want to fuck you, Ev," he murmured in my ear. His breath was hot, and I was getting hotter. I could feel the bulge of his thick cock pressing against my hip as he got closer. "But I can't, so I won't." His voice was a pained groan when he ended his sentence.

He continued, though, speaking in my ear and rolling my nipple in his fingers. "Now what I *do* want from you tonight is your best performance. Shake your ass, wiggle your tits, and make sure they vote for you.

You belong to us, so you represent us. And I want you to be the very best."

I slowly understood what he wanted me to do. A ring girl, whatever that meant, was apparently like a fight club stripper who kept her clothes on. I was supposed to use my body to get them excited. All of them.

But something occurred to me just then. If I wasn't able to win the vote, maybe I'd be off the hook. I could earn my freedom by doing nothing to gain the crowd's support.

It was as if Archer read my mind. He leaned over me and pinched my nipple again, but this time cruelly. It sent a spark of longing through to my throbbing core. "Don't get any ideas," he breathed into my ear. "If you don't win this, we're telling your little churchie friend everything that happened to her. Shake your ass, or we'll tell her family too, and your friend will be ruined."

And like that, he reminded me of how high the stakes were tonight and that I was still on the hook, destined to obey their every command.

14

I DECIDED to say fuck it, and I worked my ass off. It was my competitive nature, the thing that shot me to the top of the class in every grade, in every subject. The very reason I was going for full ride scholarships to out-of-state colleges. I couldn't back down from a challenge or do something halfheartedly even if I tried.

There were two fighters, and Francis, the referee, left in the cage. The moment they signaled the beginning of the match, the fighters started pummeling the shit out of each other. I marched around the outside of the cage on the platform, shaking my ass and wiggling my breasts like I was a pro.

If those assholes, the Kings, wanted me to be a ring slut, I was going to be a ring slut. I was going to be the best fucking ring slut Dirty Kingdom had ever seen.

I wanted to make sure the girl from math didn't win by accident. I wanted to piss Sofia off by leaning into it, and even more, I wanted Kingston to see how much everybody else wanted me.

The most annoying part about this plan was that

every time I walked past Sofia hanging off Kingston's arm in the front row, she yelled, "piggy!" or "whore!" or some variation with all of her friends. She knew I was popular, and she wanted to cut me down every chance she got. She finally shut up when I ignored her vicious taunts and really shook my ass in her face. They all did, her friends and Kingston.

The cherry on top of that strategy was that every time I looked back, I caught Kingston watching me with a withering, dark look flicking across his handsome face.

Good, I thought to myself. Fuck him and fuck the Kings for what they're doing to me here. If I'm going to be sausaged into a literal whore's costume, I'm going to rub it in their faces every chance I get.

The two other guys loved it. Archer smacked my ass each time I walked by, and Valen ran up to walk alongside me, staring up under my dress and hyping me up.

"You wearing any panties, buttercup? I'd love to find out," he called to me. I smiled down at him and flashed between my thighs, not enough to show him everything but enough to make him howl with lustful laughter.

As I as it was, male attention made me feel powerful and so sexy. I'd gone my entire life without it, being the quiet little mouse that hid in the corners and daydreamed about a life with her childhood crush.

I'd never been the kind of girl to light up men's eyes, to ignite the fire I was seeing out there now from Archer and Valen, and with the boys in the crowd from every high school around.

And from one more guy, one from Harrington Prep, our rival school for the night. It was in a town a couple hours away and catered to the richest of the rich on this side of the country. It had a reputation for housing future world leaders, international scholars, and billionaires of all stripes.

He was gorgeous, and he was looking at me with that flame of lust in his eyes. He was wearing a Harrington Prep school uniform but had loosened the tie and had the top few buttons open. He had jet black curly hair that was medium length. His eyes were glowing green, and his face was that of an Adonis. He looked Italian or Greek, and like he came from money. You could just tell with some people. Old money pulsed in their veins, and it gave off an aura.

He was up on the platform with the rest of us, and he should have been watching the fight, but he couldn't keep his eyes off of me. I walked past him after I noticed his heated gaze following me and he said, "Hey, sexy, I'm Max."

"Hey, I'm Everly," I replied and suddenly felt too shy to converse.

"Beautiful name for a beautiful girl. I hope you win tonight. I want you as Covington Tribute," he said, and I kept walking past.

I checked out the other girls and wasn't surprised by what I found. The two from Harrington were trying to perform their duties, but they both appeared on the verge of tears.

The girl from my math class was huddled in misery on the edge of the platform, looking more and more like she wanted to take a leap off it and disappear into the crowd.

To the side of me, I heard a crack followed by a dull thud. I flinched, stopped, and looked into the ring to watch the fight inside. One guy, our Covington contender, punched the other guy hard in the side of the head. The Harrington boy staggered and wavered, almost to the point of collapse.

But he recovered and came back with an aggressive advance on our contender, punching him square in the jaw and flipping his head towards me.

Blood sprayed across my face and chest, and I felt a tooth hit my cheek. I screamed and jumped back, almost falling off the platform myself.

I couldn't help but keep watching and even cheered as our guy fought back twice as hard.

He slammed his fist into the other boy's face, then ducked low and did a sweeping kick to knock him off his feet.

Francis, last year's winner and the referee, stood in the center of the cage between the two fighters and counted down. Absolute silence fell over the gathering as we all watched intently to see if the Harrington fighter would push himself up off the floor.

He didn't, and as soon as Francis held our Covington contender's hand above their heads and announced him as the winner, the entire place erupted into a fever pitch of noise and chaos.

Our side of the crowd went absolutely bat shit fucking crazy. I don't know how many of them were drunk out of their minds or high on lines of coke, but they went insane.

I didn't move from my spot, and I could feel the blood spatter drying on my flesh, tightening where it had landed. I felt dirty, but also excited about our win, even though it didn't affect me at all. It was exhilarating to get caught up in it all. I felt part of something bigger than me for once in my life. Like I was finally involved with a group.

"We did it!" Archer yelled and ran around the cage to sweep me into his arms. "Those fuckers don't have a chance of beating us this year. Our streak will remain unbroken!"

He lifted me up, holding me tight, and then pulled me towards him for a deep kiss. It was unexpected, and I gasped before relaxing my mouth and letting it happen. It was my first real kiss as an adult, and it was in front of hundreds of people who thought I was trash. None of them seemed to care, though. They were all too caught up in their own celebrations.

Archer's mouth was hot and insistent, and his hands ran down my back before they settled on my ass. He cupped it and lifted me. I dropped my inhibitions and pulled my legs up to wrap around his waist, mimicking the way Sofia had leaped into Kingston's, and I kissed him back with hunger.

Archer kissed the edge of my mouth then drew his tongue along my cheek. I was confused by this sudden move when I remembered the blood that had spattered across my face and chest. He licked me slowly with long, languid strokes, like a cat. He licked all the way down to my chest, cleaned me up and moved back to my mouth.

"I'd suck your bleeding cunt, too," he murmured against my lips. "Just tell me when, and I'll make you feel so good."

I was a bit taken aback, but the idea of it exploded in my head. The thought of him going down on me while I had my period was oddly sensual. I was always so aroused and swollen at that time, it would feel incredible to have somebody else touch me.

"I will," I sighed, and his mouth covered mine again.

And yet, pathetically, I couldn't get Kingston out of my head, even when another guy's tongue was in my mouth. How ridiculous my brain was being.

"Don't hog her all for yourself," Valen said and joined us, much like we'd been when dancing at the party last weekend—that fateful night they'd trapped me with this Devil's bargain in the first place.

I should have been angry with them, but I wasn't. It felt too good at that moment to give into my simmering resentment.

Valen kissed the back of my neck and lifted me out of Archer's embrace. I wiggled as they both held me, but Valen pulled my face to his and kissed me, too.

His mouth was softer and less demanding than Archer's. His tongue was gentle and tender, almost hesitant, as if he was waiting for me to make the moves. He was so different from the boy he'd been when he'd forced the head of his dick into my mouth in the change room. The one who had mocked me and called me spazz.

Now, he treated me like he cared for me, and that was most dangerous of all. I could believe him if he kept kissing me like this. He could tear my walls down and get inside my head. And then he could break me down and break my heart.

Everything about this was a dangerous game, and I was playing with fire. I was in way too deep and was sure I'd wind up getting burned to ash at the end of it all.

Until that happened, I could ease up on my tense existence and allow myself a brief detour into feeling good. And I was doing just that until Kingston bellowed at us from the ground.

"It's time to vote. Get her down here before she's disqualified!"

I broke away from them in sudden shame and looked down at him. He glowered with a smoldering fire that would have incinerated the three of us if he could.

Sofia caught his anger, grabbed his hand, and glared up at me. "Come on King, let the piggy handle herself."

"Yeah, *King*," I sneered and stepped away from Archer and Valen. I adjusted the ridiculous leather dress across my breasts and let them pop up, making them seem larger. "I can handle myself. You'd better handle your bitch."

"Whoa!" Valen laughed loudly while Archer snorted and clapped his hands together to cheer me on.

"What did you just say to me?" Sofia shrieked, and her cheeks went bright red. She tried to climb up onto the platform, her face twisted into anger and disgust, but Kingston held her back.

"I said you'd better listen to your King and back the fuck off. I have a contest to win," I replied with a snarky glare. I flipped my long, thick curls over my shoulder and wiggled my ass all the way to where the guy from Harrington was waiting with the three other girls.

And I kept a smile on my face when I heard Kingston trying to calm her down. I'd gotten to the bitch, and knowing I had that power felt almost as good as being kissed.

15

I HAD no idea what to expect and still had no idea how I was supposed to win anything, or if there was even a thing to win. I was all fired up tonight, and even though I was still in the dark, I wanted to win.

It wasn't even that I wanted to make the guys proud of me or that I wanted to piss off Sofia. It was more that I liked the attention. If I was being honest with myself, like brutally honest, I was already fucking addicted to being the center of attention. I never thought I'd feel like this, but it was like being drunk, only a thousand times better. Having people envying me for my body and my looks, having girls get jealous of me for being up here, and having guys want to fuck me. There was nothing like it in the world. And I wanted more.

And speaking of hot guys wanting a piece of my formally boring ass, Max, the stunningly handsome guy from Harrington, sidled up to me and looked me up and down with a lascivious look. Like he could have devoured me with one long, slow lick.

"Well, hello there, beauty," he said, and I felt the

tension as he looked about to leap on me and devour me whole. "You are a sight to behold. That ass and those tits... Fuck, I almost fell off the side of the fucking cage every time you walked past."

I laughed and touched his arm. "That would have been terrible. I'm sorry I caused you such distress."

He chuckled and said, "The only distress would be falling away from you, sexy little thing."

I blushed, pushed at him flirtatiously, and walked over to stand next to the girl from Covington.

"This is horrible," she said and hugged up close to me right away. "I wish they'd just give it to you and get this over with."

"Don't worry, I'll take this," I said. "I know how much you don't want it."

"Oh god, thank you," she replied. "I would owe you, like, so much. My name's Christie, by the way. I'm a gigantic math nerd if you ever need any help. There's only one person ahead of me in our class, you know."

"I know." I laughed. "That's me."

Her eyes widened, and she gasped before shaking her head. "You're kidding, right? No, of course not. I'm sorry for thinking you couldn't be brilliant and hot."

"No problem," I replied and felt flattered at being called hot by somebody not trying to bang me, probably for the first time in my life.

I looked over at the two girls from Harrington. They huddled close together, and neither one of them seemed like they wanted to even be here. But at this point, they didn't have a choice. Covington and Harrington were each putting up their nominees for the year-end Dirty Kingdom Tribute. There was no way out. We were all in this together.

"Welcome to the greatest moment of the year!" Max's voice boomed across the crowd, silencing them all the moment it echoed over them. It only lasted a moment or two and then the crowd went crazy, chanting and yelling with chaotic bursts of energy until they all settled together on one phrase.

"Bring the Tribute! Bring the Tribute! Bring the Tribute!"

"Get on with it, Max," Archer yelled from behind me. He was holding a bottle of beer in his hand and he lifted it up as if in salute. "We've got to get this over with so we can get fucking wasted!"

"Calm your testicular nubbins, Whitmore," Max scoffed. "There's an art form to choosing the Tribute. You know that."

"We choose Everly as ours!" Valen yelled, and kids all around him roared in agreement. They were cheering for me, actually *cheering*. It felt incredible. It felt amazing. I couldn't believe I was so wanted, so loved by the kids who'd thought I was nothing just days before.

"Do you take Everly as your Tribute?" Max asked, facing the Covington side.

The screams and calls of agreement were overwhelming, and I was the clear winner in a resounding yes vote. Just to test the waters, Max held up the other girl's limp hand and said, "Or do you take Christie as your Tribute?"

The crowd began to boo, and I felt awful for the girl. Their reaction was awful. But she had a smile on her face as she flipped them all the finger on both hands, pushed Max away, and hopped down off the platform.

The last I saw of her, she was stalking through the

crowd and heading towards the house. I envied her freedom for a moment but was drawn back into the intensity of the competition within seconds.

Max got through the Harrington girls quickly, and soon it was clear that me and a blonde, pretty girl, were this year's Tributes.

I still didn't know what that entailed at the end of the year, but I figured I'd find out before Dirty Kingdom. Until then, I would enjoy the attention and have some fun.

And I did. I pulled the leather dress down lower on my thighs so it would stop riding up and exposing my ass, and I hopped into Valen's open arms.

It was a chaotic but interesting night, but I made the choice not to drink. I didn't want any repeats of the last time I was drunk at a party, although I was enjoying the aftermath of that at the moment. Valen and Archer, however, got hammered, and Kingston disappeared with the bitch, Sofia, just before ten.

I crept upstairs later on in the evening and found my clothes. Sofia's walk-in closet was so big that it had its own door to the hallway, and somehow I found it. I was getting changed out of the awful leather dress when I heard noises coming from Sofia's main bedroom area.

I knew what the noises were, and I knew who it would be, but something came over me and I couldn't help myself. I had to check them out. I just had to. Fuck, it was a strange compulsion, but I had to see.

I opened the closet door just a crack and peeked through. Sofia's head was bobbing up and down on Kingston's dick. He was lying on her bed on his back with one arm tucked behind it like a lazy god. His other hand was down, cupping her head as she sucked and moaned.

She moved to the side to get a different angle, and I caught a glimpse of him sliding in and out of her stretched mouth.

His cock was massive. I could see the head of it bulging in her cheeks as it passed her tongue and slipped down her throat. My eyes widened as I guessed how long it was. It had to be at least nine inches, and it was thick with gorgeous veins running the length of the shaft. My mouth almost watered as I craved it inside of me with him fucking my face or fucking me hard. Either way, I wanted him to take my virginity with his monster.

I took a step back and bumped into a metal shoe rack. Sofia didn't seem to hear it, but Kingston's eyes flicked to where I was standing completely still and they locked on me. Fuck, just like my clumsy move in the change room, I'd allowed myself to be caught by stumbling.

I prayed he hadn't seen me, and for a moment I thought I'd gotten away with it. But Kingston didn't look away. A smile curved his mouth, and he pushed Sofia's face all the way down his dick while staring at me through the open door.

She gagged and sputtered, but Kingston didn't let up. He smirked and said, "That's right, Evie. Suck my cock like the little white trash whore you are. Suck it good, you bitch."

His words were directed at me, and I heard Sofia shriek on his dick, but the meat of it muffled her voice. He kept her there, forcing her to choke on it as his eyes kept me pinned in place.

I was frozen there, unable to move, and paralyzed by

equal parts horror and fascination. I wanted to watch until he finished. The visceral animal part of me wanted to see his face the moment he filled her throat with his hot seed. But the sudden realization of what I was doing hit me hard.

When had I become this depraved?

I stepped back carefully and navigated my way out of Sofia's closet, through her fancy marble bathroom, and out the separate entrance into the back hallway just by the top of the staircase.

And then I booked it out of there like my hair was on fire, when in fact it was my heart that was inflamed and my pussy that was burning up with an aching need.

On the way down the stairs from Sofia's bedroom, I ran right into Archer and Max at the bottom. They were engaged in a deep conversation about something that had happened at the last football game, and I didn't want to interrupt. I tried to sneak past them, but Max's hand snaked out and took hold of me.

"You there, beauty, where are you going?" he asked, his eyes sparkling with interest.

"She was coming to get me. She wants to ride my dick later," Archer said, putting his arm around me like he owned me. And yes, I supposed he did.

"You don't want to ruin the Tribute," Max laughed and shook his head. "That's rule number one, even before them being so deliciously fuckable. I miss the dress, though. Why did you take it off?"

"It wasn't mine," I replied and looked from Max to Archer. "What's rule number one?"

"The Tribute must be a virgin," Archer laughed. "And you know how hard that is to find these days.

That's why we came after you, Ev. We knew you'd be unbroken."

"Why does that matter?" I asked.

Max gave me a sly look and said, "You really don't know, do you?"

I shook my head in frustration. "Why won't anyone tell me?"

"They were protecting you. At least they thought they were. You see, when the top two schools compete in the Dirty Kingdom at the end of the fight season, the winning school keeps the Tribute."

"You mean she has to transfer schools? That doesn't make sense," I replied.

"No, not transfer," he replied, and had the good sense to at least appear regretful. "I mean they keep her. The Tribute is handed over to the winning school's football team for them to use however they want for the final week after the Grand Tournament."

"A week?" I gasped. "That's bullshit!"

"Don't worry, beauty," he said and ran his hand down my back, settling it in the curve of my waist. "I'll treat you right. I'll treat you gently."

Archer swatted his hand away from me and protectively guarded me by pulling me close to him and draping his arm across my shoulders.

"Don't worry about a thing, Ev," he said and lifted my hair to nuzzle my neck. "The Kings win every year. It's a long-standing tradition. We only submitted you as Tribute because we knew we'd get you back. And then one of us will claim that virgin pussy of yours. Don't you even think about it happening any other way."

"Nice try, Whitmore," Max said, and his eyes darkened. He raked them up and down my body and settled, looking at me intently. "You might have had a good run, but you haven't seen our guy Ryker fight. He's going to fucking destroy your guy. He'll rip him apart."

Archer said something back at him, and the two beaked each other off for a couple of minutes before Archer pulled me with him in search of another beer. I just wanted a ride home.

I glanced back and caught Max watching me with that predatory look I'd come to know well from these boys. Although he was gorgeous, I didn't know him, and he seemed too confident that I would belong to him after Dirty Kingdom.

In this case, the devil I knew was far more manageable than the one I didn't. And I didn't think I could handle being sent to the guys at Harrington.

We had to win, or my life would be over.

16

I GOT HOME that night by catching a ride with a girl I knew from Oakville High. She was also a friend of Penny's, so I let her tell me about their week. It sounded like Penny was doing okay, but I couldn't exactly ask her outright. It might get back to Penny, and then my cover-up would be exposed and Penny's life would be destroyed. And that would ultimately lead to my scholarship offers being revoked.

So we chatted casually. I thanked her at the end of the night, and I went inside just before my curfew at midnight.

As I was brushing my teeth and getting ready for bed, Mom came into my room to talk.

"How was your evening with Kingston?" she asked, a knowing smile on her face. "Do we need to get you on the pill yet?"

"I went on the pill last year to regulate my periods," I told her after I spit and cleaned my mouth. "Reg took me to the appointment. He said you asked him to because you were busy."

Her face darkened as if she'd forgotten about it for a moment, but then the smile returned, and she said, "Oh yes, silly me. I forgot."

"You buy them for me, remember?" I said. "You're worrying me, Mom."

"Of course I do. It must be the wine I had earlier," she said and tilted her head back and forth a couple times. "Crazy old mom, hey? But still, tell me what Kingston is like on a date. I wonder if he's anything like his father."

"You've dated his father?" I asked with a laugh.

"No," she stammered and pressed her mouth into a thin line. "My friend Audrey from work went out with him a couple times, that's all."

"I don't know," I said. "We went to a party, and he basically abandoned me. But I had fun."

"I'm glad you're going out more. This is your time to live it up," Mom said with a smile. "And somebody like Kingston Taylor could be good for you. He doesn't have money, but he has connections. I'd like to see you use those connections to make your life better."

"That's ice cold," I replied, and I looked at her a little differently after that. "I want to make connections because of love, not to improve my life."

"Love is a business arrangement," Mom said and then shook her head. "You don't see it now because you're young. One day you'll understand what I mean."

She left after that, and I fell asleep thinking about how wrong she was. The arrangement that had me trapped right now? Now that was a business deal. But real love? It would come to me when I found it. Maybe I already had. Maybe it would be one of the Kings.

Or maybe all three, a little voice whispered in the

back of my head. I blushed in the dark under the blankets but touched myself at the thought of it. Three hot, muscled bodies surrounding me in my bed.

I drifted off after I finished masturbating, a smile on my face and a million possible futures in my head.

* * *

I WENT the rest of the weekend with the Kings leaving me alone. They had intense football practices or games or whatever it was they got up to for the team.

I texted Penny and tried to meet up with her at the library so I could spill all the hottest tea now that I had some, but she was busy. I didn't exactly believe her, but I didn't understand why she'd lie about it, so I didn't call her out.

I did catch Kingston watching me one time on Sunday afternoon. I was outside watering my mom's little patch of flowers in front of the house and he was outside washing his stupid lifted truck.

I ignored him on purpose because I figured the longer I didn't acknowledge watching Sofia give him head the night of the fight, the longer I had to maintain the illusion that I was a normal, boring girl.

It was tough. Every time I glanced his way, he was shooting me smoldering looks filled with knowing fire. He'd seen me. He knew what I had been doing, and somehow he knew how hard it had been for me to break away. He knew I was hot for him, and he loved it.

After a few minutes, I was going to scurry back

inside to hide from his knowing, cocky gaze. But I decided *fuck it*. I was going to give him a little taste of his own medicine.

Just as I made my choice, Mom and the brat came out and interrupted us. The brat had a dance recital in a town about an hour away, so Mom wouldn't be home for dinner.

"I left Reg something to throw in the microwave, but I thought you'd rather make your own," she said as she passed in front of my direct view of Kingston. "We'll be back at eight."

"Oh, for sure. Good luck, Natalie," I said and hugged her quickly.

"Thanks, Everly," she replied and giggled. "I hope you had good luck on your date."

"Natalie! More focus on your routine and less on your sister's love life," Mom snapped. Natalie jumped and screwed up her face behind Mom's back, and I laughed as they walked away.

They got in my mom's minivan, and for a moment I wondered if what Kingston had said was true. Was Reg married when my mom met him? Was she a home wrecking whore like I'd been told? And in the end, did it matter? I wasn't her clone. I could live my own life.

She and Nat drove away, and Kingston got back to shooting me knowing glances. I pushed everything else out of my mind and stood up straight. I turned off the hose and stretched my arms over my head. I pretended not to notice Kingston standing by his truck with a sponge in his hand, soapy water dripping on the driveway as he watched me. I tried not to notice how his muscles rippled and played under his tanned skin when he moved or how his skin glistened under the sun now that he had his shirt off.

And I definitely tried not to notice how well his shorts hugged the round curves of his tight, muscled ass or how fucking hot he looked when he stretched over the hood of his truck to soap it all down.

I was too hot myself, so I pulled my hoodie off over my head, carefully making sure to expose my midriff as my tee shirt caught on the hem and pulled up almost all the way to my breasts. I wasn't wearing a bra, and I let the bottoms of them peek out before I yanked it off and the tee shirt fell back into place.

I turned to pick up the hose, bent over, and let him get a look at how good my ass looked in the tight jeans I'd gotten as hand-me-downs from my mom, and then I stood up. I took a look over my shoulder and he was still in the same position, staring at me as I teased him.

I turned back and waved at him, a jaunty little swish of my hand, and laughed when he jerked his head away and looked down. He was trying to pretend he hadn't just been eyeball fucking me the entire time.

I flung my hoodie over my shoulder and took the three steps up to our front porch. When I got there, I looked to the right to check on Kingston again, but I spotted something in the living room window.

Reg was standing just behind the curtain, trying to hide himself in the shadows. On his face was a look of naked lust. And his eyes were locked on me.

I shuddered and opened the door, but when I got inside, he was nowhere to be found.

It happened so fast that it felt like I was imagining it. But it triggered such an intense reaction in my stomach that I wondered what else was buried inside of me.

What other secrets had my own brain locked away for my mental health.

I couldn't face any of it just then, so like a coward, I ran upstairs and locked myself inside my room doing homework until I heard the sound of my mother's van in the driveway and could feel safe again.

Nothing had ever happened between me and Reg, so why did I feel that way?

Would I ever know?

* * *

THE NEXT WEEK AT SCHOOL, Sofia was relentless. She was horrible to me every chance she got, and the way she stalked me, she made sure there were multiple chances.

Monday, she and her friends cornered me in the girl's change room before PE and roughed me up, mocking me for being the Tribute, trying to tell me all the horrible things that it entailed.

I tried to explain some of it to Penny that night on the phone, but how could I let her know that I'd agreed to their game without letting her know how they had gotten me there in the first place? She still didn't know what had happened to her that night, and I didn't want to be the one to tell her.

"It sounds like you're just really popular," she said, and I wondered if she was jealous of me and my newfound social status. I couldn't let her know that it wasn't earned, and that in the end, I was still just boring old me. Even if I did shake my ass for a crowd and make out with hot football players on the weekend.

On Tuesday, I splurged and bought an overpriced lunch at school. Mom had paid me for looking after Nat the brat, and I had some extra cash floating around. Instead of depositing it all into my college savings account, I figured I deserved something special.

I was standing in the drink line after paying for my salad. I had the empty paper cup and was waiting behind people for my chance to fill mine. I didn't even see her coming, but Sofia caught me off guard. She passed by with her little cheer team entourage, swung her fist, hit the bottom of my tray and slammed it upwards. My paper cup toppled over and hit the floor, but my salad bowl rose up in a perfect arc, flipped, and dumped down the front of me.

I'd gone for extra vinaigrette dressing that day. It coated the front of my hoodie, spilled down the collar between my breasts and left me smelling like a sub sandwich for the rest of the day.

And if that wasn't bad enough, the entire cafeteria had seen it. Every one of them had erupted into laughter and cheered for Sofia. My rage side simmered, but I knew if I lashed out I'd have another demerit added to my record, and that could ruin my scholarship chances.

So instead of standing up to her, I took the cowardly way out, although one could argue it was the sensible way. I went back to bagged lunches from home again.

This time, I wasn't going to eat them alone in the change room, not after last time, so I hid under the bleachers surrounding the football field and had some success on Wednesday. Everybody left me alone, and I even had a nice text chat with Penny. She was perking up and told me a funny story about her little fluffy white dog taking a big poop on the nosy neighbor lady's lawn.

Then on Thursday morning, I was walking to my locker when I heard Sofia yell, "Have a nice trip, bitch!"

She pushed me as hard as she could, catching me unaware and unprepared for when she hit my backpack with her full weight. I flew forward and landed on my hands and knees on the floor of the crowded hallway.

"Look at that, the spazz can't even walk!" one of Sofia's cheer clones chortled. I should have been embarrassed when the hallway erupted with laughter, but it didn't even hurt me by that point. I was over giving any fucks what any of them thought.

Later that day at lunch, I got away from my locker and the rest of the school really fast. I snuck through the small gym and went outside where I sat in my hidden bleacher spot. I was hunched over my lunch like a waif in a Dickensian film, eating my sandwich and humming a song, when Archer and Valen found me.

"I thought I smelled a sexy little whore down here," Archer said with triumph when he discovered my hiding spot. When he said whore, it didn't make me feel dirty like it did coming out of Kingston's mouth. Archer said whore like it was something to be proud of. As if taking a lot of dick was a special skill. Kingston said it like I was riddled with disease and deserved to die a slow and painful death.

"There's our buttercup," Valen said, his smooth voice full of warmth and seduction. He was like listening to melted chocolate dripping over a strawberry. All luxury and deliciousness. "Just when I was craving a tasty little treat, here you are."

They were sweaty and wearing gym clothes. They'd just been out on the field, running laps. I'd heard the coach yelling at the entire team, including Kingston. He'd been calling them pussies and saying they'd never win the playoffs with their weak-ass plays. High school football drama at its peak.

I could smell them before they even got close to me. They were pungent, like sweat and teenage hormones raging out of control. Like they wanted to fuck me hard, right then and there.

I can't even lie. It was sexy as hell. I wasn't one for sniffing armpits or anything like that, but damn. Being that close to two perfect specimens of masculine gorgeousness did something for a girl.

"Hey, guys," I said and got up off the ground. I brushed the grass off my pants and offered an awkward smile. "I'm just hiding out, eating my lunch in peace."

I blushed and held up my sandwich.

"That looks like shit. How can you eat that?" Valen asked and reached out to take it from me. He tore into the spot where I'd just been eating and chewed it slowly. "The only thing that makes this edible is knowing your perfect little cock-sucking lips were just on it."

He tossed it to the ground when he was done.

"Hey, that's my lunch!" I cried out and glared at him. "That's all I have."

"We'll get you something in the caff," Archer said. "You're too good to eat dry bread, Ev, darling."

He grinned at me and grabbed my wrist, pulling me towards him. "But first, I need a taste of your mouth. You're so sweet and delicious."

Before I could react, his lips crushed mine, and he was all hard mouth and demanding tongue, taking my breath away. His scent filled my nostrils, and the taste of the sandwich played along my tastebuds. His rock hard muscled body pressed against me while I could feel his cock growing with each pass of his slippery tongue. He made a growling sound in the back of his throat and reached down to cup my pussy through my yoga pants.

"Save some for me," Valen rasped, and stepped behind us, trapping me between the two of them like the aroused filling in their horny sandwich. "I love the feel of you, buttercup. I love the way your ass feels against my cock. I can't wait to fuck you one day and claim this tight little hole as my own."

His breath was hot on the back of my neck, and he shoved his hands down into the waistband of my pants, under my panties, and grabbed my bare ass. He pressed his hard dick against me while he kissed the back of my neck and the flesh there, exposed by pushing my hair to the side.

In the front, Archer pushed his hand past my waistband and under my panties to my bare flesh. I melted in his hand and felt liquid hot as he pressed his fingers into my molten slit.

He found my clit and began to rub it as we kissed, and I groaned, losing all sense of decently or self-restraint.

I could have fucked them both at their command. I realized that the moment his rough finger made contact with my burning, sensitive flesh. I was in heat and crazy for them. Both of them. I wanted them to fill me up and fuck me hard, like I was a fire craving their gasoline.

They somehow turned me so I was sideways between them, and Valen began to kiss me, but Archer's fingers stayed pressed against my clit. Valen's hand moved between my thighs from behind, and I gasped as he found my entrance. Not the hole he wanted to claim, but my virgin pussy. It was slick with hot juices, and he carefully slid his finger inside.

Archer's fingers on my clit, Valen's finger inside of me, Archer's lips and teeth on the back of my neck, Valen's mouth crushing mine with his passionate demands.

It was the perfect snapshot for a mind blowing first orgasm. Well, not *the* first. I'd masturbated like a crazy woman since I was pretty young. But it was the first time I'd orgasmed like that at the end of somebody else's fingers. By somebody else's hand.

And in this case, *hands*.

Pleasure bloomed in the heated core of my center, then blossomed outward in waves, flowing over me in hot lava flows. Like a volcano of lust exploding down the mountain of desire.

I felt it in every cell of my being, in every beat of my heart and every pulse of blood pumping through it.

And when it finally slammed head on into me, I let out a hoarse cry against Valen's mouth and squeezed my eyes shut. Bursts of light exploded behind my lids, and I couldn't catch my breath as it left my body in shallow, panting moans.

The two of them kept the pressure on, squeezing me tight between their hard bodies, their massive thick cocks pressing against me as I rocked my hips back and forth. I was greedily sopping up every ounce of sensation from each of them that I could glean.

And then, with a great shuddering exhalation of breath, I was done. I stood trembling as my body was drained of the tension, as it was released through each shuddering breath.

They stopped working on me and pulled out, broke away, and looked down at me like they were two proud teachers looking at their favorite student.

"What?" I asked, as they watched me with matching smiles.

"You're gorgeous," Archer said. He lifted his finger to his mouth and sucked it slowly, winked at me, and said, "Delicious, too. Like sweet virgin nectar."

"Yes, you can taste your pure juices. You haven't been ruined by any dick in there." Valen grinned after sucking his.

I felt my cheeks heat up, and I was searching my mind for some quick-witted comeback when I caught movement out of the corner of my eye.

I looked past Archer and saw Kingston stalking away, his hands balled into fists and a tense anger to his stride.

And I couldn't help but feel good that he'd seen us here. I hoped he'd watched the whole thing.

Payback, like me, was sometimes a bitch.

17

After that day under the bleachers, Archer and Valen decided to do something against the rules of Covington's strict social hierarchy. They took me under their wings and offered me protection in the cafeteria.

And they started buying me lunch. I couldn't afford the kind of fancy meals they made for the rich Covington kids (other than a simple salad), but they decided there were no more homemade PB and Js for me.

"We can't have the Tribute eating peasant food." Valen chuckled and slid over a tray with a plate holding a salmon puff pastry, a side salad, and a fancy, beautiful dessert on tiny cake.

"God, no, only the best for our little pet," Archer said and offered me a cold pressed blueberry and acai juice. The Covington catering staff had made it in the kitchen that morning, and you could taste it.

Everything the rich did seemed to be better, even their high school lunches.

Another thing the rich did better than any other

social class was bullying. The mean girls at Oakville High had nothing on the horrible bitches scrambling for attention at Covington, especially the queen bitch. And by that, of course, I was talking about Sofia.

It might have been the intense orgasm at the hands of Archer and Valen. Or it might have been becoming visibly attached to them in the school social hierarchy. But I'll admit it, I got a little bit too cocky. I won't lie, the afterglow of the big O lasted days, and their attention gave me an attitude that was bound to get me into trouble eventually.

And it did.

The couple of days after the bleachers, everything was okay. I was lulled into a sense of being safe because Sofia didn't have me in her sights. Valen and Archer were busy around me, walking me to classes and hanging out with me on breaks. They were introducing me to some of their friends, like other football players and their girlfriends, and I felt like everybody liked me.

Friday afternoon was a good reminder that Sofia didn't forget. She hadn't forgotten about me at all. She'd simply been lying in wait to get her chance.

It happened after the last class of the day. We had been in PE together, and she'd never shown any signs of bitchiness to me because our teacher was eagle eyed and extremely against any sort of bullying.

The class was starting a swimming section in the Olympic-sized pool on campus. I was thrilled for such luxury. I loved swimming and loved that the rich spared no expense for their precious offspring.

The school had given me a swimsuit when the year first started, and I had kept it in my locker since then.

We were all meant to wear the same thing, so none of us would show up in a string bikini or a Speedo.

At the time, I hadn't even considered the implications of what it meant. That one day I'd have to strip naked in front of Sofia and her friends.

I was horrified when I got into the change room and made this discovery. I waited until everybody else had finished changing and pulled it on in the in the corner by myself.

The suit itself was much more revealing than I was used to, and I didn't like the way it tugged up on my hips and dipped too low between my breasts. It was also black with hot pink stripes along the sides, giving me the illusion of curves where I normally didn't notice them. In my mind, it drew too much attention to my body, and even though I'd been fine as Tribute at the fight night, being seen at school was deeply disturbing.

I edged out to the pool deck after everybody else and stood in the back as the swim coach discussed our evaluations. By the time they got to me, everybody was already in the pool and paired up or in groups.

I was able to work with the coach and slip into the water without being noticed. It was perfect. I actually had an enjoyable time doing laps up and down without the hateful eyes of Sofia and the bitch crew on me. Coach was thrilled at my skill level, and she even told me I might make the swim team if I practiced hard enough. I was excited about that. It would look great on college applications and beef up my scholarship hopes.

After we were called out of the pool, I once again held back. I rinsed off after everybody else and smiled to myself when I got back to the change room and it was essentially empty. I could change alone. All in all, my first swim class had exceeded my expectations.

However, the only hitch was that it was the end of the school day, and I had to hurry to catch the city bus back home. I opened my locker and reached in to grab my clothes and felt nothing but smooth metal and a single, empty hook.

My heart lurched, so I opened the door wide, looked inside, and found it completely empty.

Confused, I stepped back and checked the number, assuming I'd gotten it wrong. It was mine, number 26, third from the end row nearest the toilet.

"Fuck," I exclaimed, and looked around for some clue as to where my things had wound up.

I saw nothing that gave me any indication, but I walked around anyway. I heard nasty giggles from the doorway, but when I looked that way, there was nobody there. I rushed over, looked down the hallway, and whoever had been spying on me was gone.

I didn't have my bus pass, my phone, my ID, my wallet, or my clothes or shoes. In short, I was fucked.

I took a towel, wrapped it around myself and walked around the corner to the lost and found bin. It was essentially useless, but at least I found a pair of oversized Nike track shoes, a ridiculously large pair of men's Gucci sweatpants, and a men's large Covington hoodie.

They all smelled musty and stale like they'd been there a while, but it was better than walking home in just my swimsuit. I went to my locker, grabbed my backpack with school books and water bottle, and decided the head home even if I had to hoof it.

I left the school, and it was almost empty. Nothing

cleared the campus out like a Friday afternoon. I thanked my lucky stars that all the Covington kids were gone, because I didn't know what I would have done if I'd been caught walking through the streets in these drab, oversized clothes. I mean, I know I usually wore hoodies and yoga pants, but these were over the top ridiculously large. But at least this way, I could blend in with other street people and nobody would notice me.

I hunched over, my shoulders tense from humiliation and anger, and slunk towards my neighborhood. The dark, angry part of myself vowed revenge, and I thought about it as I walked. I plotted all the horrible things I could do to Sofia and her friends, but my mind kept tracking back to one thing that would hurt the most.

Steal Kingston Taylor.

I had to do it. I had to crush her heart.

I kept walking in misery, thinking of ways to alleviate the pain of the oversized shoes that were surely causing a blister. I would have stopped and asked somebody to borrow their phone, but I couldn't remember a single number. Not even my mother's. *Fucking technology.*

Every time I heard the sound of a loud engine or saw a jacked-up polluto-mobile black truck, I would pray it was Kingston. I'd even take Archer's little sports car that was hard to get in and out of and didn't even have a spot for my backpack.

Or Valen's motorcycle, the one the Kings called his crotch rocket. He would speed into school on it with it buzzing like the vibrator he promised it would be if I'd ever climb up behind him. I would ride it like a champ right now, if it got me out of this mess.

I couldn't help but feel ridiculous and depressed. I'd been stupid thinking I was safe from Sofia just because the guys who were putting me up like some prize trophy for the Dirty Kingdom had fooled around with me and jerked me around by the heartstrings.

I was ridiculous, and it was time I got over myself.

I walked quite a few blocks and stopped when I got through the main street down the centre of our town. It was very busy this time of the day, and I waited at the crosswalk for the light to change.

As I was standing there, I stretched and pulled the hood off my head, watched a flower delivery van drive by, and then stepped back out of fear when a speedy little BMW came racing up and stopped next to me.

The passenger window slid down and the driver looked across the seat at me with a wide smile on his face. "I thought that was you. It's the Tribute!"

I realized it was Max from last weekend, the boy from Harrington Academy who'd been hanging around the fight at Sofia's place—and also the one who had angered Archer so much.

"Hey there, you found me!" I said brightly, realizing this would upset the Kings more than anything else. Maybe then they'd get a handle on their bitch, Sofia. Maybe Kingston would tighten her leash and keep her away from me if I sent them a message that other people wanted me.

"I wasn't aware I was supposed to be looking," he laughed. Behind him, a minivan laid onto their horn, making me jump. "Shit, I can't hold up traffic. Listen, do you need a ride somewhere?"

"Yes!" I exclaimed. "Please, you'd be saving my life!"

"Then I guess you'd owe me," he grinned, a cocky little smirk of self-gratification. "Quick, hop in!"

I opened the door and slid into the passenger seat. It was all smooth, buttery leather and ice cold air conditioning inside, and I exhaled in relief the moment the door closed beside me.

"It's so hot today," I said and dropped my head back onto the seat behind me. "You really are a lifesaver."

"Why are you out here and where are you going?" he asked, looking at the road in front of him. He wrinkled up his nose and added, "What's that smell?"

I didn't want to make it any worse by making myself seem like a victim, so I said, "There was a big spill in the lab. My clothes had to be bagged up and thrown away. These were all they could find for me to wear home."

"Was it your fault or are you a chemistry nerd?" he asked, and I froze in panic. I didn't know what to tell him that would keep him interested. I didn't even know why I wanted him interested, other than the fact that he was devastatingly sexy and clearly friendlier than the Kings and their push-pull bullshit.

"A bit of a nerd," I said with a blush. "I enjoy school. I know, not exactly something that makes me seem mysterious and sexy or anything."

"You're sexy enough to me, and I love smart girls," Max replied. "Besides, you're the most alluring Tribute I've ever seen."

"The other girls were pretty," I replied, but I couldn't help it. I liked that he was buttering me up. I was so easy, apparently, but it was rare I got that much attention without a bunch of strings attached.

"Pretty? Maybe. Not like you, though." He glanced

over at me with a cocky grin. "You're the kind of girl I'd fuck even if you weren't Tribute."

"Oh wow, how romantic," I snorted.

"It's true. I'm a blunt man, beauty. I tell it like I see it. Something I learned from my father. And you? I see you as mine."

"Don't you have to win the fight first?" I asked. "I can't exactly be anybody's if they lose."

I glanced over and looked at him from the corner of my eye. I liked the way his mouth curled into a smile at my flirtatious attempt to goad him into showing off.

He didn't take my bait. He might be slightly more mature than Kingston and the Kings. Max simply let out a dry laugh and shook his head.

"You don't know how badly I want to fight your guy," he said. "I can't. So I've found the next best thing, a hurricane in a barrel named Ryker. He's going to destroy your Kingston, and you will belong to me."

"I don't want to belong to anybody," I bristled.

"Why are you doing this anyhow?" he asked. "What do they have on you?"

That hit too close to home, and I winced before going quiet and looking out the window. I hoped he'd let it go once he got the hint, but he kept going.

"Isn't that enough reason to accept me winning?" he asked. "They're forcing you into Tribute. I would never do that to a girl like you."

I watched as we neared the turnoff for my house and I said, "Down this way."

I finished giving him directions and soon we were in front of my place before anyone was home, so I didn't have to face any awkward conversations with my mom.

"Thanks so much," I said with a smile when he stopped his car. "Maybe I do owe you."

"I'm serious," he said as I opened the door. I paused and looked back.

"About what?"

"You'll be mine. You might as well get used to the idea, because I'm going to have my way with you whether you like it or not."

For a moment, a dark look flickered across his face, and he appeared dangerous. Then it passed, and he was handsome Max from Harrington once again.

I shivered, nodded at him, and closed the door.

I walked towards the house, and at the steps I turned back to find him watching me.

Along with Kingston staring from across the yard.

I waved at Max and blew him a kiss. He sped off, and I fished around under the plant pot next to the door to get myself the key.

Once inside, I let the tears come, and their heat burned my cheeks until I found solace in the shower.

I had to be on guard at all times, everywhere I went. I could never let Sofia do this to me again.

When had life gotten so fucking complicated?

I had the answer right in front of me, but I wasn't sure if I wanted to face it.

Life took a downturn the day Kingston fucking Taylor came back to town.

And it seemed hellbent on dragging me down with it.

18

The next morning I was in my room when my mom yelled up to me I had a phone call. I was annoyed, wondering who the hell would call me on the house phone, when I realized all over again that my cell phone had been stolen.

"Coming!" I called down to her, thinking of a hundred excuses I could give her for why my phone was gone. She'd given me her old one, and I'd promised to take care of it or I was going to lose it for good.

It also had thousands of photos on there, but those were also in the cloud, so they weren't gone forever. But still, I wanted my fucking phone back.

"It's Penny," she mouthed as she handed me the cordless receiver. She raised her eyebrows, and I knew she'd ask me later about my cell.

"Hey!" I said. "You got my message!"

I'd resorted to old-fashioned sliding into her DMs to let her know I wasn't ignoring her if she tried to call.

"Yeah," she said, and she sounded off. I could immediately sense something was up.

"Are you okay?" I asked.

"I'm fine," she replied, and her voice was flat with no emotion. "Listen, I just called to let you know I can't make it today."

"But I haven't seen you forever. I feel like we haven't had time to catch up lately."

"Yeah. School is just so busy. You know."

"I do. I have so much to tell you. When can we hang out?"

"I'll shoot you a text," she replied.

"I lost my pho—"

The line went dead before I even got the words out, leaving me feeling rejected by my one friend in the world.

I thought about writing her another message, but what could I say? I wasn't able to tell her too much of anything, and I was sure part of her was jealous of the fact I was at Covington. Maybe she'd even heard about me with the guys and thought I was too slutty for her now.

I would never know because she had hung up.

"What was that I heard about your phone?" Mom asked, popping out from behind the door frame for the kitchen.

All the lies that had been running through my head seemed to poof out of existence at the same time. My mouth hung open and my eyes were probably something like a deer's in headlights.

But before I had to confess anything to her, the doorbell rang, and she turned her head towards the front door. "Who could that be?" she asked.

She walked over to the front door, opened it, and

Kingston Taylor was standing on our front porch, a bag in his hand and a warm smile on his face.

"Mrs. Preston," he said, using my mom's new married name and not my last name, Hayes. "I should come over more often, you look lovely."

My mom stammered and looked down at her pink crop top and tight jeans and said, "You're too kind, Kingston. But I appreciate it."

"Oh, I'm serious," he said, catching my eye and giving me a smirk. "You're seriously a MILF and a half."

He winked at my mom, and I could practically see her vibrating with excitement at his words. He knew exactly what it took to get on my mom's good side. Just a little old-fashioned, over the top flattery.

"Why are you here?" I burst my mom's bubble by interrupting. "What do you want from me?"

"Maybe he's here for me, sweetheart." Mom giggled and shook her hair out. She was in her late thirties and looked fantastic. Men hit on her all the time, but so far she seemed to be pretty loyal to Reg.

That could change when a hot guy like Kingston hit on her, though. Maybe she had a thing for *hunky studs*, as she liked to call them.

"That's a distinct possibility," Kingston said, winking at her again with this sexy little flirtatious grin that drove me crazy. Was I jealous of my own mother?

"Okay, okay," I said, and reached for Kingston's arm. "Let's get this over with."

I grabbed his wrist and tugged at it until he followed me up the stairs to my room. I wanted him alone so I could confront him about Sofia and get him away from my mom's flirting. Mom stared at us as we went up the stairs, watching until we turned the corner and got behind my door.

She didn't say a thing about me having a boy in my room, so I guess she knew me well. Or she assumed somebody like Kingston would never be attracted to somebody like me.

"What's this? Can't keep your hands off me?" Kingston asked as soon as I closed the door. "Do I still make you that hot, sweet little Evie?"

"Fuck you," I said and snatched the bag from his hand. I dug through it and found my clothes and my phone from yesterday. I dumped them into my laundry basket and grabbed an antibacterial wipe for my phone. "You need to put a short leash on your bitch. This kind of thing is uncalled for. Do you know what could have happened to me?"

I was seeing red. My hands shook as I rubbed Sofia's greasy fingerprints off the surface. It was dead, so I plugged it into the charger with an angry shove.

"What are you talking about?" he asked and raised his eyebrow. He seemed genuinely confused.

"Your bitch. Your whore. Your stupid cunt girlfriend. You know what she did to me. You were laughing about it with her," I snapped.

I crossed back over and looked up at him, thrusting my jaw out in my old friend, that simmering rage.

"Wait, what did she do to you?" he asked. "What happened?"

"Like you don't know. She left me in my swimsuit, alone in the school. I had to take filthy clothes from the lost and found and walk home. Max picked me up and gave me a ride, so at least I have somebody on my side."

"Max is not a good person," Kingston said in a low voice. "You need to stay away from him."

"How about you keep your cunty little bitch-faced slut away from me and I'll handle my own shit?" I spat.

He recoiled as if I physically slapped him, and he reached out to take my wrists in his hands. I struggled against him and fought to get free, but the more I struggled, the tighter he held me.

"Let me go," I exhaled in frustration. "Fucking let me go."

"Or what?" he growled and leaned over me. His normally warm brown eyes had darkened so much, they were almost violet, and they locked on mine in a challenge. "What are you going to do about it?"

"I'll.... I'll..." I searched my brain for anything to hurt him with. Something I could say that would anger him so much that he wouldn't know what to say about it. "I'll fuck Max! I'll give him my virginity so I'll be disqualified from being Tribute!"

His eyes narrowed, and I could see a small twitch form on the edge of each of them.

"I think we both know that isn't gonna happen. It's not possible," he said in a dangerous, low voice.

"You can't predict the future," I said and refused to look away. "Anything could happen. Anything at all."

"You must have forgotten what happened in the past. That little incident that brought us together, that made you mine," he replied, referring to Penny's assault. He towered over me again, seeming to grow several inches in height as his dark energy increased. "Is that what happened yesterday, Evie? Did you fuck Max?"

"No!" I snapped, caught off guard. "Why would you even say that?"

"Did you let him dip his finger in your sweet little cunt, like Archer and Valen under the bleachers?"

I wanted to protest and deny it, to tell him that would never happen, but I couldn't back down. Kingston's initial rejection when he left, the continued abandonment of what I'd thought was our budding romance, and now the way he treated me filled me with rage, and I couldn't extinguish it.

"I was going to deny it, but I guess you will never fucking know, will you?" I hissed and put my hands on his chest to push him away. He still had me by my wrists, and it only made me fall against him.

I lost my balance completely, and he caught me, held me upright, then set his blazing eyes on the swell of my breasts over my little tank top. "You said it yourself," he told me with a fevered intensity that forced my breath to catch in my throat. "You can't predict the future. Not even you know that."

"I know I'll never let you touch me that way," I replied, but even as I said the words, I stopped believing them.

He pushed against me in one sudden movement, and my legs caught on the edge of my bed. I fell backwards and landed on my comforter, bent at the knee, and flat on my back.

Kingston followed me, hovered over me, and for a moment I thought he was going to force my thighs open with his knee and take me right then and there.

I wanted him to. I wanted it so badly that I stopped breathing in anticipation of it. I wanted him to tear into me and force himself on me, to take my virginity from me like he owned me. Like it was his. Like it had been all along.

Instead, his eyes lit up with a devious sort of planning, and he slid his finger down my quivering stomach to the top of my shorts. He pulled them down, and I parted my own thighs, letting them fall open for him. For my King.

"You want this, don't you, Evie?" he asked, slipping his hand inside where he cupped the mound of my pussy. "You fucking want this."

I exhaled slowly and nodded my head. I didn't care if he knew. I wanted him to know, so he'd do something about it.

Kingston bent down and kissed me like I needed to be kissed. Exactly how I wanted to be kissed. My second time having a first kiss with him, and it was just an intensely hot as the first time.

Only this time, he knew what he was doing. And he cupped my face in his hand, the hand that had been holding my pussy, and squeezed it just tight enough to let me know I wasn't going anywhere.

He settled down on his elbow and kissed a trail down across my abdomen to the smooth plane where my thigh met my body.

He tugged at my shorts with frustration, his eager movements tangling his fingers in the buttons. I helped him pull them and my panties down so I was exposed to him at last. He was still holding my face in his hand while he was between my legs, but his hand fluttered down my cheek and moved lower. He settled on my throat.

He squeezed my neck and kissed my mound, then parted my slit with his tongue and drew it along my clit in one long, lazy swipe. My body ached for him. I ached for him. Everything was on fire for him, and his entire being filled my head with lust and desire.

"Oh fuck," I moaned, and he squeezed harder, cutting off my voice. I rasped out a hoarse groan, and he forced his tongue deep, stabbing my clit and sending my head into explosions of pleasure. Staccato bursts of ecstasy.

I wanted to cry out, but my voice was still constricted, so I let out as much as I could, nothing more than a whisper.

He was relentless, an expert in his application, and I tried to fight off the images of women he'd practiced his technique on before this moment. The others he'd pleasured with his mouth.

He was on his knees now at the end of the bed. He had my thighs spread wide, and he sat up, releasing my throat.

"I want to see your beautiful cunt, Evie," he whispered, his mouth slick with my heated juices. "I want to see your face when you come, my perfect little slut."

I tensed up at the use of the word slut. I didn't love the way he saw me now, not when I thought about how sweet he'd been back when we were kids. When our love was pure.

But before I had a chance to say anything, he was back between my legs, eating me like a starving man. His tongue was darting, and his rough hands gripped my thighs, holding them apart. The flashes of pleasure grew more and more intense with each pass across my swollen clit, and I finally couldn't hang on any longer.

I fell deep into the ocean of bliss and gasped as wave

after wave rocked over me, leaving me breathless and floating on the sensations flowing through me.

It was endless and beautiful, the orgasm I had on Kingston's mouth. My pussy fluttered and quivered, and I let out a low moan, like I was begging him to slide his thick shaft inside me and join our bodies as one.

The swells of joy receded, and the waves lost their peaks of intensity. Kingston slowed his long, deliberate passes across my cleft, and eased off his attention to my over-sensitive clit.

The waves in my head rolled lower and smoother until I came crashing back into my body and into my mind. I closed my eyes and let myself float for a few moments, just to experience the way he made me feel.

He finally stopped all together, pulled away from me, and gave my lower lips one last kiss. When I came down from my orgasmic high, I was completely limp, like a noodle, and I exhaled one last long, shaky breath. He kissed my inner thighs, and I felt him chuckle against me.

"Oh my god," I said and struggled to sit up, but my head was spinning and my pussy was throbbing. "That was..."

"Amazing?" Kingston asked and popped up from my pussy with a cocky grin on his face. He reached out and took my hand, helped me up, and pulled me to him for another kiss. I tasted myself on his tongue, and I smelled myself on his skin. He didn't seem bothered by any of it, though. He seemed to thrill in being coated with my juices. I loved how sexy it made me feel, as if I'd marked him as mine. Claimed my territory at last.

"Yes," I exhaled when I had a moment. "Insanely good."

He opened his mouth as if to speak again when there was a knock at the door.

"You kids thirsty?" Mom asked from the other side.

"Uh, yeah," I replied, and my eyes widened in horror. We pulled apart immediately, and Kingston stood over by the door, his face glazed and shining with my scent.

I pulled my shorts and panties up, rearranged myself, and sat on the edge of my bed.

Mom opened the door with a tray. Kingston surprised her by taking a glass, downing the lemonade, and saying, "Ah, refreshing. Just what I needed."

He raised his brow, smirked, and set his empty cup back on the tray. He gave me a wink, ran his fingers through his hair, and left my room, my scent covering him now.

My heart was still pounding when Mom grilled me on everything I knew about Kingston Taylor. She asked so many questions, I could barely keep up.

But unfortunately for her and for me, it seemed like I still knew nothing at all.

19

Life was different after that. It was like there was the time before Kingston Taylor ate my pussy and the time after it happened.

I don't know if he softened towards me after that, but he didn't seem to hate me as much as he had before. I got looks of heat and desire mixed with the occasional scowl instead of pure disdain or anger.

School went okay for me. Covington was a very well-funded place, and I did well in all of my classes. I added an extra course in World History to help my chances at a scholarship, which meant I had no free time at all. Time marched on, though, and even Sofia grew tired of harassing me.

It felt like the Tribute stuff and being bribed by the Kings had been a crazy dream, because none of them really talked to me that much through the month of September and into October.

Penny had been too busy—or too busy avoiding me—to see me at all, and I was lonely without her. It felt like I had peaked with attention from Archer and Valen, then Kingston going down on me, and now I was old news again.

I still craved the high I got from all their attention and wondered if it would ever feel as good as it did the night at the fight.

I was pretty depressed and feeling sorry for myself on a Saturday night when my mom knocked on my door. Why was I always depressed on Saturdays? My entire life, Saturdays had been my day of exhaustion, retreat, and depression.

This time, I was pleasantly surprised by the person who showed up. In a repeat of the last time, Kingston was in our house looking for me. He was standing there behind her, looking annoyed that I was wearing sweatpants and a hoodie on my bed while I stuffed my face with Doritos.

"You are going to lose any chance you have of keeping him if you keep doing this on date nights," Mom said through a clenched jaw. I could see how much this meant to her. She made her entire identity about pleasing men and hadn't been able to fathom her virgin daughter not dating in high school.

I mean, hell, she had me just after graduation, so she was probably expecting to be a grandma by now.

"He didn't tell me," I grumbled and sat up, brushing crumbs off the front of me. My hair was an insane mess of tangled curls all wound up on top of my head, and my makeup was non-existent.

"I thought you'd be ready," he replied, raising an eyebrow. "Didn't Archer tell you?"

"No," I replied, and stood up. "Nobody tells me anything."

"I'll leave you two to figure things out. You just have a good time, and don't be too late," Mom giggled and playfully pushed at Kingston's arm. "Unless you want to get into trouble with me."

"Not with you," he replied, being polite as hell. I knew what kind of thoughts lay beneath his charming exterior, and I was sure my mom picked up on them, too. Maybe he would fuck her if she was younger and not married. Kingston didn't seem to have a type. As long as they were willing, from what I heard about his time in New York.

She finally left, and I stood there glaring at him. "What am I supposed to do?" I asked.

"Whore yourself up. Make yourself look fuckable. It's fight night, Evie."

"I don't have anything to wear, though," I replied.

"You don't need to wear something as trashy as last time. That was for votes. Just look hot enough that every guy there wants to fuck you. That's all. It's not rocket science."

He walked to my closet and pulled it open. He dug around and tossed a couple of things out at me. One was a simple black dress that I'd forgotten I owned. I bought it a couple years back, so it was probably too small now.

And along with that was a bright red scarf my cousin had sent me for Christmas last year and a pair of high-heeled black leather sandals.

"These should do," he said. "Tie the scarf around your waist, it will look fire."

"Since when are you a designer?" I asked with skepticism.

"Since I know what makes dudes want to fuck you," he replied. "Hurry it up, people are waiting."

I didn't move because I didn't like the way he was talking to me. I put my hands on my hips and stared at him.

"Put it on, Evie, or your friend's little group fuck video is going viral."

A fist clenched in my stomach, and I remembered how I got into this entire situation in the first place.

He was right. If I didn't obey, she would be ruined. And it's not like we were even best friends these days. I barely talked to her lately, but I couldn't be the reason her life was destroyed. She would literally wind up homeless and without a family supporting her. She wasn't strong enough to survive such a thing.

So I did what any good friend would do. I squared off my shoulders and gritted my teeth. I glared at him and held out my hand.

"Fine, give it to me and I'll get changed."

He handed me the dress, and I turned to go into the bathroom, my one luxury as older sister, an en suite, but he grabbed my wrist.

"I don't think so, Evie," he said, and his voice flipped a switch to dark and dangerous again. It took on that husky rasp it had on the day he'd gone down on me. The day he'd tasted me. "You can get changed in front of me. I want to pick out your underwear, too."

"Oh," I stammered and opened my lingerie drawer. He drew his hand across them and settled on a bold black and bright pink combo my mom had picked out for me.

"These are sexy," he said and dropped them into my

hand. "Now get dressed before I lose my patience. People are waiting."

I slipped off my clothes and was naked before him in an instant. I was doing up the clasp on the new bra when I decided to poke him a little.

"Who's waiting, your little whore bitch girlfriend, Sofia?" I asked and scoffed. "You sure do like to jump when she yanks your chain."

A tic formed in his jaw muscle, and he didn't say a word. He just watched me with hooded eyes, like a hawk watching a little field mouse.

I pulled on the panties, doing it slowly because I might as well get the maximum reaction if he was going to put me through this.

"What, cat's got your tongue?" I smirked and shimmied my hips. "Or does Sofia own your mouth now, too?"

"She doesn't own anything," he grumbled. "She's barely my girlfriend."

"But she *is* your girlfriend," I scoffed and pulled on the black dress. My arms got caught, and for a moment I felt panicked as I struggled to get through the armholes. He reached over and helped me adjust it until it was settled on my body perfectly.

"No, just a girl I fuck," he said and smoothed out the front of the dress and adjusted the slash of red across my center. He tugged it up to look like a bodice, and I had to admit, it was fire. "This looks good on you. See? I was right."

"You have an eye," I replied and looked up when I was bent over to strap my sandals onto my feet. "Why are you with her then?"

"She helps pass the time, and she sucks my dick like

a pro," he replied without emotion. As if she could be any glory hole in any bathroom in any town. Like she was nothing to him.

And I found it infinitely curious. Finding cracks in his relationship amused me. It made me feel like I had a hidden secret that nobody else knew.

"Why are you suddenly so interested in my relationship status?" he asked me as we were on our way out.

"Just wondering, I guess," I replied, and I couldn't help it. My eyes darted down to his cock and then back up to his face.

"Wondering what?" he asked and grabbed his crotch, cupping it in his hands. "Wondering how much of this monster you could cram down your throat?"

I raised my eyebrows in shock and shook my head, but part of me was immediately imagining him standing over me, fucking my face and running his fingers in my hair like I'd seen him do to Sofia in her bedroom.

I wanted that.

God, what a slut I was. The Kings had chosen well when they'd targeted me. I had this entire secret world inside my darkest corners that was begging to be released. A hidden Everly that wanted to be used by Kingston. But it didn't stop there. I wanted to be used by his friends, too.

Of course it took an overachiever like me to take things next level. It wasn't enough for me to break out of my shell and fuck the football star, Kingston fucking Taylor. I had to lust after two more guys, making me a dick-hungry whore like my mother, apparently.

"You're thinking about it," Kingston chuckled. "But

alas, you'll have to wait for another time, Evie, we're late."

I loved it when he called me Evie. It always connected us through time back to when we were kids, when I'd been his little Evie and he'd been my little Kingston. He'd always hated being called King, and I'd never liked Everly.

We said goodbye to my mom then left the house. We got into his truck, drove to pick up Archer, and wound up at another ridiculous monument to American capitalism and greed in the form of a mansion. I didn't even know there were houses like this in Oakville. I guess people like me weren't invited to them that often.

And again, like Sofia's place, there were no parents in sight and a fighting cage had been set up on a hastily built black wooden platform on the expansive lawn in the back yard of the mansion.

"Aren't there any adults around?" I asked Kingston when we strolled in, moving through the crowd like we belonged there. Almost like we were royalty.

"Not a single one. This is Adam's place, and his parents are in Asia for business. We had the guys set up the cage here so we could fit in another fight before Christmas break."

"What about the neighbors?" I asked, looked around at the hundreds of drunken kids, taking note of the DJ booth overlooking the event at this one.

"Adults in Oakville don't give a fuck how we get ready for Dirty Kingdom," Kingston laughed. "You're not that naïve, are you? Who do you think is behind the whole tradition?"

"I don't know, who?" I asked.

"Fucking *everyone*," he replied, extending his hands

in a wide gesture. "From the bottom to the top and back down again. Everybody who's anybody has a stake in this tournament. The money being exchanged in betting alone would pay for this house and then some."

"People bet on the football games?" I asked. I'd heard about that already, at least a little. There had been an expose last year by our town newspaper about it.

"Yeah, that," he said. "But also the fight. The actual tournament. Dirty Kingdom. You have to get used to hearing the name because you're part of the game now, Evie."

"How are the bets made?" I asked, looking around for anyone I knew. I vaguely recognized some of the kids from my various classes, but the majority were strangers to me.

"Why are you asking so many questions?" Kingston asked, stepping back to get a long look at me. "You're not planning on telling anyone, are you? Because if you are, I guarantee they're in on this."

"No, not at all," I stammered, and I really wasn't. The only thing that interested me was how much pressure I'd feel at the end of it all. I knew the guys had all reassured me that they would never lose, but what if I was forced to go with the other school for a week? Who could I call for help?

"Good. Because nobody in this state, or maybe even in the whole damned country, would lift a finger to do a damned thing about the tournament. When I say it goes to the top, I mean all the way up," he said, and for a moment his face softened. His eyes looked like my Kingston from our youth again. He seemed tired. He ran his hand through his hair, ruffling it up, and sighed.

"Believe me, there is no way out of this. If there was, I would take you and we'd—"

"King! Babe!"

Sofia's screech burst into the bubble of intimacy that had formed around us, like a mini time capsule taking us back to when it was just Evie and Kingston, before the world became chaotic and dangerous.

Kingston's eyes flattened into that reptilian stare he kept as a mask, and I lost him all over again.

"Hey," he said, and held his arm out so Sofia could fit underneath. She wrapped her arms around his waist and shot me a look of pure triumph.

"Still trying to fuck my man?" she scoffed. "Too bad he wouldn't touch your dead fish pussy with somebody else's dick. And what the hell are you wearing? You look like a cheap slut."

"Yeah, I think that was the point," I replied and glared at Kingston for not standing up for me. Again. "And I wouldn't let your *man* touch me, not if he was the last dick on earth."

She opened her mouth to screech at me, but Archer and Valen saved me from the harpy by showing up, bringing a wild, chaotic energy with them.

"There's our sexy Tribute," Archer said, sidling up to me. "Hope you've been thinking about us the way we've been thinking about you."

"Of course she has. I'm sorry we've been neglecting you for football, my sweet," Valen said on the other side of me. "Come, let's get you a drink and get the night started."

I let them drag me away from Sofia and Kingston, and when I looked back, he was staring at me as she yammered away at him.

His eyes had gone back to my Kingston from our youth, but this time, there was something in them that surprised me enough to make me draw in a small, sharp breath.

They were filled with pain.

20

"What's happening tonight?" I asked, taking a bizarre-looking drink from Archer. He had basically poured a bunch of mix into a red Solo cup and topped it off with *way* too much vodka.

I held it to my lips and drained several long gulps, just enough that my stomach heated up and I felt that soft cocoon glow of happiness that came with alcohol.

"You'll be our ring girl again, gorgeous," Archer said. "So don't fuck it up. We have a lot riding on this."

"What he means is that you look really fucking hot," Valen added and touched my arm gently. "But this does add to our overall total point score for the final match. So if you score higher based on the judges' decision, then it benefits Covington at the end of the year."

"Who are the judges?" I asked, looking around for fight officials.

"Nobody knows," Archer said. "They hide in the crowd. It could be anyone."

"This is all really confusing," I said, taking another

drink. "I guess you have the advantage of growing up with all of this."

"Our families never participate, just orchestrate," Archer said and frowned. "You understand that, don't you? The division here between us and... well, you and Kingston. Those like you."

"What do you mean, *like me*?" I asked with dark, defensive anger. "Are you being an asshole or going the extra mile to be a classist piece of shit, too?"

"He didn't mean it like that," Valen said, soothing my flash of indignation. As I've said before, sometimes I reacted like that and I didn't know why. I couldn't contain it. At least I didn't run away and hide in a tree like I did last time. "What he meant was that our families are the founders, your families aren't. And Kingston has been training for this since he could take a punch. For years now."

"He's been fighting that long?" I asked, confused.

"Why do you think he never came back to his father's?" Archer asked. "His mother took him away to avoid all of this entirely. She didn't want him to follow in dear old dad's footsteps and compete for Covington."

"But he went to football camp," I replied, more confused than ever. I drank more, finished the cup, and watched as Valen made me another one.

"He went to football camp part of the time. He was training for this fight during the rest of his time away from school," Archer said. "He's been ready to destroy our competition since day one. He came out of the womb ready. He's our savage fighter, our Viking warrior."

"It almost sounds like you have a crush on him." I

laughed, but Archer's eyes shaded over as he withdrew his enthusiastic assessment of Kingston's abilities.

"I'm just excited to make money off this fight," he said, but I felt like his cover had been blown. Was Archer Whitmore bisexual? If he was, then why did it make me want him even more?

"We all have crushes on Kingston. I mean come on, you'd have to be dead to not realize he's the alpha male in this little group of bitches," Valen said with a sardonic laugh. He raised his beer as a toast. "Here's to the leader of our pack."

Again, I was as confused as hell. But it could have just been the vodka. Sometimes around these two I felt like I was watching something I wasn't supposed to see, like getting a sneak peek behind the curtain of a stage production.

I noticed movement on the platform near us and looked up to find Max grinning at me with the girl from Harrington Academy standing next to him. She was dressed in a short black leather skirt and white tank top and looked terrified.

"Hey, beauty," he called to me. "Get your tight little ass up here."

Archer nudged me. "You heard him, that's what you're here for."

Valen and Archer picked me up by the waist and lifted me onto the platform next to Max. The older guy, Francis, was inside the cage again, ready to emcee the fight. I still didn't know why these fights were happening, but when I looked out across the expanse of the lawn, I realized the crowd was even larger than last time. They were happening for some reason. It just wasn't clear to me yet.

"I hope you've been keeping yourself pure for me," Max said in my ear when he squeezed my shoulder in a quick hug. "You know, I think about it a little more than normal. I might be obsessed with it, the thought of taking your virginity."

I wasn't thrilled with the idea of being forced to go with him if Covington lost, but the vodka had heated me up from head to toe with a special concentration of hot desire pooling in my pussy.

I throbbed at the thought of being taken by him, like some kind of crazy bitch in heat. He was incredibly good looking and possessed such a cocky self-assurance. I couldn't help but be attracted to him.

I could almost see myself pulling a train, the urban legend that goes around every school from time to time. That one girl who fucked the entire football team. I wanted to be her for a moment, to release my inhibitions and have a trail of hard, thick dicks lined up to tame the darkness inside my head.

But the moment passed, and I concentrated on Max instead, seeing that he was in front of me.

"You'll have to earn it, like anything else in life worth working for," I purred and leaned into him. He chuckled and lazily drew his finger across my bare shoulder to push back a thick lock of hair. I hadn't done much in the way of makeup, and my hair was down and hung in loose curls around my shoulders and down my back.

"You look fantastic, by the way," he murmured into my ear, just close enough for me to feel the heat of his breath on my skin.

"Thank you," I said and almost told him about Kingston being the one to choose the outfit but I didn't.

Dirty Kingdom 161

I looked down into the crowd for him and his bitch girlfriend, Sofia.

I found him in the third row with a group of Sofia's friends and some players from the Covington Kings. He was staring at me with an intense scowl on his face as he watched me with Max.

So I let myself go again, let the vodka flow through me and energize me for the crowd. I hammed it up, shook my ass, and blew kisses to football players from Covington and other schools.

And the entire time I did, Kingston Taylor's eyes didn't stop tracking my every movement.

At last, it was time for the fight, and a muscled guy from Sinclair Prep (a few towns away) jogged up to the platform, leaped up in one bound, and strode into the center of the cage. The crowd cheered, and he walked around with his hands up, smacking them together and hitting himself on the chest. Very primitive and very hot.

All at once, though, the crowd went silent and parted to reveal a tall, broad shouldered, incredible specimen of male perfection. He had to be six and a half feet tall, had black hair with half of it dyed green, and had beautiful tattoos decorating both of his arms up to his shoulders and across his gorgeous chest.

He was a beast, and he was magnificent.

"Who is *that*?" I asked as he walked with purpose through the group of kids, looking on either side of him, occasionally raising his hand and smiling at somebody he knew. He was like royalty, our very own Prince of Dirty Kingdom, a man with greatness pumping through his veins.

"That," Max said with a sly smile, "is my secret

weapon. That is Ryker Fortis, and he's going to destroy your little friend, Kingston."

My stomach twisted at the thought of Ryker and Kingston going head to head. They were closely matched physically, but where Kingston had the cleaner cut bad boy look perfected, Ryker oozed dangerous vibes. If Kingston was playing with matches and dry tinder, then Ryker was like playing with a bonfire next to an open can of gasoline.

"He looks tough," I said, and as Ryker passed through the people gathered closest to the platform, they all began to talk and then cheer again. Like he'd been a minor god amongst them, they offered him deference.

"He is tough. I found him in some coal mining town down south," Max scoffed. "Can you believe that? Nothing but white trash and trailer parks and this scrapper who'd been fighting his way to survive his entire life."

I flinched at the way he said trailer parks and white trash, thinking of my own humble beginnings and happiest memories playing in my grandparents' trailer and with my friends from the park.

Even now, I was probably white trash compared to Max and the people he hung out with. Another thing about the very rich, they could afford to be judgmental and degrading to others. They could call down an entire group of people without even the slightest fear of reprisal.

"Now don't get me wrong, he's nice to some of us, but it was tough as hell to get him to Harrington on a full scholarship. He wasn't exactly our usual type, if you know what I mean," Max continued. "When push comes to shove, he's fucking insane. He's caused us a lot of damage and drama over there at Harrington. He's been fighting and fucking half the student population and inspiring the other half to line up for it."

"Have you done it or are you in line for it?" I asked and raised my brow.

"I'll never tell," Max said, and I did a double take. What the fuck, was everybody horny as hell tonight, or was there an entire level of sexual exploration happening just under my nose?

I didn't have time to respond because Ryker joined the other fighter in the cage and began to walk around with his hands up, riling up the crowd and beating his chest like a beast. His eyes were wild, filled with a crazed energy that was both so seductive and off putting.

He was sexy as anything I'd ever seen, but he kinda scared me. Maybe I liked that, I didn't know. I did know my body responded to the feral way he behaved, and my pussy vibrated for him, hummed a siren song for the beast of Harrington. I would have fucked him right then and there and asked you, "Kingston who?" if you'd told me I was nuts.

"You're up," Max said, not taking his eyes off Ryker. "Parade that fine ass around and get people cheering for the fight. Covington has nobody in this one, so you could get them cheering for my side if you'd like."

"Maybe I will," I said and found my eyes drifting towards Ryker as well. His charisma was so fucking intoxicating.

I glanced down to where Kingston was holding court with the guys from Covington and found him staring straight at me. Only Sofia matched his intensity with the way she was watching my every move with a sour expression pasted to her face.

I decided to pretend they didn't exist, so I wiggled my ass around the platform and really put on a performance this time. Then the fight started, and I could barely look away. Ryker was incredible. He was relentless with his punches and kicks and moved like a classically trained dancer when he was leaping away from the other guy's fists.

His gorgeous body was soon covered in a light sheen of perspiration that highlighted every ripple and every cut in his lean muscle. The other guy was dripping with sweat and having trouble catching his breath by round three.

By the fifth round, the other guy was sagging every time he backed up against the cage during a break or a moment of relief. Ryker was still hyped up and hadn't even begun to breathe hard. He was the epitome of peak physical perfection.

And as much as I was concerned for Kingston if these two ever met, I couldn't help but admire Ryker for all his skills. I felt like I was getting a look at one of the greatest fighters in his early years, like seeing a Lady Gaga performing in her high school auditorium.

There was just *something* about him.

I kept walking around, and the crowd loved me. For the second time in my life, I felt popular and powerful for a huge mass of people. Even Sofia's taunts didn't bother me. She and her friends called me a piggy, spazz, whore, all the usual, and it barely registered. I was too high on adrenaline and distracted by the man beast, Ryker.

"Yes, I told you," Max said as I came around and

Ryker went at the other guy with a series of brutal blows to the head. "I fucking told you he's my golden ticket!"

Max grabbed my hand, twirled me around to face him, and slammed me against the outside of the fight cage.

The breath was forced out of my body as he pressed himself against me, got half an inch from my face and said, "I told you this will be mine soon enough."

His smooth hand released mine and flashed down to the hem of my dress. He tugged at it, slid his hand underneath, and began to force himself between my thighs.

I snarled and shook my head, pushing at him, but there was no point. Max was just too strong.

"Let me go!" I screamed and shoved my hands against his chest even harder, but to no avail. He was insistent on taking what he thought was his. "Get the fuck off me!"

I felt the cage rattle behind me and somebody was thrown against it, almost hitting me through the metal mesh of the structure. Ryker filled my peripheral vision, and I turned my head to find him staring at me. He reached down, picked up the guy by his collar, and held him against the cage behind me.

"Let her go," he growled, and the crowd went silent. Max's hand pawed at me, trying to go higher between my thighs.

"I fucking said let her go," Ryker repeated himself, and I realized at last what was happening. He was talking to Max.

"Come on, Ryker." Max chuckled, but his hand stopped moving upwards. "We're all friends around here."

"You heard the girl. She said *let her go*," Ryker growled again, more aggressively. "If you don't release her right now, as soon as I'm done with this punk, I'm coming for you."

Max gulped, pulled his hand out, and stepped back, letting me go. I turned to face Ryker to thank him, and I gasped when I saw how gorgeous he was up close, but also how insane he looked. His eyes were on fire with battle lust, and he was covered in the other guy's blood. His chest and face were spattered in it, and he was rolling something fleshy around in his mouth. I glanced down and saw the tip of the guy's finger missing. Instead of gagging, I was in awe of his masculine strength. He was a warrior.

I opened my mouth to finish my thoughts and reply to Ryker, but behind him, the other guy was staggering to his feet. With some kind of sixth sense, Ryker knew it and whirled around, delivering a kick to the other guy's already bloodied face.

The other guy sailed backwards and landed on the floor of the cage with a bone cracking thud. He stayed down this time, his eyes glazed over and his breath coming in shallow panting motions.

Ryker stood over him, his hands raised in victory, and bellowed like a monster. The crowd fell into madness, screaming his name and going over the edge with excitement at his performance. Max sidled away from me, but I couldn't walk away. I was pinned to the spot, watching Ryker with awe.

He turned back to me, a wide grin on his blood-covered face, and said, "Get your ass in here, princess. I want you by my side as I celebrate."

I had no idea what his intentions were, but I did

know I wasn't going to tell a man like Ryker anything but yes. So I dashed around the side of the platform and joined him in the cage.

He was even more stunning standing next to him, smelling his musky scent and hearing the raw power of his voice.

I could almost feel the weight of Kingston's jealousy on me when Ryker touched my shoulder. And nothing else that night felt any better than that.

21

It was exhilarating to be next to Ryker, even though I felt sick to my stomach when I saw how defeated the other guy was. I supposed he'd clean himself up and be fine, but still, he was bleeding from his nose and the tip of his finger, and he held his side as if he had cracked a rib.

"What's your name, princess?" Ryker asked with a bloodied grin. His teeth were stained red from the other guy's spray.

"Everly," I replied, still gripped with shyness.

"Well, hello, Everly, I'm glad you're here. Have you ever seen how I celebrate my victories?" he asked, still grinning like a madman. On the floor in front of us, the other guy groaned.

"You're not serious, are you? You can't fucking do this," the defeated guy said, trying to stagger to his feet.

Ryker pushed him back down, and I shook my head for no. I hadn't seen him before tonight and had never seen him fight.

"Well, you're in for a treat, princess," he said, and the

grin dropped off his face and was replaced by a look of intense purpose. He flipped the waistband of his shorts down, popped out a protective cup, and handed it to me. It was still warm from contact with his body and I was still confused.

Then somebody in the crowd yelled, "Make him suck it!"

And I realized what was going on. Ryker proceeded to pull out a monster dick to match his monster size, and I couldn't look away. Just like him, it was glorious and over the top. It was pierced up the shaft and had a thick barbell across the tip. His elaborate tattoos circled his thickness in black Celtic designs and a scrolling snake. The head emerged at his cock head, its eyes the jewels on the ends of the barbell.

I couldn't help but stare. I was part horrified because I'd never seen anything like it—hell, I'd barely seen anybody's dick ever, let alone one like this—and part aroused because holy shit, it was impressive. I couldn't help but wonder what those piercings would do if he were inside of me.

"You've got the best seat in the house, princess," Ryker said with a grin as he began to jerk himself a little to get it hard. "How about you help me out here?"

I stood, unable to move or respond. My mouth hung open, and I wanted to touch it, to jerk him off, but I didn't know how the Kings would react. As much as I loved fucking with Kingston, I felt like this was going over the line.

I was saved from having to choose when the guy on the floor in front of us moaned, drew his face back in horror, and began to babble. He was begging Ryker to let him go without doing this, and I'd caught on what *this* actually entailed. I wanted to see it happen. As sick as it was and as dirty as it made me feel, I wanted to see Ryker force himself down the rich kid's throat.

"You knew what you signed up for," Ryker scoffed. "Every one of them begs me to go free, but this is the best part of the fight. In ancient times, warriors of many different civilizations would rape their enemy leaders to assert their dominance. I feel like this is letting them get off easy and letting me get off—a double benefit. It releases my pent up energy and forces him to fully accept his defeat."

I nodded and watched him stroke himself, unable to look away as his dick grew even bigger. It was massive, much larger than the ones I'd seen. Although where Ryker's had raw, feral beauty, my Covington guys had beautiful, cultured dicks. Large and impressive in their own rights, just lacking the carnival side show features that Ryker's had.

"Okay, enjoy the show," Ryker announced after he was rock hard and throbbing. There were huge groups of people gathered around the platform, watching and talking excitedly over this, the second half of the show.

The guy on the ground stood up but Ryker pushed him slowly to his knees. Tears dotted the guy's eyes, and he looked ready to bolt. He opened his mouth to plead his case again, and I noticed a missing tooth. He was a rich kid, and this felt justified. I felt like Ryker and I were on the same team, coming from white trash to beat down on the wealthy who despised us. This guy here was one of the fighters with money who did this for sport, not for survival, like Ryker. One who was soft and had been coached just enough to feel like he could hold his own in the ring.

I tried not to feel sorry for him, but he knew what he was getting into when he agreed to fight Ryker, apparently. Ryker was a force of nature, the kind of guy who was unstoppable once he got going, leaving a path of destruction in his wake. And he might wind up fighting Kingston at the finale of Dirty Kingdom. I tried not to think of it, not because I didn't want to see Kingston suck a magnificent cock like that (I kinda did), but mostly because I worried about his safety in the ring with an insane, brutal fighter like Ryker.

"You wanted this!" Ryker announced as he took a fistful of the defeated guy's hair. "This is what all you rich fuckers are after! You want to feel alive. You want authenticity. You want to feel like you're connected to the beating pulse of the planet. Well, rich boy, it doesn't get any realer than this."

And he thrust forward, pushed through the guy's lips, past his teeth and down his throat. The defeated fighter gagged, and a tear leaked from his eye as he took his defeat. Ryker fucked his face slowly, giving everybody a chance to get a good look. Phones were left at the entrance to this party, so nobody was recording openly, but I was certain somebody was getting this digitized for the archives.

"You might think I'm gay," Ryker said to me as he released the guy's hair. He was deep down the fighter's throat when he said it, and I loved the way he stood. His hips were thrust forward, but the rest of his body was so cocky, so relaxed. "But don't worry, princess, I'm not. So get your sweet self over here so I can play with your gorgeous tits."

"Oh, I don't think I'm allowed—" I stammered and

looked around. How was I supposed to tell a guy like Ryker no?

Lucky for me, I didn't have to. A strong hand snaked out and encircled my wrist. I was whirled around and pulled backwards into Kingston's arms.

"Keep your hands off her, she's the Tribute," Kingston growled and wrapped his arm around me protectively.

"What are you doing?" Sofia shrieked from below, next to the platform. "Get out of there! Let that hillbilly trash have the little whore!"

"You want a go at this?" Ryker asked Kingston. His eyes flicked down to the guy on his knees, sucking him off. "You'll get your turn at Dirty Kingdom, don't worry."

"Come with me, Evie," Kingston murmured in my ear. "Stay away from him. I don't want him touching you. I can't stand the thought of it."

"Kingston, get your ass down here right now!" Sofia whined. "Get away from her. Everybody can see you up there making a fool of yourself."

"You sure you don't want to help me out here?" Ryker asked me, fixing his eyes on me. He gave me a slow, lazy smile and added, "I could eat your cunt while your man there is admitting defeat."

Kingston tensed, and his arms tightened around me in reflex. I loved that his first instinct was to protect me, to hold me tighter, as if he could save me from the world.

"You'd do yourself a favor to know who the fuck you're talking to," Kingston said with a menacing tone. "Not only am I going to fucking ruin you at the end of the year, I'm going to claim the Tribute as my own."

"Kingston," Sofia cried out as if betrayed. "Uggghhhhhh!"

The noise she emitted sounded like a cow with a stomachache. I smiled to myself about it.

Ryker's eyes flicked down my body and back up to Kingston. "I'll bet she tastes real sweet, like peaches 'n cream. Am I right about that, Kingston Taylor? The man I'm gonna have on the end of my dick one day."

Kingston's hand squeezed mine harder when he mentioned eating my pussy, and I knew the same image flashed through his mind as well as mine. My legs open, me on my bed, Kingston's face buried in my throbbing heat.

"Fuck you," Kingston said with warning and stopped backing up. He stood taller, too, before he kept talking. "Chances are we are gonna meet up in the end, at Dirty Kingdom. And chances are I'm gonna kick your ass from here to Harrington Academy and back again. You'll never touch Everly. Keep your filthy fucking hands off her and keep her sweet little cunt out of your head!"

With that, he turned to leave the cage and took me with him, his arm around me as if I was some delicate little thing that needed to be saved from Ryker's devilish grasp.

I looked back once to find Ryker watching me, his mouth twisted into a gorgeous, laughing smile. Then he winked, looked away, shuddered, and shot his load in the defeated rich guy's throat and pulled back.

I got one last look at his monster before Kingston jumped off the edge of the platform and turned around to reach for me. It was softening but still massive.

The rich guy was hunched over on his hands and

knees, throwing up, and Ryker laughed. The crowd cheered. And for a moment I felt like I was in some alternate reality. As if I could blink my eyes and find myself snuggled in my bed watching romantic comedies online with Penny. I still didn't understand how I'd even gotten here.

But I was pulled out of it when Kingston turned, still holding my hand. Sofia launched herself at us and tried to jump into Kingston's arms. He stepped to the side and she bounced off him and right into me. He nudged her off me, caught me in his arms as I stumbled, and lowered me gently to stand next to him once more.

"What the fuck were you doing in there?" she screamed in his face. "Why the fuck were you defending this whore? This spazz? Everybody saw it, King. Fucking everybody!?"

Kingston looked down at her, curled his lip and said, "You need to back all the way off, Sofia. I'm done with your little games and bullshit. Everly is a friend, and I had to protect her from that fucking animal."

"That's right," Ryker laughed. He stood above us on the platform, his dick tucked back into his shorts and a cocky grin on his face. "I'm a fucking animal, and I fuck like an animal. Want to give me a ride, rich girl?"

He was looking at Sofia, and she glared at Kingston with incredibly hot rage. She looked up at Ryker, fixed a smile on her beautiful face, and said, "Sure. Let's go hang out and see what happens."

"You snooze, you lose," she spat at Kingston as Ryker jumped down and stood next to her.

Ryker only had eyes for me. He said, "Next time, princess. I'll have your pussy for lunch, whether it kills me or not. You'd better take care of what's yours."

He said the last sentence to Kingston, who twitched as if he wanted to deny that I was his, but he didn't voice it.

Ryker and Sofia left through the crowd, and I laughed out loud.

"What's so funny?" Kingston asked, his voice a low huff of indignation.

"You just dumped Sofia for me," I replied, and turned to look up at him. "Does this mean you're still interested in my peaches 'n cream pussy?"

His face darkened and his eyes contained a thunderstorm in miniature as he processed everything that I'd just said. My heart was trapped in my throat as I waited for him to respond, part of me wondering if I'd pushed too far. Maybe he would tell me to fuck off, that he only felt sorry for me, and that's why he pulled me from Ryker and kept me safe.

And for a moment, I thought the thunderstorm was going to clear and he would flash me his gorgeous Kingston smile, the smile I'd known since we were kids, the one that always lifted me up and made me feel like I was the centre of his world.

But his eyes grew stormier, and he released me. "I'm just protecting the Tribute," he said with an arrogant curl of his lip. "Even though I know your little *secret*, we have to maintain the *illusion* of your purity."

I was shocked into silence, and by the time I opened my mouth to respond, he was stalking away through the crowd of kids with his shoulders hunched over in anger.

Kingston fucking Taylor, the most frustrating and horrible guy I'd ever known.

* * *

"I'm sorry I haven't been talking to you much lately," Penny texted me a few days later. "I've been so busy at school."

"Me too," I texted back. How could I possibly quantify everything I'd been up to in the past few weeks over text? "Wanna hook up irl?"

In real life, I know, shocking. Actually meeting up with a friend instead of texting. I waited for her to finish her response. I could see her typing on the other end.

After what felt like an excruciatingly long time, she finally got back to me.

"Busy this weekend. Maybe next weekend? Pizza?"

"Sounds great, let me know when and where."

I put my phone down with a smile and got back to my schoolwork. I was doing some extra credit reading for my AP World History class. I was reading about ancient warrior cultures when I came across a single sentence that spiraled me into an intense memory of Ryker making the defeated rich guy give him head.

"Often after a victory in a battle, Selythian warriors would force themselves upon their defeated enemies. This mostly took the form of oral sex, forcing the man to fellate the warrior as an act of ultimate humiliation. Sometimes it went farther into physical sexual aggression to drive home the complete and utter domination of one group over another."

He had been right. Ryker hadn't been making it up. I was shocked. He'd given me the vibe of a guy who didn't enjoy learning. Somebody who would rather fight than read a book. And yet, here it was.

Damn, maybe there was more to Ryker than I first imagined. Maybe there was an intellect beneath the beastly exterior.

I didn't think I'd ever find out, though. As much as Ryker was an animal in the cage, he didn't have Kingston's single-minded focus on winning. And I knew at that point Kingston would win. Even if he said he didn't want me, he would fight for me as the prize.

And that filled me with smug satisfaction and a lot of stomach twisting fear.

22

We went through another couple weeks of the Kings ignoring me, but this time Sofia barely looked at me. I chatted with Penny here and there, but we weren't able to get together like we'd planned.

It felt strange. I was just the same old boring Everly in my oversized hoodie and baggy pants, but inside I had changed. Everything had changed. I'd seen and done things I'd never even dreamed about, but now that they were in my head...

I wanted more.

I hated to even admit that to myself, because it made me feel like the whore I'd been named by Sofia and even Kingston.

It still seemed to me like Sofia and Kingston had broken up and she was too busy skulking around, licking her wounds, to take it out on me. I didn't see them together at school ever these days, and the Kings spent each lunch hour either on the field at practice or off campus hanging out at Archer or Valen's place.

And then, after two weeks of nothing, Valen cornered me on a Friday morning as I was getting my books out of my locker. I was leaning down, intent on digging my scientific calculator out of the bottom of my locker, and I didn't notice him coming.

"Hey, buttercup," he said and lifted my limp braid off my shoulder. "We need to talk."

"What do you want?" I asked and stood up. "I have to get to class."

"You'll have time for class," he smirked. "This is just a head's up. We need to meet you after school."

"After school? Come on, I have to study," I replied with a groan, but inwardly I was flattered that they were suddenly paying me attention again. Not that I'd ever let them see it. I was too irritated by their neglect to let them know I was so horny for them all.

"This is important. We're planning a Halloween blowout at my place and have to go over your costume," he said and grinned. "We've got a good one picked out for you."

"Is it a theme party, or do I get to wear something on my own?" I asked.

"You'll see," he said and leaned forward to tug at the front of my hoodie. "This thing is really fucking ugly, by the way. The Tribute should dress a little nicer than this."

"I wasn't aware of the rules," I replied and tried to push his hand away. "Nobody tells me a damned thing around here."

I didn't know why I was so bitchy to him. Probably just those tender feelings at being ignored for so long after the last fight night.

Dirty Kingdom

He narrowed his eyes as if he just clued into something and said, "Shit. You're right. We need to write you up some rules or something. We'll get back to you on that, but rule number one will be don't dress like a homeless shelter reject."

I could have kicked myself at that point. I'd just given him an idea, and it was a bad one. Providing me with more rules and regulations for me to obey.

Fuck.

He dropped my braid back onto my shoulder, gave me a wink, and turned to leave. I would have taken a lot longer to enjoy the view as he sauntered away, but I really *was* late for class.

Still, I got a good eyeful of his gorgeous ass packed tight into his jeans, and I thought about how it would feel to be in his arms, to have him using that big, muscled body to fuck me hard and long.

Oh man, what the hell is wrong with me?

I hurried through the hallways, avoiding my fellow students, and made it to class on time. The rest of the morning went by without a hitch, but at lunch, Sofia took notice of me again for the first time since Ryker's fight.

"Hey, whore," she said as I walked by with my bagged sandwich and apple with a drink from the vending machine. I'd come to a compromise: no more hiding out with my food from home, but no fancy Covington meals unless the guys were buying. I would eat in the corner of the cafeteria and people watch, learning about the inner workings of the school's social hierarchy that way.

"Hey slut," I quipped back and immediately

regretted my mistake as her foot snaked out and caught my ankle. I felt myself falling before my body even reacted to it, so by the time I had my hands out to brace the impact, I'd already hit the floor. My wrist twisted with a sharp crunch, and my bagged lunch went skittering under Sofia's table.

"Oh shit," one of her friends winced, and the rest tittered nervous laughter.

I held my hand up, and it dangled at an unnatural angle. I wiggled my fingers, though, so it wasn't broken, but it hurt so fucking bad and was beginning to swell even as I looked at it.

"What the hell did you do?" I hissed, unable to control myself. I looked up at her from where I was still splayed on the floor and kept talking, even though I knew I should have stopped. Riling her up was probably not going to end well with me. "Is this because Kingston dumped your ass at the last fight night? Don't blame me if you have a sloppy cunt that doesn't keep him happy!"

I shrugged my shoulders and struggled to get up. I got to my feet at last, staggering as I held my wrist with my other hand.

"You fucking bitch!" she shrieked and launched herself at me from the cafeteria table bench. She landed against my chest, and I instinctively pulled my hand up to block her. She wound up hitting my strained wrist again, and I yowled in pain and anger.

"Get off me!" I yelled and tried to shove her, but my strength was gone, and using only one hand made me ineffectual. "Leave me alone!"

"You think you have a chance with Kingston fucking Taylor?" she sneered in my face, her spittle flying through her lips and peppering my face. "You think he'd want anything to do with your nasty, disgusting, stretched out pussy? I've heard the rumors. So has everyone. It's bad enough you took a train from the soccer team at the Oakville party, but now you're totally fine being passed around as the Kings' team whore."

"As long as Kingston is first in line, I don't care," I replied in a cold, calm voice. It bothered me, though, that people might have been talking about me like that.

I saw the flames of rage flare in her eyes and she let out a noise like a wounded animal combined with an enraged gorilla. She took her hands, placed them on my chest, and shoved really hard.

I fell back and lost my balance, twisted around, and fell on my ass. I hurt my wrist again, and I cried out in pain, unable to articulate the feelings that had exploded in my chest. Mostly anger. In fact, it was almost all anger, but threaded through with a healthy dose of pain.

She followed me to the floor and grabbed hold of my hair, tried to pull me up again to slam me down, but I used my good hand and punched her in the stomach.

She let out a grunt of agony and let me go, then pinned my good arm and swung her other hand back to hit me. I reached up with my bad hand, pushing through the shards of pain threatening to shatter my concentration, and gouged at her face. I drew my nails down from her forehead to her chin. The only thing I could think of to keep her at bay.

She made another noise of anger and hatred, held her face in her hand to frantically feel for blood, then drew it back to hit me again. I closed my eyes and braced for impact, my wrist sending spiraling agony all the way up my arm to my shoulder and into my chest.

But it never came. I felt her body lifted off me, and my eyes snapped open to find Kingston standing over us, his hand gripping Sofia by her upper arm, holding her off the ground.

"Let go of me, you bastard," she snarled and twisted in his hand. "This is bullshit. Stop protecting your whore!"

"Stop acting like a sociopath, Sofia. Rein it in or somebody will tell your daddy that you've been ruining the Newton family name out here in public," Kingston growled and lifted her to her feet. When he released her, she whirled around and glared at him.

"Fuck you! And fuck all your Kings!" she exclaimed.

"Seem to me that you've already done that," he smirked. "Plus that fighter from Harrington. Tell me, did he fuck your ass like our quarterback did?"

She stopped altogether, looked up at him, then sucked in a gasping lungful of air and spit in his face.

All around us, people exclaimed in shock at what had happened. All eyes were on the two of them, and the way the muscle in Kingston's temple began to twitch, I half expected him to start raging.

But instead, he said in a low, dangerous tone, "I suggest you get the fuck out of here and leave Evie alone, or your family will find out what you look like when you're bobbing on the end of my dick while my team bros pull a train on your ass."

She gasped, held her hand to her chest in horror, and said, "You wouldn't!"

"Try me," Kingston replied and held her steady, like a bug wiggling on a pin. They were locked in a standoff, so I slowly got back up to my feet and watched with intent interest. I didn't open my mouth but waited this time to see what she'd do.

"Fuck you," she said at last and whirled around to storm off. She shot me one last look of withering disdain before she left.

Kingston took a wet cloth handed to him from one of the cafeteria ladies. They loved him and always gave him extra dessert for being so cute, something that he played up and something that came in handy in cases like this. He used it to wipe the spit off his face, handed it back to the lunch lady, and shook his head at me.

"Why do I always seem to get pulled into your bullshit, Evie?" he grumbled without a trace of humor.

"I didn't ask you to," I replied and glanced around. Everybody had lost interest and was back eating and visiting before the next bell rang. "Why does it always seem like you're sticking your nose where it doesn't belong?"

"And what? Let you get your ass beaten by bimbo Barbie over there?" he demanded. "We need to get you to the school nurse to get that looked at. It might be broken."

"I can do it myself," I replied, bristling at his annoyed energy. I didn't want Kingston to hang around if he didn't want to be there. "Just get the hell out of my way."

"Why do you always have to be like this?" he said in a strained voice and put his arm around my shoulder, leading me out of the cafeteria towards the nurse's office.

I struggled, then gave in, relaxing against him as we walked. "Like *what*?"

"*So* fucking stubborn."

I had no reply because the only thing I could say was that it was him. He brought it out in me. Kingston fucking Taylor made me crazy, but I didn't know if it was crazy in hate or crazy in love.

23

"Let me get that for you," Valen said, taking my backpack from me when I was leaving school. "Did you drive today?"

I handed him my bag and an extra heavy history textbook, grateful to ease the burden off my sore wrist. I couldn't help it, though, I rolled my eyes and said, "Are you kidding? I take the bus, dude. I'm not exactly rolling in Covington cash even if I'm at your school. You know that. White trash, remember?"

I saw him flinch at my words, and he frowned. "I don't think that, buttercup. I've never thought that about you. Trash is a state of mind, not how much you have in your bank account. And you've got a presence about you that makes it obvious you're far from being trash."

"Thanks for the sentiment," I scoffed. "But if you saw my house, you might think otherwise."

"I've seen your house," he stated as we walked together down the hall. "I've been to Kingston's place, remember?"

I didn't remember. In fact, I barely thought about

the guys over there at all. It seemed like they would spend more time at one of the gigantic mansions and not Kingston's little place.

"Did you know I once thought our house was a mansion?" I smiled. "When we first moved there, I was so young and stupid. I really thought it was the biggest house I'd ever see."

"Oh wow," he laughed and raised his eyebrows. "So what do you think now?"

"I think it's a little shit shack, and I can't wait to get out of there," I replied.

"Are you having trouble with your family?" he asked and opened the door for me. I was suspicious about why he was being so nice to me when normally they only seemed nice when they were drunk or horny. They all must have found out I'd sprained my wrist, but luckily, after a couple of painkillers and some ice, it was feeling much better.

"I don't know," I said. "It's not like they're abusive or anything, I just feel like I don't belong there."

How could I put into words that I felt a strange disconnect between myself and the rest of them? Or that Reg made me feel so uncomfortable, even though he'd never done anything to me that would explain it. He was a jerk and favored the brat, but he still loved my mom and my sister and provided me with food and shelter.

How could I say anything about all that?

"I get you," he said. "I feel like that with my family."

"Do you have any siblings?" I asked.

"No, it's just me," he said, and for a moment a flicker of sadness rippled across his handsome face. He drew his thumb across his sensual, full lips in a gesture of contemplation, and I wondered what his home life was like. It seemed like I wasn't the only one with problems. "And I'm afraid I'm a disappointment for dear old mom and dad. When they're around at all, that is."

"They travel a lot?" I asked.

"You might say that. They spend most of their time at our London apartment or the estate in Madrid."

I noticed his slight British accent became more pronounced when he was relaxed. I liked it.

"You're left alone?" I asked.

"I wish. I'm left with a house full of loyal keepers," he sniffed. "They report every failure and every problem right back to my parents."

"I'm sorry," I said. "It sounds like it really sucks."

"It does indeed."

"This is me," I said and nodded my chin towards the bus stop that was empty. Almost no other kids took the bus like a peasant, like me.

"Not it's not," he laughed. "You're coming with me. We want to have that costume meeting at my place. Do you need anything before we get there?"

"Like what?"

"Oh, I don't know," he grinned and looked at me with a sly look. "A latte, a burger, or maybe condoms and a jug of lube?"

I laughed and grimaced. "Ew, what would I need lube for? If you're doing it right, I should be wet enough."

I almost choked on my scandalous words, but they spilled from my lips before I realized what I'd said.

He looked over at me, heat in his eyes, and said, "The hole I'm thinking of fucking needs lube, buttercup."

"The hole? What do you... Oh wait, oh my god, are you serious?"

He was talking about doing anal. *Oh my god, he was talking about butt sex.* I had no idea how to respond. I wound up sputtering and almost choking on any further reply.

"I see you might be a virgin after all," Valen laughed. "Only a virgin would get that panicked at the thought of me taking her ass."

"It's not exactly something I've thought about," I replied.

"I have," he said with a devilish grin. "And this here is me."

He gestured as we approached a sleek black Audi sports car. He opened the passenger door, got close to my ear and said, "Might I say, you'll probably be thinking about it now. A *lot*. Promise me you'll save it for my pleasure, though. Let me be your first."

He dropped my backpack into the space behind the passenger seat and stepped back for me to slide in. As I moved past him, he cupped my ass and said, "Don't worry, buttercup, we'll go slow."

My face was furiously hot by the time I took my seat. But he was right. I was thinking about it when he got in and we began to drive.

We didn't talk any more about that particular topic on the way to his place, but we did talk about family problems and our hopes and dreams for the future. He surprised me by telling me he wanted to go into the arts, and I confessed my desire to get a full ride scholarship to for history at an Ivy League school, or at the very least, a state school far from here.

When we got to his place, Archer and Kingston were

waiting for us in front of Valen's massive mansion. Kingston's lifted truck was parked in the driveway, its big tires and rough exterior looking very out of place.

We went inside and found them sitting at the back of the first floor in a large, well-furnished rec room.

"There she is, our little Tribute," Archer said, patting the seat of the couch next to him. "Come sit here, Ev. We need to talk."

"About the costume?" I asked, my eyes flitting to Kingston. He was sitting in a chair, and I couldn't read what he was thinking. I was worried he was still angry with me and confused as to why. *Why does he hate me so much, and why is he completely convinced I'm such a whore?*

"The costume, yes, among other things," he said, and patted the couch again. "I'm sorry if I made it seem like a suggestion. Get your ass over here, Tribute. Now."

The mood in the room had changed, and I vacillated between obeying them and telling them to fuck off. I hated being told what to do, and it wouldn't kill them to just ask nicely for once.

"Do we need to remind you that you're in this thing really deep now?" Archer said, raising an eyebrow. "We'll either ruin your friend or release footage of you. Either way, it's going to destroy somebody's life."

"What video do you have?" I demanded. "Doing what?"

"*So* many things," Kingston replied. "Seriously, Everly, you think I would pass up the chance to film you sucking cock like a pro under the bleachers? And that's just the start."

"Did you film yourself going down on me?" I snapped, my anger rising too fast for me to quell the tide. "Did you get a good video of you licking my clit and making me come?"

"Wait, you went down on her?" Valen asked, sounding betrayed. "What the fuck, dude?"

"Yeah, what the fuck, Kingston?" Archer exclaimed. "That wasn't part of the plan."

"What plan?" I asked, look at each of them. "What are you guys playing at here?"

"Nothing," Kingston said, but he was being guarded and sullen. I knew the look well. He was lying about something.

"What is it?" I demanded, standing my ground with my hands on my hips. These guys were up to something, and I wasn't going to like it. I just knew.

"Tell her," Valen said. "Just fucking tell her."

Kingston motioned to the two other guys, holding his hand up in a stop gesture. Archer and Valen both squirmed on the couch, and I sensed that they were uncomfortable with the situation.

"Tell me," I said, and glared at Kingston. "You owe it to me at least."

"Tell her, then," Kingston said, but I sensed he'd already censored the others. I wasn't going to get the full story, but at least I'd get a hint.

"You're our project," Archer said with a sigh. "A challenge for us. To turn you from an ugly duckling into the girl every guy wants to fuck."

"Why all the secrecy?" I asked. "That's it? It's not such a big deal."

"We didn't want you to freak out," Archer said. "That's all."

The way the three of them looked at each other indicated otherwise. It felt like there was more to the story, like they were hiding something darker beneath the surface of their intentions. I wasn't going to get the answer I wanted out of them, so I let it go. I had no other choice.

After that, I capitulated and sat next to Archer. Valen took his spot beside me and the two of them sandwiched me in as we discussed the rules of Tribute and costume ideas for Halloween.

The rules weren't as bad as I thought they'd be. Anything you'd expect from a group like them. It seemed as though they'd been written in previous years and now applied to me as this year's Tribute.

I was to always obey them, always dress in a manner that showed off my beauty, and take care of myself. I was to be at their beck and call and be available night and day whenever they asked. I didn't stop them to point out how difficult this would be, considering I had extra coursework, no money for new clothes, and strict parents. There was no point arguing with them.

When we were finished going over the rules, we talked briefly about Halloween costumes. I wasn't that interested, considering I hadn't been out at Halloween in years. I decided to let them come up with something on their own.

When the little group chat came to an end, Archer promptly unzipped his jeans and pulled out his cock. I nervously looked over at Kingston then back to Archer and tittered, "What's going on?"

"I need you to suck my dick," Archer said and reached up, weaving his hands in my hair. He grabbed hold of the back of my head to pull me down into his lap. "I've been dying to fuck your pretty little mouth since you got here. Remember, you *can't* say no."

I hoped Kingston would say something, like demand that I start with him or tell Archer to stop all together. I'd been thinking about reciprocating and giving Kingston a blow job ever since he'd gone down on me, but he seemed too distant and angry to let me do such a thing.

And now, he didn't even flinch at his friend's demands, so I let Archer pull me down and slam his thick cock into my mouth.

And let's face it, I wanted it. I won't lie. Being wanted by Archer and Valen was good for my ego. But mostly I wanted to anger Kingston even more. I felt like if I kept doing these things, obeying his friends and being a little whore with them, then he would be driven to react. He would be driven to uncork the feelings that simmered inside of him every time we were together.

Maybe I could find out why he thought I was so slutty and why he was so fucking angry at me. I didn't deserve either of his judgements, but him bottling it up meant I would never know why he felt that way.

The moment I started bobbing up and down, Valen reached around under my hoodie and slid his hand up to my breasts. He pulled at me, so I shifted myself until I was on my hands and knees on the couch, sucking Archer's thick shaft and straddling Valen's knees.

I looked at Kingston out of the corner of my eye and he was watching from his seat, a dark look of contempt clouding his handsome features. He was visibly disgusted with me, and I wanted to cry when I saw it.

And then that stubborn streak of mine took over, and I thought, *fuck it*. If he's going to sit there hating me for this, the very thing they wanted me to do, then he could throw his tantrum and watch me enjoy it. And I did enjoy it. I mean I'd have to be dead inside to not feel good when two hot, rich, sexy as fuck studs like Archer and Valen wanted to play with me. I'd have to be stupid to not take this chance and express myself sexually when I could.

I might never get another chance with gorgeous men like this, and since this was my first time doing it, I wanted to do it well. Given my social upbringing and background, chances were more likely that in the end I'd find myself hitched to some middle manager type who hated his job and started drinking the minute he got home.

Or even worse, I'd wind up having a litter of kids and head back to where I came from, the trailer park. I'd become the very thing I despised and fulfill whatever prophecy Kingston saw for me when he called me a white trash whore.

So I gave in and sunk deep into the depravity of the moment. I let it happen and made the conscious choice to enjoy every damned minute of it.

They brought me to the heights of desire again, my third, fourth, and fifth orgasms at the hand of somebody other than myself. Archer and Valen were experts in making me feel at this point, and I was becoming an expert in giving them head after doing it a couple of times.

The only dark stain on the bright afternoon with the Kings was Kingston's glowering bad mood. He kept me just enough on edge that I didn't fully plunge into the deepest end of the pool of lust. There was always part of me that watched him, like one eye focused on him so I could always monitor what he was thinking.

He was the clear leader in our group, and he was clearly hiding how much it bothered him to not join in.

He was going to drive me over the edge into madness if he didn't let it all out soon. If he didn't tell me the source of his disgust for me. Why he thought I was such trash. I mean, other than me giving head like Sofia at a football game after a few wine coolers, that was.

But the thing was, as much as I wanted to hear it, I worried about the pain it might cause me when I saw myself through his eyes.

After that day, I would give anything to go back in time and have my childhood friend in my life to be innocent and able to trust. To let it all go and start over from the beginning. And make Kingston fucking Taylor love me the way I was meant to be loved.

24

From that point on, with the rules laid down, things were clearer for me. And spending time with them allowed me to learn more about their personalities.

Kingston was the leader, of course. He was alpha through and through and was hot and cold from hour to hour. His mood swings drove me crazy, but underneath all the anxiety-inducing behavior, he was still my first love and the boy I'd lost so long ago. I couldn't ever completely give up on him.

Archer was the consummate bad boy and didn't have wide arcing mood swings like Kingston. He was essentially either horny and aggressive or horny and sweet. You might have guessed, his default setting was, yes, horny.

Valen was the sweetheart of the three. We had the most in common with our strange relationships with our parents and our sensitive, loving hearts. He was also pretty horny, so there was that underlying consistency with him as well.

Valen offered to take me shopping for some new

things in a city nearby. A place that had a high end mall with some expensive shops. Somewhere I'd never been before. It was much too rich for my blood. I made up some lie about needing to do research in the town's library for an extra credit project, and Mom totally bought it.

Nat the brat didn't. She watched me with narrowed eyes and her suspicious nature on full display.

I avoided her for the rest of the day by hiding in my room talking to Valen over video chat.

"There's no way I can afford anything," I told him, my worry getting the best of me. Of course, the shopping trip was on his dime, but I had to be certain.

"It's on me, buttercup. I'll pick up the tab," he said. "You need to look good for us. You're representing Covington and us Kings, we can't have you out there looking like a homeless cat lady."

"Wouldn't a cat lady need a home, though?" I asked, smiling into the camera.

"Good point." He laughed. I loved making him and Archer laugh. They always seem surprised by it. Most of the girls they usually hung out with would probably rather obsess over looking good and landing a wealthy husband than being clever and focusing on wit. "I guess you look like a homeless bag lady? Is that even okay to say anymore, though?"

"I think if we're being progressive, we could say a lady without a house who collects bags. But only environmentally friendly bags."

He laughed again, and we set up a time for him to pick me up in the morning.

It was a Friday night, and I desperately texted Penny again after talking to Valen. She had ghosted the fuck out of me, and I wasn't having any of it. I didn't care if we went to different schools now, or we were both so busy it was difficult to carve out time. I needed my friend. I wasn't going to let her get away without a fight.

She didn't respond, so I sent a few more and then gave up. For the time being. There were two weeks until Halloween, and this would be the first year since Kingston left that I wasn't planning a theme costume with her.

Last year we'd gone as CO_2, I was the carbon molecule. She was the double oxygen molecule and when we stood next to each other, we held painted sticks to represent bonds. We'd thought it was hilarious, but it hadn't won us any costume prizes or anything at school. We didn't care. We had fun, and our chemistry teacher, Miss Sanders, had brought us cupcakes the next day to congratulate us for being clever.

Neither one of us had even dared to suggest we leave the house that night. I'd stayed over with her and her crazy religious family and we'd huddled under her covers watching scary movies and eating too much chocolate.

I missed those times. I missed my friend.

This year was so different, I hardly recognized who I was anymore. I was going as something I despised. Penny and I had always openly mocked slutty costumes, and we'd play a game where we'd take the most random profession and turn it into a woman's Halloween costume. Like slutty veterinarian or slutty school custodian.

And now I was going to wear a slutty costume. I was going to be a sexy prisoner and the three guys were going as cops. I tried to tell them about the systemic problems with policing in our country and how this was the wrong message to send, but Archer had held his finger to my lips and said, "Shhh, Ev. We didn't pick you for your opinion, we picked you to look fuckable. Remember that."

I'd rolled my eyes and playfully pushed his shoulder, but I'd gone quiet afterwards. His words felt heavy and had put me in my place.

I watched a movie alone to pass the time while I did some homework. When it finished, it was around nine, and mom and the brat were off for an overnight trip in another town. She was entered in a dance competition first thing in the morning, so they had left after dinner. I realized it was just me and Reg alone in the house.

And again, Reg had never done anything overt to freak me out, but being around him always put me on edge. I was so uncomfortable knowing he was just downstairs watching TV.

I was hungry and needed a sandwich and a glass of milk, one of my favorite late night snacks. I practically lived on PB and Js. It was the one thing I could make quietly and know that I wasn't using up any expensive ingredients. Just peanut butter and jam on bread.

The TV was playing some old cop show, Reg's favorite kind, and he didn't even hear me heading into the kitchen. I made my sandwich, grabbed a Coke, and turned to head back upstairs. Reg was standing in the doorway, watching me.

"Oh shoot, I didn't see you there," I said after I jumped. "What's going on?"

"Do you want me to make you a drink?" he asked, eyeballing the Coke.

On some nights when I was anxious about life and

mom was away, Reg would let me have alcohol. I knew it wasn't legal, and I knew it wasn't the best thing for me, but normally I liked it. I liked feeling illicit, and I liked the warm fuzzy feeling I got when I flopped into bed afterwards.

The problem was that it usually knocked me out for too long. After just a little hard alcohol, Reg's whiskey, I was down for the count until the next afternoon. I didn't know what was different about his alcohol, but it seemed to hit different from the stuff I had at parties. I had to get up pretty early to meet up with Valen.

"Not tonight," I said. "A friend is coming to pick me up at eight so we can do some research at the town library in Martindale. Thanks for the offer, though."

"Does your mother know about this?" he asked, his face dropping into a deep scowl.

"She does," I fibbed. She knew. She just didn't know who it was with or the real reason I was going. "She said as long as I left enough time for homework it should be okay."

Reg was silent for a moment then pressed his lips into a grim line. He took a breath and said, "You sure you don't want something to help you sleep?"

"I'll be good," I replied. "I'm going to stay up and get some work done tonight. That extra credit history course is kicking me in the butt."

Irritation rippled across his face, and for a moment I thought he wasn't going to get out of my way. I stood next to the fridge, balancing the can of Coke and the sandwich in one hand and gripping my phone in the other.

But then he smiled and relaxed. The tension fled the

room, and he said, "We're really proud of you for working so hard. Keep it up."

Then he stepped to the side and let me pass.

I didn't let myself feel afraid until I was alone in my room. Once there, I set the things down on my nightstand, sat on the edge of my bed, and cradled my head in my hands. I was wearing my fuzzy panda bear onesie, and although it was oversized and fit loosely, I still felt slutty. Like a whore.

And I didn't know why. I didn't understand how that could happen here in the safety of my own home.

But a little voice in my head whispered that I did know. It was because this wasn't my home, and I wasn't safe here.

I had to get out as soon as I could.

※ ※ ※

Valen picked me up on time, and Reg was gone when we left. It was probably just a weird one off encounter, or maybe he had already had a few too many drinks, I told myself.

As soon as Valen began to spoil me rotten and we had the best time together, the thing with Reg was gone from my head. The day was just too amazing for any ugliness to linger. We'd bonded over stories of feeling like outcasts in our own homes, and he'd opened up to me about liking me more than he thought he would when he first saw me. I felt like I was Valen's girlfriend in Martindale, and I didn't want the day to end.

It had to, of course, and when we got back into Oakville, we drove straight to Archer's place once again.

Kingston and Archer were waiting for us, and Valen asked for one of the help to bring in my clothing purchases.

"You have to model them for us," Archer insisted. "Let's see what the Valen bought. He does have pretty shitty taste in clothing, so this could be good."

"I'm not going to wear them if you're just going to laugh at me." I bristled and narrowed my eyes.

"Just fucking show us," Kingston said, irritation giving his voice an edge. "We need to know how you're going to represent us at school."

"Represent you?" I laughed. "I know you have your little set of rules and all, but I'll wear what I want. End of story."

"Then why don't you stick to oversized hoodies and leggings?" Kingston growled at me.

"Why don't you two either fuck or lay off each other?" Valen exclaimed in frustration. "Seriously, this back and forth bullshit between you guys is ridiculous. Kingston, you obviously have a massive boner for Everly. You can't stop looking at her and act like you're going to tear the head off any guy who even looked at her."

"Except for us," Archer told me. "He'd let us have you, remember that. The three of us love playing with the same toy. It adds spice to the mix."

I raised my eyebrows and widened my eyes. I wasn't exactly innocent anymore. I'd seen a few things and had fooled around with them. But the thought of all three at one time, going all the way?

It was intimidating and intriguing. Would I be able

to handle them all, or would I be too distracted to do anything? Even now, I didn't know how well I'd do with them. Sure, I felt like a whore sometimes, and I knew they expected me to perform, but what if I couldn't get them off? What if I didn't know what I was doing when it came down to it? Then I'd be disappointing three guys at one time instead of just one.

Ugh, why did this all have to be so sexy and so scary?

"Of course, he wouldn't chase us away from you," Valen said with a grin. He put his arm around Archer on the couch and winked at me. "Then he wouldn't have anyone to finish him off if you were busy occupied with another one of us."

"Wait. What?" I asked.

"Nothing. He didn't mean anything by it." Kingston growled dangerously and glowered at the two of them on the couch. They were like his sidekicks, and he was the main character. I wanted to be included in Kingston's story, I longed to be part of it. "Now get your fashion show finished. I have plans to discuss with them, and you're not needed for it."

I frowned, unhappy with the way he spoke to me, but I refused to let him see it. I was often disappointed by Kingston and had to learn to hide it, or I felt like he'd have the upper hand.

I didn't know if that was normal, to feel like I was constantly at war with the guy I wanted so desperately. It was a fine line between love and hate, as they say, and Kingston and I dance along it continually. Ours was razor sharp, threatening to cut both of us open if we slipped.

I picked up one of the bags, and instead of looking for somewhere to change, I thought, *fuck it*. I was already so close to the edge of danger, I might as well dive in headfirst.

I undressed slowly, deciding then and there to get naked in front of them all. I slipped my shirt off, shimmied out of my bra, and pulled my pants off. I kicked them to the side and edged my panties down over my hips and dropped them on top of my pants.

Three sets of eyes were locked on me, hunger in each of them. The power I felt commanding their attention was addictive, and I put on quite the show, slipping into a beautiful little black dress.

I spun around, braless and without panties, and held my arms up. "What do you think, my Kings?"

"You look incredible, buttercup," Valen said with a wide grin. He was leaning forward on the couch, his hands on his knees, watching me closely. "That's one of my favorites."

"You should always go bare underneath," Archer said appreciatively. His eyes raked me up and down, and he licked his lips in lustful hunger. "I could get at your sweet little cunt wherever we were at."

"What do you think, Kingston?" Valen asked, not taking his eyes off me. "Is our Tribute fuckable, or is she fuckable?"

Kingston let out a rumble in his chest, like a deep sigh mixed with a sound of appreciation. "It looks good on you, Evie," he said begrudgingly, then crossed his arms and again curled his lip in disgust as he looked me up and down.

"Are you sure? You look like you're going to spit on me," I replied. "Should I try on the next one?"

"Whatever you want," he said and sat back in the chair. I never knew how he actually felt about me in moments like that. His compliment sent me flying high. It gave me a thrill, and I couldn't believe I was that excited to hear him approve of my dress. But when he looked at me like that, I felt sick to my stomach, like I'd done something wrong.

"The red one," Valen said, sitting on the edge of the couch. "That one makes you look so beautiful, and so fucking sexy."

I let myself forget about Kingston and his judgmental ways and slipped on the red dress. It was Chanel and cost more than my mother's car, but Valen had insisted on it. He'd picked out a pair of Louboutin heels with their matching red soles and said I looked like a runway model in them.

"Fuck yes," Archer agreed and pulled me down onto his lap. The red dress edged up around my thighs, and his hand crept between them. Valen leaned in and kissed my neck. I let them touch me, not just because I loved being between two muscled, hot guys, but also because I loved the way it made Kingston shift uncomfortably in the chair across from us.

If he wasn't going to tell me how he really felt, I was going to drive him crazy until he did.

Besides, the best thing about spending time getting to know Valen and Archer was growing closer with them. The closer I felt to them, the less power Kingston had over me. And the more my feelings grew for the others.

Life was complicated for me now, but I couldn't help but scoop it up and devour everything thrown my way. I was in love with how I felt and possibly falling in love with the Kings.

25

After the shopping day, I dressed like I belonged to the Kings. I dressed like I belonged at Covington because I finally did.

Nothing Sofia could do was a bother to me anymore, and nothing she did to me could change my new position of power at the school.

I'd defeated her and her crew by leaning into my position as Tribute, and with me having public support by two of the three biggest bad asses around, I was untouchable.

Kingston dumping her skank ass helped me a lot, too. He wasn't exactly Mr. Friendly with me, but he had nothing to do with her. Plus, even though he seemed to resent it, he started driving me to school. I was thrilled that I didn't have to take the bus, and every once in a while, it felt like we were just good friends again.

But most of the time, it felt like I was just his property. I was the Tribute, and he was a Covington King, and I was there for his pleasure alone. Like an automaton, a sex machine just for him and his friends to use and discard.

"Your skirts are getting shorter," he noted one day when I climbed up into his truck with his help. "Nice red panties."

"Oh my god," I exclaimed and yanked the hem of my little Gucci plaid skirt. It was adorable, brown and white plaid, and I'd paired it with a white Miaou blouse and knee high Mascha brown boots.

Sometimes I couldn't believe how much Valen had spent on me, and sometimes I had to sneak out of the house in my long raincoat so my mother didn't see how much my wardrobe had improved.

"Not that I mind looking," he said, and shut the door behind him. Ever the gentleman, he helped me into his truck every morning, but this was the first time he'd mentioned me looking good. Maybe I was wearing him down slowly.

He climbed into the driver's side and patted the seat next to him. "Slide over here and suck my cock on the way to school," he said matter-of-factly.

"What?" I sputtered and shook my head. "No. You can't just dive in like that without asking."

"I can do anything I want. Remember the rules?" he replied, looking at me with purpose. "You going to break a rule and risk your friend's reputation? Or what about yours? It's just going to take one video of you gobbling Archer's knob under the bleachers to guarantee you don't get a single scholarship for college. Besides, Evie, I know you like it."

"Fuck," I grumbled as he put the truck into gear and pulled out of his driveway. He'd hit too close to home with his last observation.

He started to drive and patted the seat again, this time with more force. I weighed his words in my head, and although I was pretty sure none of them actually would call Penny's parents or release a video of me at this point, I wasn't a *hundred* percent sure of it. And Kingston was the strictest of the three, for sure, when it came to wanting complete obedience. "Okay, fine, get your dick out."

"That's your job, Evie." He chuckled and undid the top button on his jeans with one hand while he was driving.

I leaned down and finished with the rest of them, pulled his growing cock out of his pants, and stroked it slowly with one hand.

I propped myself up so I could get to it and dropped down, licking and kissing the smooth head until the whole thing grew rock hard and hot in my fingers. Kingston began to breathe faster, and I felt a surge of power course through my body. Here I was, the complete center of his world with his dick in my hand and his focus directly on me.

I'd wanted to do this. Fuck, I'd wanted this so bad. I'd been thinking about it ever since he'd buried his tongue in my pussy and made me come like that. I'd wanted him in my mouth, and I'd wanted to drink him down. But not exactly like this, perhaps—not with him demanding it like I was a servant, and not in the cab of his stupid lifted black truck.

"Come on, Evie, suck it like you do with the guys," he groaned and gripped the steering wheel with white knuckles. "You know you want it. I see how you look at me. I see how much you want this. And I've seen you deep throat both their cocks before. Do it like that."

I wasn't about to argue with him about the difference between wanting him and the love we'd once had versus wanting his dick in my mouth. But having his dick in my mouth wasn't negotiable, so I licked my lips and opened wide as I slid the throbbing head past my tongue and down my throat.

I couldn't help it. I gagged. He was much thicker and much longer than Valen and Archer, and maybe I wanted to please him more, so I was trying harder. I wanted to get him off, to make him feel the way he'd made me feel that day in my room. The night I'd met the beast, Ryker.

I moaned against Kingston's cock and wiggled my hips, aching for him to slide inside of me. For him and the other Kings to take turns taking me hard. Archer and Valen would love to join in, and all three of them would be worshiping and pleasuring me.

I whimpered at the sheer scandalous nature of my fantasies. My cheeks flamed hot as I let my imagination run wild. And yet there was a part of me that scolded me for letting even my fantasies delve into such depravity. A part of me that wished for a simpler time when I could wear oversized hoodies and have lunch at Oakville High with Penny and get ignored by every boy around. A time when the world wasn't so complicated and I didn't feel so much shame for wanting dirty things to happen to me.

"I fucking knew it," Kingston said, his voice breathless and drawn out. A low, thick drawl filled with lust and longing for me. And like that, he snapped me back to reality. And the reality was that I had Kingston fucking Taylor's thick dick in my mouth, and I was going to drink his cum before school even started.

And I didn't care what my inner prude decided to tell me. That was fucking hot.

I sucked him with more force, cupped his balls, and enjoyed their weight and heat in the palm of my hand. I felt vital to him just then, necessary and wanted. He spun the wheel of the truck and hit the horn. I heard the turn signal click on and off and felt the truck slow down.

"Faster, Evie, we're at school," he grunted and threw the truck into park. "Come on, fucking suck it. That's good, you're so good at this. I knew you were a little whore, but I didn't know your mouth was so fucking hot. I'll bet your little cunt is even hotter."

I was encouraged by his words, and he lifted my hair away from my face so he could watch my performance. I bobbed faster, up and down, my mouth making wet sucking and slapping sounds as his precum filled my mouth, salty and thick.

And then he grabbed a handful of my hair, tensed up, and shoved my face down his throbbing rod. I choked but forced myself to take it all. I opened my throat and felt his cock twitch and jump as it swelled and pulsed a load of hot, thick cum deep inside of me.

"Oh fuck, Evie," he drawled again, this time slower and filled with admiration. "Fuck, you're good at that."

I swallowed and felt him soften in my mouth. I slurped up slowly, let him fall out of my lips with a wet plop, and looked up to smile at him. His eyes were focused on me, and for a moment, I swore he was going to say something sweet. Like he loved me, or he wanted me.

But just as he opened his mouth, stroked my hair tenderly, and looked into my eyes, somebody slammed the truck window and I heard, "Holy shit, that was fucking wild!"

"Wooooooh!" a bunch of guys cheered around us, and Kingston's hands pulled away from me as if burned and he put them behind his head like he was relaxing.

I lifted my head to find the entire Covington Kings football team gathered around the truck watching me give Kingston fucking Taylor a blow job in front of the school.

"She's a hungry little bitch," one boy yelled, and a few more hollered and agreed.

"What a fucking pro!" another chortled and banged the window. I saw phones out, recording the whole thing, and I couldn't believe I hadn't caught on. Shame and anger flared inside of me, but I was helpless in the face of their excitement.

Kingston pushed his dick back into his pants and did up the buttons. "I think the show's over," he told me, and that cool, detached cruelty was back. "I need to get to class a little early, so hop out of here, please. You could flash your sexy red panties and give the team a show if you want."

"Not likely." I shook my head and sat up. The group of guys around the truck moved out of the way when I opened the truck door, and for once, Kingston didn't help me out. He got out of his side and stalked away.

I felt discarded but wouldn't let him know it. I straightened my back, squared off my shoulders, and hopped down with as much dignity as I could muster.

One of the younger football players dove down and lifted my skirt quickly. They all laughed, and he yelled, "Red! I just knew they'd be red."

I had to brush it off like I wasn't dying of humiliation

inside. "Whatever, losers. Look all you want because you know you can't touch this."

I swung around and lifted the front of my skirt, showing off the bright red silken panties I was wearing that morning. They responded exactly how you'd expect, howling and laughing, hooting and calling my name. I even heard a couple declarations of love in the mix.

I turned around and sauntered towards the school, ignoring the rest of them but catching Kingston's eye as I passed by him and Archer and Valen. He seemed proud of me. Smug and proud. As if I'd done something right, for once.

I'd hang onto it, like I hung onto every positive interaction I had with him. One of these days, he would crumble like sand in my fingers and express his love for me, but until then I had to collect each and every little offering like precious stones beaded along the strand of a necklace.

"Hey, wait up," Valen said, jogging over to my side. "That was pretty sexy. Can I get a look, buttercup?"

"If you ask nicely, maybe later." I grinned, and he casually draped his arm around my shoulders. Archer joined us on the other side and slid his hand down my ass until it rested, cupping me possessively.

"I heard there was a hot little pair of panties over here." He chuckled, and I nodded at him with a wink.

The three of us walked into the school like that, and I knew the things they said about me. I heard the whispers. I even knew exactly what Sofia herself had spread around the school. That I was a slut, a whore, that I was fucking them all at the same time. Even though I knew, I didn't care.

I felt good. They were handsome, and they were into me. I wouldn't mind banging them hard and fast at some point, and they were key to getting my Kingston to love me again. So I would proudly walk between my two Covington Kings and be their Tribute, because without them I was nothing now. Just a depressed girl in an oversized hoodie with no friends.

At least now I was never lonely.

26

It was a week before Halloween, and the guys still hadn't settled on a group costume idea. I was getting tired of the group chat filled with them debating the finer points of dressing me like a whore or a queen. At least they'd dumped the prisoner idea after I'd stood up to them again about what a tone deaf costume it was considering our current political climate.

But finally, I couldn't stand it anymore, so when we were sitting at our usual lunch table one day I said, "What about both?"

"What do you mean, both?" Archer asked. He was picking at my fries, dipping them one at a time in my ketchup and eating them.

"I mean, we go as a queen and her consorts," I smiled. "That way I'm a queen and a whore, I could be the dirty little slut who fucks all her men."

"All the king's men," Valen laughed. "I like it. This just might work. We could worship you, and I'm sure we could get you into something very sexy."

"What do you think, could I be your queen?" I asked

Kingston, hating the hesitation in my voice. Why did I, even now, always want and need his approval? Valen was my tender King, Archer was my horny, over the top King, and Kingston was very distant and ever disapproving.

Fuck my daddy issues. They left me vulnerable and needy. I hated that I still wanted to please the most aloof of the bunch.

Kingston's eyes finally flicked to my face. Then he dragged them slowly up and down, settling on my chest. I was wearing a tight pink cashmere sweater and a grey pencil skirt with the cutest pair of black heels. All designer, and all purchased by Valen during our big shopping trip. I took a deep breath and saw his eyebrows go up as my breasts expanded.

"Yeah, we could make it work," he said. "I'll worship you, our little whore queen."

"Perfect!" Valen exclaimed. "I am so excited about this. Let's contact... what's her name?"

He turned to Archer and snapped his fingers. "That designer your father was fucking. What was her name?"

"My father isn't fucking anyone," Archer said, bristling as he narrowed his eyes in a threat. "Not even my mother at this point."

"Okay, okay, we'll maintain the squeaky clean Whitmore family image in front of the outsider," Valen laughed. He shook his head and added, "What's the name of that designer your father was, well, let's call her your father's protégée?"

"Maria Sinclair," Archer begrudgingly told him.

"Archer's mother is a model and his father is rich," Kingston said to me as I watched them go back and forth. "Archer's mother is never here, and his father mentally checked out moments after Archer was born. Such are the lives of the rich and famous."

"Your mother is a model? She must be beautiful," I said, ignoring all the family drama I'd just found out. I wanted to distract Archer; he seemed agitated.

"She's beautiful because she's a coke addict," Archer replied with one eyebrow raised. "You're beautiful because you're you, Ev. Always remember that. Your beauty is from within. My mother is a well moisturized skin suit draped over a skeletal frame."

"Enough of your family bullshit, let's talk to Maria and get Everly fitted for her costume," Valen said. "I mean, I know you're a massive pussy and feel the need to cry about it like a little bitch, but I'm tired of hearing about your asshole parents."

"Like yours are so much better," Archer snapped. "Do you even have parents? Or did some bitch whelp you and abandon you on your own, little dog? I haven't even seen them in a couple years."

"They fucked off the moment they had me," Valen said with a grin. "But unlike you, I am completely mentally adjusted despite their staggering parental neglect."

"You two are pathetic," Kingston said, and shook his head. "Seriously, cut this shit out."

I loved it when he took charge. I couldn't help it. He was powerful, and he was in control. It just goes to show how money didn't dictate power, even in a place like Covington. Power was the way a guy handled himself, especially around other guys. I could see that now.

"What should I wear?" I asked, distracting them again. They were getting heated with each other and I wanted to prevent any arguments among them. If I couldn't distract them with my body, I could keep them talking to avoid them fighting.

Sometimes I felt more like a den mother than a Tribute.

"We'll get Maria to work it out," Valen said. "Don't worry, you'll be the queen of everything. The most beautiful girl at the party. By far."

"She will, no matter what she wears," Archer agreed. "Right, Kingston?"

He pointedly stared at Kingston until Kingston had to nod his head and reluctantly say, "Yes. Yes, she will be fucking incredible. She's *always* fucking incredible."

He didn't take his eyes off me when he said that, and I felt a shiver snake up my spine at his words. Everything he said to me was magic. Everything was like heat coiling around my stomach and sparking a thrill of desire inside of me.

I just wished he didn't sometimes hate me so much that it hurt.

* * *

The designer came up with the most extraordinary dress for me that I almost fell over the first time I tried it on.

I didn't know how I could possibly explain the elaborate and beautiful gown to mom and Reg, so I asked Archer if I could keep it at his place. We were all basically hanging out there every chance we got, so it was the most logical place for the four of us to get ready.

It was odd, being around them like I was one of the guys at times. They hadn't done much fooling around with me since I gave Kingston head in the front seat of his truck. They'd stuck to flirting and dirty talk filled with promises of things to come once Covington won Dirty Kingdom and my virginity belonged to them.

Other than that, they didn't force themselves on me again and didn't treat me that badly even. It was as if Kingston's dick down my throat had put me off limits. I wasn't free to fool around with anyone anymore, not if Kingston had marked me as his.

But the fucked up part about it was he hadn't. He never made a move afterwards. He shot his load, smirked at the Covington Kings, got multiple high fives from the entire team about it. And then acted like nothing had happened.

Waiting for him to act was frustrating. I could feel the tension in my skin every time we were near each other. Like I was pulled tight, a drum hide stretched taut across my own skeletal frame. If Kingston pushed me away, I would break apart and clatter to the ground.

The day of the big Halloween party, I texted Penny to see if she would come with us. I was giving her one last chance, because she'd been avoiding me too much lately. She claimed she was sick and had been for the past two weeks, but I didn't know. Sometimes I worried she thought I was a snob, or she found out about the slutty things I'd done with the guys.

She didn't get back to me this time and left me on unread, so I got ready to head to Archer's. Kingston was driving me there, and I could see him from my bedroom window, pacing by his truck, waiting for me.

I took the stairs to the first floor and found mom and

Natalie pulling on Natalie's dance costume, a unicorn fairy princess.

"Shouldn't you have another horn for that?" I teased her and gave her a nudge.

"What do you mean?" she asked and laced up her winter boot.

"Two horns, you know. Like a cow?" I grinned.

She squealed and slapped my hand away. But it was all in good fun. "I'm dancing in the school play tonight," she told me. "It's one of the lead roles."

"That's amazing," I replied, and squeezed her quickly. "I'm proud of you."

"Whoa, somebody write this down. You two are being nice to each other," Mom laughed.

"You'd better take a picture," I replied and nudged Natalie again. "It's not going to last long."

"Heck no, it won't last." She giggled and pushed me back.

"What's going on in here?" Reg bellowed as he stormed into the foyer. "I'm trying to watch the game."

Reg was in a foul mood. You could see it on his face, the way his eyes narrowed and the wrinkles at the side were deeper, guttered, and spidery. His jaw clenched and unclenched.

"Oh Reg, they were just fooling around. The girls are getting along for once. We need to celebrate it," Mom said, her voice lowering in that gentle manner she used to calm him during his moods. She'd used that same voice on him since I was a kid.

"I just want to have a nice afternoon to myself," Reg said, calmed by her tactic but still pouty. He was agitated, but his angst had eased off.

"I understand that. You work hard," Mom said and

rubbed his shoulder with her hand. "Maybe Everly could help you out, make you some snacks."

"I'm leaving," I said. "I have plans tonight."

"She has plans," Reg said, and glowered at me. "Of course she has plans. Haven't you noticed your girl coming and going at all hours lately? She's been spending too much time with that Taylor kid next door."

"Ohhhh, Kingston Taylor is hot," Natalie said and nodded her head as if to give me her approval. "Good going, big sis."

"Thanks," I said. "And besides, Reg, when have you ever cared what's going on with me?"

He sputtered and was about to launch into a raging attack on my character or an assault on my value as a human being... the usual Reg rant kind of shit. But Mom stepped in, put her hand on his chest, and shook her head.

"No," she said simply in a low, threatening voice. "Not my girl."

I took that as my exit opportunity and ducked out the door before anymore weirdness unfolded. Mom never stood up to Reg, but she'd gone into full boss bitch mode for me for a hot minute, and I didn't know why. I guess even she had her limits on how much shit she was willing to take.

Now I just had to find mine.

* * *

"You look fucking amazing," Valen said and stepped towards me as I came down the stairs at Archer's mansion. I'd spent over an hour with hair and makeup, the people they'd hired, getting ready for the party, and I felt like a queen.

The three of them were wearing rococo court costumes, mostly simple waistcoats with frilled shirts poking out from the cuffs and the neckline. They had tight riding breeches that emphasized each of their sexy asses and highlighted each one of their thick, muscled thighs. I could practically count the veins in the outlines of their dicks, too, they were that tight.

My dress looked like something off a movie set, I looked like Marie Antoinette but sluttier. It had a deep, scooped neckline and the bustier was laced so tight that my breasts popped out over the top like two perfect little globes.

The dress was light yellow and had gold embroidery patterns along the waist and overskirt, but the underskirt was short and puffy, expanding it in a sexy swish when I walked.

My hair was coiled into an elaborate braid under a tall, stacked, blue-black wig that was threaded throughout with bright gold lace.

I felt incredible, and I couldn't believe it was me when I looked in the mirror. I felt like a different person.

"You are stunning," Archer exclaimed and pushed past Valen to pick me up and swing me around, his hands encircling my waist. He set me down, and I felt breathless.

"Thank you." I laughed and looked over at Kingston, who was standing there in a gold brocade jacket that matched my dress. Valen and Archer were wearing off-white, like the matching bookends to Kingston and me making up the power couple.

I felt like we were a couple, but after spending this long with Archer and Valen around, I felt more complete with all three of them. I couldn't imagine having just one of them all the time. It would feel unbalanced and lonely in a way.

"What do you think, *King*?" Archer asked as he leaned down and nuzzled my exposed shoulder. "Is our Tribute fuckable or what?"

"Definitely," Kingston said, standing up. His eyes were blazing with unknown force—lust or anger, I couldn't tell. But he crossed the room to me swiftly and stood in front of me. He looked down, drew his finger across my collarbone and said, "She is fuckable. And I can't wait to be the one to have her."

I shivered at his touch and nodded my head in agreement.

27

"Party!" Archer yelled as we tumbled out of the Range Rover and onto the front steps of Philip Rolston's mansion. Phillip, aka Philly, was one of the players on the Covington Kings and according to Archer, he threw the best bangers around.

The Range Rover was Valen's. His private driver was dropping us off and would wait for us to go home afterward. I couldn't stay too late. Mom and Natalie were staying overnight at her school's traveling dance performance in a town nearby, but she would check on me to make sure I wasn't breaking curfew.

Hopefully, I didn't forget the time and miss it, and if I did, I hoped Reg was passed out and wouldn't notice me sneaking in hours late.

"Let's get fucking lit!" Valen hooted as we raced up the front steps. I was laughing breathlessly, and Kingston hooked his arm around my waist, lifting me off the ground as we raced.

I giggled and kicked, but he tightened his grasp and wouldn't let me go.

And I loved it.

There were kids everywhere, from all around the state. This truly was the spectacle of the season, and I was thrilled to be there, dressed like this and with these three.

As soon as we got inside, Archer went off in search of drinks, Valen got distracted by a friend, and Kingston was dragged off to settle a bet about football.

I was left in the middle of a massive room with triple-height ceilings and expensive, modern furniture and art. There were costumed rich kids as far as the eye could see, and for a moment I felt glad that I wasn't here with Penny. She would have felt out of place in one of our usual handmade costumes.

And then I immediately felt guilty over feeling that way.

"Hey, sexy," Max said, coming behind me. I would recognize his voice anywhere. "Why are you here alone? You could get snatched up and taken away if you're not careful."

"I'm a grown woman. I can take care of myself," I bristled. There was something about Max that rubbed me the wrong way. He was attractive and intelligent, but something was off about the way he spoke. Everything felt like it had a double meaning and I was missing the joke. Or I was the butt of the joke. Either way, I didn't like it.

He was wearing a Joker costume and stood next to me, too close, to speak.

"You're hardly grown, princess," he whispered into my ear and grabbed my ass. "You still have time to fill out all the way."

I was about to say something snappish to him when

Archer returned with drinks. I grabbed one and gulped it in one go to take the edge off my discomfort, and Max practically did the fifty meter dash to the backyard to get away from Archer.

"Was that douche bag bothering you?" he asked and took a long draw from his beer bottle. "Give me the word and I'll rearrange his face for you."

He watched Max make his way through the crowd with a dark look on his face. He wanted to fight. His body was drawn tight, like a bow ready to release an arrow. I was the one holding the string. I could loosen my fingers and set him free to beat Max to the ground.

I contemplated it for a moment, enjoying my power. Rolling it around like I'd roll a fine wine around on my tongue the way the Kings had taught me during some of my lessons in Archer's mansion.

But in the end, I decided against it. I wanted to have fun, to explore my newfound place among Covington society, and maybe fool around a little with my Kings.

"No, let him go," I said and put my hand on Archer's forearm to calm him. "I want to dance."

"After a couple more," he said and held up another drink. I took the cup and drained it, ignoring the bitter taste of the vodka, and then drank another.

A sexy song came on, and I wasn't about to wait. I grabbed Archer and began to grind against him to the beat, closed my eyes, and really got into it. The lights dimmed, and the DJ played another right after it, something with a deep, sensual bass that got the vodka flowing through my body and loosened me up.

Valen came back and found us, brought me another drink or two, and joined in. The three of us kissed and danced while I twisted between them. I'd kiss Archer, then pivot and kiss Valen, and back again over and over until the entire night was filled with the crush of their big, muscled bodies, the scent of them, the feel of our luxurious costumes brushing my leg, and the taste of their drinks on their lips.

I was sweating and exhausted after an hour of it, and the crowd on the dance floor was growing with each song, making it harder and harder to dance in my big gown. My wig was itchy, and I contemplated tearing it off my head.

"Can we go outside?" I asked during a lull in the music. "I'm so hot, I need some fresh air."

"Of course," Valen said, but Archer raised his brow and gave me a wolfish grin.

"You are hot. Fucking hot."

I laughed and exited the house with one on each side. I was holding onto them, because when we hit the cool night air, my head felt like it had grown ten sizes and was hovering above my body.

"I think I had too much to drink," I said and lifted my hand to my forehead. "I feel dizzy."

"Only one cure for that," Archer said, that wolfish grin back on his face. "More booze!"

"And more kisses," Valen added. He was ever the romantic. Archer was ever my party animal. I loved the balance they brought into my life.

If only my skulking bad boy alpha wolf, leader of the pack, Kingston would come around more often I would be complete.

"Shit, I see somebody I have to talk to," Valen said suddenly, and he darted off through the crowd on the wide marble veranda.

"Why don't you take a seat here, and I'll go hunt

down something to drink and maybe a little something to eat?" Archer said, helping me sit on a beautiful delicate metal bench tucked into a rosebush. There were no blooms now, of course, but the foliage was still green and it felt like a little hidden room in the midst of the overwhelming number of people at the party.

I waited by myself for a few minutes, passing the time people watching and enjoying the costumes. I thought I saw a glimpse of Sofia dressed as, big fucking surprise, a slutty cheerleader with her cheer crew in matching costumes. There were lots of really creative ones, too—monsters and cosplay comic characters, even full furry suits and complicated ones that needed more than one person, like the centaur near the snack table.

"Greetings, Tribute."

I looked up and saw Ryker there, dressed as a Roman gladiator and looking fucking fine as hell.

I flashed to a vision of his dick, the piercings and tattoos and the way he'd forced the loser to give him head. It was an uncomfortable memory, and I was flooded with guilt at how much I liked it.

"Uh, hey," I stammered, and my throat tightened before I could say anything clever.

He flopped on the bench next to me, suddenly seeming too large for it. His body was massive, a block of muscled, tattooed, hot guy in costume that barely covered anything.

He smelled divine, and his skin glistened. I could envision Ryker spreading coconut oil or something on his skin before coming out tonight, and I realized I was more of a slut than I'd ever known. I had no boundaries. Even with the three Kings to fill my life, my head couldn't stop imagining all the different ways I'd like to explore Ryker's body and find out if he was as wild with a woman as he was in the cage.

"You like shit like this?" he asked and gestured outwards. He was leaning back with his long legs stretched in front of him, and he casually draped one arm on the bench behind me.

"It's okay," I replied. "I've never been to a party like this before."

"Have you been drinking?" he asked.

"Yeah, is it obvious? I don't usually drink, either. I think I'm a lightweight, so I wind up sounding really stupid really fast."

"I don't think you sound stupid at all," he said, looking over at me. "I was just thinking how stupid your handlers are to leave you tipsy and unattended at a party like this."

"Handlers?" I snorted. I brushed my hand towards him in irritation. "I don't have 'handlers.' They aren't handling me."

"Oh, are you going to tell me they're your boyfriends?" he asked, raising one eyebrow in a mocking way.

I was quiet as I tried to figure out how to explain it to him. They weren't exactly my boyfriends, but they weren't my handlers. That was bullshit, and it offended the hell out of me for him to say it.

"You're wrong," I replied evenly. "They're not my boyfriends, but they're not my handlers. They're... We just... I like spending time with them."

"Tell yourself whatever you want, princess." He chuckled and leaned close enough that I could see the way his thick, black lashes flicked when he blinked. I could see the flecks of gold in the deep brown eyes and a single green patch under the pupil of his left one. "But they'll never treat you right if you're sitting here by yourself and are okay with it."

"You're trying to tell me you wouldn't leave your girl alone?" I replied and shook my head. "I don't believe you."

"Believe what you want," he said and moved even closer. Our lips were almost touching, and I could feel his breath on my mouth. "But I'm telling you, if I had a girl like you, I wouldn't let you out of my sight. I wouldn't trust a single one of these fucking predators here. I wouldn't trust anyone to keep their hands off you."

His eyes were intense and lit bright from within, and I believed him. I believed his sincerity with every ounce of my being.

And then he leaned even closer, put his hand on the back of my neck as if claiming me as his property, and brushed his lips against mine. Sparks exploded the moment we touched. My blood raced around my body and whirled inside my head like a hurricane out of control.

"Get your fucking hands off her!"

Kingston's voice split my ears, and I jerked away to look up at him. Ryker didn't move but kept his hand on my neck and his face close to mine.

"She was left here unattended," he said without looking at Kingston. "I was treating her the way she should be treated, like a delicious little princess. The queen of the party, and worthy of attention."

Then he looked up with a challenging smile playing across his lips. "If you're not going to treat her like the Tribute, you don't deserve to have her at all."

"She's ours," Kingston growled dangerously. "I'm only going to say it one more time. Get your fucking hands off her."

Ryker laughed, released me, and stood up. He was eye to eye with Kingston but was wider. His shoulders were broader, and he exuded a feral power that scared me on Kingston's behalf.

"Or what?" he asked, a direct challenge to Kingston. "Why don't you tell her what happens to the Tribute? Or are you too much of a pussy to man up and let her in on the biggest secret of all?"

Kingston flinched and took a single step back. He looked at Ryker and said, "Stay out of Covington business, and again, keep your fucking hands off our Tribute."

"What are you going to do about it, tough guy?" Ryker laughed, openly mocking Kingston.

"Or I'll tear them off your fucking body," Kingston replied.

I'd had enough. I wasn't going to let testosterone and booze fuel their fight on my behalf, not tonight. They could battle it out in the cage at Dirty Kingdom if it came down to that.

I jumped up and took a step between them. My puffy skirts dragged across both their legs, and I reached up to place my hands on each of their chests.

"Enough," I said in a serious voice. "This is a party, meant for fun. If I'm the queen, then you must obey me when I tell you to get along."

"I'll get along with him if he sucks my fat cock," Kingston growled, grabbing himself in the crotch. He meant for it to be an insult, but he'd forgotten what kind of guy Ryker was, the kind of crazy he was dealing with.

Ryker stepped back, looked Kingston up and down, and said, "Not my usual type, but I might give it a suck. Pull it out."

I thought the vein in the side of Kingston's head was going to explode, and he ground his teeth while staring Ryker down.

I thought I was going to have a fight on my hands for sure, but Archer reappeared just then, balancing a couple of drinks in his hands.

"One for you," he said and handed me a red Solo cup. He looked at Ryker, then Kingston, and back to me. "And one for... holy shit, either of these dudes. What's going on here?"

I laughed, and before I could reply, Ryker grumbled, "Nothing. Fucking nothing." He turned to me, drew his thumb along my jawline and added, "Remember, you're worth more than being left alone at a party, princess. You are worth more than being their Tribute."

And with that, he stalked off into the crowd where he was met with admiring fans and plenty of girls in slutty costumes. I'd been hoping he would express an interest in me, as crazy as that sounded, but I was forgettable as soon as he had others hanging off him.

"That was fucking embarrassing," Kingston said in my ear as he gripped my upper arm with his massive hand. His fingers dug in, and he added, "I know you're a little whore, but at least pretend to be a virgin until Dirty Kingdom."

I didn't know what to say to that, but my anger reared its ugly head, and I had that rage rush through me—the rage that got me into trouble with my family at times, the rage I thought I had under control.

It was like somebody else did it, and I was watching from afar.

But I lifted my red cup, threw the drink in Kingston's face, and stormed back into the house.

I was tired of being humiliated, tired of being disrespected, and most of all, I was tired of Kingston fucking Taylor being the one to do it.

28

Once inside the house, I became aware of how angry I was, but also how tipsy I felt. The lights spun around me, and the floor swayed as if made of jelly. The techno beat of the dance music throbbing in the living room felt like a pulse, pushing me through the halls and through narrow passages behind the kitchen and dining room.

I came out into yet another massive room that was crammed shoulder to shoulder with people, and I stumbled around looking for the exit. I just saw tall windows overlooking the outside party area, so I'd somehow managed to come full circle, but on the inside of the mansion.

"Everly!" Somebody called my name, and I whirled around, looking for the source.

"Over here, piggy," Sofia called and waved at me. Her gaggle of slutty cheerleaders giggled and gathered around her. I tried to move away, but it was too crowded to get away. They made their way towards me, looking more like a gang of geese than sexy cheerleaders, with the way they seemed threatening and huddled together.

"I'm not doing this, Sofia," I said and held my hand up. "I'm going home. So you did it, you scared me off."

I made a sarcastic gesture with my hand and made a spooky noise to show she'd done nothing, that I was going on my accord.

"That's not what I want, psycho," she hissed and stood in front of me. "I want to see you hurt."

"Yikes, who's the psycho then?" I laughed and looked at her friends. One of them tittered nervously with me.

"Tiffany, what the fuck?" Sofia blurted and slapped the girl on the arm. "Listen, bitch, I was coming over here to kick your ass, but I actually have a message for you."

"What's the message? You're going to kick my ass if I don't leave or something fucking stupid? Yeah, I know, and I am leaving."

"No," she replied and rolled her eyes at me. "Listen, Kingston asked me to find you and give you a message. He said you seemed upset, and he wants to talk to you."

"Tell him I'll meet him by his truck," I said, realizing I needed a ride home. I would have walked, but the little silk slippers I was wearing weren't exactly made for a hike, even if it was just through city streets. It would have taken me a couple hours to get there.

"Listen, bitch, I'm not your little messenger," she hissed and slapped at the tall, beautiful wig I was wearing. It tipped over and toppled off my head onto the floor where she promptly stomped it under her feet.

Her cheerleaders giggled, and my head felt better immediately. But still, it was annoying as fuck.

"Are you being serious? I really can't do this right now, Sofia, so if you're trying to fuck with me, please hold off until another time."

"No, I'm being totally serious. You know I won't fuck with King," she said, and the way she drawled out his name into a whine set my nerves on edge. "I don't want to do anything to make him angrier with me. I want him to like me again. So that's the message."

"I don't know..." My voice trailed off, and I gave her the old side eye, trying to detect any setup. As far as I could tell, she was being sincere, and I did know she wanted to get back with him pretty badly.

"Please," she said, her eyes pleading with me. "We're not going to be besties or anything, but do this one small thing for me."

And against my better judgement, I nodded and got her directions. Apparently, Kingston wanted to meet me upstairs where it was quieter and where they had lounges set up in some of the guest suites.

I found the room with the blue door that she'd told me about at the top of the stairs and to the left and pushed it open. It was dark inside, with LED lights lining the entire place where the walls met the ceiling. It was set to the lowest level in a light blue to match the door.

"Kingston?" I asked, stepping inside, my wide rococo skirt brushing against the doorjamb. "Are you in here?"

The door was pushed closed behind me, and strong arms grabbed me from behind.

"No, he's not, but I am," Max said, slobbering into my ear on my left side. "Fuck, you're hot. I've been dying to find out what's under that sexy little slut queen costume all night."

"Let me go!" I exclaimed and struggled in his grasp, but he had me pinned pretty tight with just one hand. My wrists began to ache, and pain shot up my arm into my shoulder. "Fuck, Max, let me go!"

"You want it, that's why you came up here," he exhaled in my ear. "The message was clear, sweetheart. It was fucking clear. Come through that door and you belong to me for the night."

"That's not what Sofia told me!" I cried out and twisted to get away, but he was strong. His muscular hands tightened grip the harder I fought.

"She said you'd say that," he breathed into my ear. "You're saying exactly what she said. She said you were into this kind of thing."

He kissed my neck and slurped his tongue up and down until he settled on my earlobe. I could hear his breathing in my ear, and the slippery noises his tongue made were sickening. I gagged and felt my stomach lurch from all the alcohol swishing around inside, combined with the disgusting sensation of Max's mouth on my flesh.

"Max," I groaned and leaned away. "Max..."

"That's right, you're getting into now," he said, mistaking my groan of warning for one of pleasure. "Come on, babe, give it to me."

His free hand reached down and tugged at my skirt and lifted it until I was exposed from the back. He slid his fingers under the slip of my panties and prodded towards the slit of my pussy.

I gagged again, and tears sprung from my eyes, threatening to spill over.

I opened my mouth to scream and give it one last push to get away from him, but the door swung open, and light from the hallway flooded us, brightening up the scene.

"Of course, this is where you are," Kingston said from the doorway. "Sofia told me what was up and I didn't believe her, but I should always fucking trust my gut."

"Help me!" I cried out and twisted to look back at him. "Please, he's forcing me!"

"That's exactly what the little whore likes to say." Max leered and jerked me harder back against him. "She likes it rough, but you already know that, don't you?"

"Let her go," Kingston said in a low tone.

"You wanna go first? I don't mind watching, as long as I get my turn," Max said.

I struggled again, and Kingston caught my eye, narrowed his, and crossed towards us. He grabbed Max by the collar and lifted him off the floor. "I fucking said let her go."

His jaw was clenched, his teeth were gritted tight, and his intent was clear. Max let out a squeak and wiggled like a little Joker marionette. If I hadn't been so filled with adrenaline and fear, I would have laughed.

"I was just about to leave," Max said, his voice high pitched now, and all at once, he released me. I stumbled away and fell into Kingston's arms, grateful that I was finally saved.

"Get the fuck out of here," he growled to Max, and Max backed away slowly.

But he stood up straight and became emboldened the moment he thought he was out of fist range. "Defend the Covington Tribute all you want, but you know she wanted me. And you know I'll have her after Dirty

Kingdom. And then she'll rake her nails down my back and forget your name when I fuck her tight little cunt."

The moment the words were out of his mouth, he realized he'd fucked up. It was too late, though, because Kingston was already in action. He held me with one arm and pulled the other back, let it go, and slammed his fist into Max's face.

Max screamed, and blood immediately spilled from his nose and down his face. He made a wet, garbled sound, and he brought his hands up to staunch the bleeding, but it didn't help. Blood poured through them and he said, "What the fuck, Taylor? What the fuck?"

Kingston shook his head and roared, "You want another one? Get the fuck out!"

Max turned and ran, blood trailing on the floor behind him. Kingston watched him leave then slammed the door behind him.

"Holy shit." I exhaled and looked down. The edge of my skirt was spattered in a fine spray of blood. His nose had exploded onto my beautiful dress. "That was intense."

Kingston had his back to me, and I walked over and reached up to touch him. I wanted to thank him for saving my ass, for being there for me. For being my Kingston, from second grade, all the way to just now.

When I touched him, he flinched and jerked away from me. I drew back in hurt, but he turned around to gaze down at me. "What were you doing up here with him?" he demanded. "Why were you whoring yourself for the Harrington douche bags?"

"I..." I stammered, confused. "I wasn't. What are you talking about?"

"First, Ryker had his hands all over you right out in plain view. And now I find you up here with Maxwell Harriot, the disgusting little trust fund cunt who runs the whole fucking thing this year."

"Sofia tricked me into coming up here," I replied and put my hand on his arm, desperate to convey my innocence. "She said you wanted to see me up here. Or else I never would have come up."

"You're a *whore*, Everly," he snapped, and pushed my hand away. "You've been a whore like your mother for years, probably, but I gave you a free pass to become Tribute because I wanted to fuck you. I wanted a taste of your white trash pussy. That's it."

"Why would you say that?" I asked. "That's so horrible. Why are you being like this?"

I turned to leave, overcome with anger and grief, but he stepped past me and blocked me from leaving.

"I'm being like the kind of guy you want," he said, his voice so low I could barely hear it. "I'm being the kind of man a slut like you craves, the kind who takes what's his and doesn't take no for an answer."

He reached down and tore the front of my dress. The sudden act of aggression shocked me into silence, and the silken fabric fell apart like it was melting off me. My breasts heaved out, unbound, and I began panting in fear. "What are you doing?" I gasped.

"What I should have done weeks ago," he rasped and cupped my breasts in his hands. I wanted to push him away and tell him to fuck off. I wanted to tell him no, that I didn't want him like this. I didn't want him when he looked at me like this.

But I couldn't. I wanted him so badly that I

physically couldn't deny him. I couldn't tell him no, and I couldn't stop him even if I tried.

I'd been waiting for this moment my whole life, and we were too far gone to ever come back from it.

I was still terrified by this new face of Kingston, this aggressive, violent face that was more feral than I needed and more terrifying than I'd ever known from him.

He dipped his head and took one of my breasts into his mouth, sucked my nipple until it puckered, and rolled the other one between his finger and thumb. I drew in a sharp breath and ran my hands through his thick, dark curls. I arched my back and felt his hands travel all across my body.

He stood abruptly and lifted me up into his arms, swung me around, and carried me towards the bed.

"Kingston, no," I moaned. "This is too fast."

"I've already waited too fucking long for this," he rasped, and he dropped me on the thick comforter. I covered my breasts with my hands and he shoved my skirt high up my thighs to my hips.

"Please, don't," I whimpered. "Not like *this*."

"You've wanted it, too," he said. "I've seen the way you look at me. Hungry for cock, desperate for attention. *My* attention. You've been thinking about this from the first moment I kissed you."

He pressed his knee between my legs and shoved them open, climbed between them and dropped over me. He kissed me, but not the way I wanted to be kissed. Not the way I needed to be kissed. His own hunger consumed him, and he became somebody unrecognizable to me.

He was no longer my Kingston, the boy I loved from

the first day I saw him defending me on the schoolyard. He was now an aggressive stranger who thought I was nothing more than a filthy little whore to be used and abused like any one of the reams of girls who were humped and dumped by him and the Kings.

He was the worst example of every kind of man I hated, the ones who had leered at me or tried to force me over the years. Not the kind of man I thought he was. I felt sick to my stomach, but still... There was that part of me that wanted it. I wanted Kingston fucking Taylor any way I could get him. I wanted this. I wanted him to be my first, because this might be my only chance.

He kissed my lips hard, stabbed his tongue into my mouth, then pulled back and kissed down my neck to my chest. He took one breast in his mouth again. He rolled my nipple in his teeth, and the pain mixed with the pleasure and hurt so good I let out an unintended moan.

He kissed further down, pulled my brocade dress apart completely, and lifted the skirt higher. His hand slipped between my legs and cupped my pussy. His thumb pressed against my slit and slipped inside. He found my clit and drew it back and forth across my sensitive flesh until I was quivering in his hands.

I thought he was going to go down on me again, and I spread my legs wider in anticipation of his hot, hungry mouth on my pussy. I ached for it.

But he made a swift motion upwards and wound up between my thighs again. But this time, he was ready to fuck. I pushed at his chest, and he reached down to undo his pants. I felt him pull his cock out, and its throbbing thickness pressed against my soaking wet slit.

I wanted to tell him no, but all at once, this incredible feral urge came over me, and I wanted him inside. I wanted him to savage me, tear into my flesh, and possess me until I dissolved in his fingers like sand under the waves.

I clung to him, and he rasped in my ear, "Say it. Tell me you want it."

"Fine, I do. Fuck, I want you, I've always wanted you." I exhaled and pushed at his chest. "But not like this, I need you to go slow for my first time."

"Oh, come on, Evie," he replied in a long, rolling growl. He pressed harder, and I began to open for him. God, how I wanted him inside of me, but I wanted him to love me first.

I tried to push him away so he'd go slow, but he kept bowling me over like a train along the tracks. There was no stopping him as he finally took what had always been his.

He pushed harder, and all at once, he was inside. I was torn, and he was buried deep. Pain exploded inside of me, radiating out in hot shards of agony as Kingston fucking Taylor took my virginity from me—not how I wanted it, but he claimed it as his despite my pleas. "We both know this isn't your first time. I've seen the pics."

I tensed up, tears of pain and emotion pouring from my eyes, and gasped, "What pics?"

He didn't stop.

29

His hips pounded against me, and his cock tore my virginal pussy apart. I couldn't make him stop, and I couldn't stop myself from clinging to him.

"All of them. All the fucking pics," he said, and he kept fucking me, hurting me. The physical pain was replaced with mental shock, and I couldn't understand what he was saying.

"Stop," I gasped, and pushed back even harder against his chest. "Please, I don't know what you're talking about."

He paused above me, still inside me, and the shards of pain gave way to a dull ache. His face was twisted in cruel intent, and he shook his head. "Stop playing coy, Evie. Stop fucking pretending like we both don't know what you've done. Now shut the fuck up and let me fuck your tight little cunt."

"You're hurting me," I moaned, not recognizing my own voice. It had a low, animal sound of pain and confusion.

"And you're pissing me off," he replied and dropped

down to rest his weight on one elbow. He covered my mouth with his again and slid deep inside me.

I pummeled at his chest and tried to wiggle away, but his massive, muscled body pushed me into the mattress and immobilized me. I was desperate to escape him and salvage my body, but as I struggled, something started to happen.

The shards of pain became that dull ache, and with each thrust of his hips and each pass of his massive, thick cock, the dull ache gave way to warmth, and it started feeling good.

Really good.

My struggles turned into movements that matched his motion, and soon our bodies were in perfect synchronicity. I wanted him deeper and harder. I ran my hands down his back and desperately pulled his shirt out of his pants so I could feel his bare flesh under my fingertips.

I groaned against his lips, and he kissed me slower, the way I wanted it. His angry thrusts grew slower and more controlled as he pistoned in and out of me with increasing deliberation.

"This," he said against my mouth and plunged forward, "is what I've been wanting."

"This," he repeated and growled, a low breathy sound against my neck as he pulled back. "Is what you've been wanting."

He slid back in, an agonizing inch by inch, until he bottomed out and split me in half while filling me fuller than I'd ever been. It was as if he was reaching me in places I didn't know existed, touching my very soul from the inside of me.

He twisted his hips, and I gasped with unexpected

bliss. He cupped my face in one hand, and at the same time, he eased himself, slippery and wet, in and out of my tightly clenched pussy. He said, "Fucking look at me, Evie. Look into my eyes while I fuck you."

I opened them up and stared at him above me, looking down with fever heat in his eyes. "Oh god," I exhaled, and he eased out, back in, and repeated his exquisite sex until I bubbled over with pure joy and could no longer contain myself.

"I can feel your cunt," he said. "My tight little queen. My perfect little whore. Evie, my love."

My head exploded on the last word as the floodgates opened wide and my body joined with my emotions, knotted together like corded roots pushing deep into the earth.

Kingston's words, his scent, the weight of his body on mine, the taste of his tongue in my mouth. All of it combined into the perfect whirlwind of ecstasy and rapturous release.

"Yes," I cried out. "I'm yours."

"Mine," he growled and thrust up one last time, hard and deep. He paused while I reached the pinnacle of my excitement, let it wash over me and crash into my mind. It all was too much for me to contain anymore, so I let out a cry of release, a surprised noise, and I came.

I was lost in it, the sensations. A cork on the ocean, a feather on the wind. I had no control over what I was saying or doing, and I dug my fingernails into Kingston's back, gouged down to his hips and clung there. I drew my legs up and locked them around him, pulling him impossibly deep, so far into me that I no longer knew where I ended and he began.

We were one.

"Evie," he rasped, and his eyes blazed with the ferocity of his own orgasm. "My beautiful Evie."

I felt his hard cock pulse and surge, and then his hot seed flooded my pussy, pushing me even farther into the orgasmic bliss that was consuming my very essence.

It was intense, a hurricane of sensations at the end of Kingston fucking Taylor's cock. The boy I'd loved for years, the one I'd hated for weeks, and the one I'd owned for hours. For he was mine as much as I was his. And I laid claim to him now, body, heart, and soul.

I was his. He was mine, and together we were the perfect alpha couple, the leaders of our misfit band of Kings.

And together, eventually, we would rule the Dirty Kingdom.

I fell back and went limp as the energy left my body and I slowed down. Kingston followed and dropped down, released my face, and kissed me gently while still inside.

"I love you," I said, emboldened by the soaring heights of my feelings for him.

"I love you too, Evie," he replied, and he kissed my lips, my face, and my eyelids. When he noticed my still damp, tear-stained cheeks, he pulled back and swiped one away with his thumb. "Why are you crying?"

"It hurt," I said with regret, as if I had failed him somehow by being a virgin. As if it was my fault all of this had happened. "You hurt me."

"You've done this before, though," he said, looking down and knitting his brows together. "This wasn't your first time."

I drew in a quivering breath and said, "Of course it

was. I'm sorry, I've never had sex before. I tried to tell you."

He was still and silent and searched my face, looking for a lie. He shook his head, just the slightest movement, and said, "But I've seen the photos. You have done this before. And what about the abortion?"

"What photos? Abortion? I've never been with anyone, Kingston. You were my first."

Fear flared inside my chest, but it was followed a knee-jerk irritation because of his doubt. I didn't like that I had to defend myself, and I wondered what the hell he'd seen to make him doubt my truthfulness in the first place. Had this been why he was convinced I was a whore all along?

"Are you—" He cut himself off and shook his head again. "Evie, my father showed me pictures. A bunch of you and Reg, and three pics with my father."

The bottom fell out of my world, and the air went out of the room. I could no longer hear the bass beat from the party down below or the beating of Kingston's heart in his chest. I could hear ringing in my ears and feel the tightness in my stomach as it began to roil.

"What the fuck are you talking about?" I asked in a quiet voice. I was unable to speak louder than a whisper as realizations exploded in my head.

The times I'd been alone with Reg. The nights he'd insisted on paying for a hotel room for Natalie and mom so they didn't have to drive back from a dance recital.

I'd been so jealous of them, of his care and attention.

But those had been the nights he'd let me have a sip of his bitter alcohol. I'd felt so special and grown up.

And those had been the nights I'd blacked out. I'd slept until the next afternoon and I'd woken with a pounding head, feeling exhausted despite my sleep, and with an aching body even though I'd done nothing the night before.

"Oh fuck," Kingston said, and his voice had the opposite reaction. It grew louder, bolder, as he added, "I'll fucking kill them. I'm going to fucking kill both of them for this, Evie. I swear, I'll fucking kill them for this."

Reg had been drugging me. Drugging me and assaulting me, and I couldn't think or breathe. I had to get revenge, and Kingston would tell Archer and Valen and they would protect me.

But how would that help me when my entire world blew apart? How was I supposed to finish school or find somewhere to live or tell my mom?

How could I face Nat the brat and let her know what her father had done to me?

Reg had destroyed everything for me, and I didn't know how I was going to pick up the pieces now.

30

His rage heated him up, and I could feel the simmering fire just below the surface of his skin. A fever of anger on my behalf.

"Where are these pictures?" I asked in my tiny voice. "What do they show?"

"They're on my laptop," he said. "I found them in my Dad's office on a thumb drive. I was so mad, Evie. So fucking mad at you. I'm so sorry, babe. I'm so sorry, princess. Please forgive me."

He laid his head on my chest, and I had no choice but to comfort him and forgive him. "Of course I do," I said and stroked his hair, making soothing sounds as if he was a great beast in distress. "I forgive you. You couldn't have known."

"It showed them between your legs, but now that I think about it, I wonder... Were you were drugged."

"Did they... Were they... *fucking* me?" I asked, horrified at the image but confused because it had hurt so hard when Kingston had taken me just now.

"No. They were *tasting* you," he said, and his voice

broke. "Please don't make me describe them to you. Just know that I'm going to fucking kill them for you. You'll never suffer again. I'll protect you, Evie, I promise. I love you so much."

"I believe you." I sighed and closed my eyes to inhale the warm scent of his musk, to feel his heartbeat against my skin, and run my hands through his hair. "And I love you."

I unhitched my mind and let myself float along this moment of bliss. But then something hit me and I pulled away from him with a jerk.

"What is it?" Kingston asked, looking down at me.

"*What* abortion?" I asked him. "You mentioned an abortion."

"Over in Ashton," he replied with a frown. "One of the guys from the team was there with his girlfriend getting birth control at that clinic. You know the one."

"Yeah," I replied. Ashton was the perfect distance for anonymous birth control and gynecology visits for kids from Oakville. We all knew *that* clinic.

"He said he saw you there. Well, he didn't see you, but he heard the abortion clinic side call your name," he told me. The clinic was divided into two sections, a side for regular checkups and short appointments, and a side for more complicated procedures, including abortions. But he wouldn't know that. Guys like him wouldn't think about the IUD insertions or pelvic exams. They just knew it as the abortion side.

"That's ridiculous," I exclaimed, and pulled back even more. He rolled off me, and I broke free to push up onto my side. My breasts tumbled out, and Kingston stared at them like we weren't talking about me being assaulted and somebody obviously using my name to end a pregnancy. I didn't mind. I mean, I wanted him to look. But I was too tied up wondering who had been pregnant and why they'd gotten it taken care of. And why my name in particular?

"I know, Evie," he said, and looked back into my eyes. "It's just what I heard. And it is ridiculous."

"When was it?" I asked. "And how would I even get there? You know I don't drive, and there's no bus to take me."

"It was the weekend of the Ryker fight," he replied. "I remember because I fucking hate that guy. Philly told me he heard your name called but didn't see you. But even that made me so fucking mad. Just the thought of you with somebody else's baby inside you drove me crazy."

"It wasn't me," I replied, and my mind raced a thousand miles a minute. Was somebody trying to get me in trouble, or was somebody using my name because they needed to? It's not like Everly Hayes was common, and it's not like I was well known or anything. "Was it Sofia? Maybe she wanted to fuck with me and knew he'd be there."

"No," Kingston replied and looked away. Shame flickered across his gorgeous face and he said, "She was with me. That was the weekend I dumped her ass, but not before I fucked it a couple more times."

"Ew, gross." I shuddered and made a face of disgust. "I can't believe you were ever with her. She's so nasty."

"She was chosen for me," he said. "For my image, my return to Covington. That's all. But it wouldn't have been her."

"I wonder who then," I said, going through everyone I knew.

And then I realized who it was. Somebody right in my face all along, the person who had gotten me into this entire mess in the first place.

My best friend, Penny. I felt sick when I thought of her going to the clinic alone, and I wanted to text her immediately to find out what had happened. To help her right then and there.

But it was nearing midnight on a Saturday, and she'd be in bed by now. Besides, this wasn't a text conversation. This was something I had to do in person.

"I think I figured it out," I said and then told him why I suspected Penny.

"So she wasn't doing it to hurt you," he said.

"No, to protect herself. If she was caught by her family, she would have been kicked out onto the streets. You know they're religious crazies. That's how you tricked me into all of this in the first place."

"It's so fucking unfair, Evie," he said, his anger rising again as his entire body tensed. He clenched his jaw and his fist, and his gorgeous eyes sparked with frustration and pain. "You girls do nothing, but you get blamed for everything."

"Tell me about it. Try living this life. It fucking sucks sometimes. There are days I wish I could run away and live in a nunnery surrounded by cats and books."

"But then you'd miss out on this," he said and leaned over to kiss me again. This time it was so careful, as if he thought I was breakable. Desire swirled through my body and collected in my core, where it heated my throbbing, aching pussy.

Kingston's anguish was on his lips in the way he touched me. He wanted to protect me, but he wanted to ravage me. He, like me, contained a duality of forces.

The desire to behave, and the desire to let go and release the dark side.

His hands trembled as they moved down my body, and he was so slow and careful as he cupped my wet heat that I almost bit his lip and forced him to finger fuck me.

But I let him go slow and move in his exquisite way across my body. He kissed me along my neck and down my breasts and lifted my skirt again. He dipped his face low and dragged his tongue across my slit, lapping at my soaking wet, freshly fucked cunt, his seed mixed with my virginal blood.

Kingston didn't hesitate. He stabbed my clit and licked me steadily, devouring my blood sacrifice and his own cum like he was starving for it. It all combined into a sexy, risqué moment, and I built up for another epic, mind shattering orgasm.

Just as I was heading towards the crashing peak, he pulled away and flopped onto the bed next to me. His cock was out of his tight costume pants still, and it was rock-hard, thick, and tall. It jutted out almost a foot from his body, and it was gorgeous.

I could see my blood mixed with his spunk drying on the tip, and I couldn't help myself. I was fired up from his teasing mouth, so I dove onto his cock, pulling it into my mouth between my lips so I could suck him clean.

I could taste the sweet musk of our combined fluids, and it was incredibly fucking hot. He tugged at me and said, "Get on top, Evie. I want to see you ride my cock. I want to see your tits bounce when I fuck you from below."

He pulled me down to him and we kissed, our

tongues sliding and slippery. Blood, saliva, cum, and pussy all blending around into a delicious mixture that spoke of sex and pleasure. He reached down and grabbed my hips, lifted me up, and helped me settle over the top of his cock.

I felt the head press against my entrance, and I took a deep breath to prepare myself for one more time with Kingston's thick shaft filling me up and splitting me open. Burning me alive from within.

"Easy, Evie," he said, his voice soothing and caring this time around. "Go slow. It's gonna fucking hurt."

His cock head spread my lips and pushed inside again, but this time I was in control. It stung at first, where he'd torn me the first time with his brutal thrusting, but I took a breath to relax and draw him inside.

It was exquisite torture, the agony quickly giving way to ecstasy as I slid down his thickness. I hit as far as I could go and paused, still leaning forward with my mouth on his.

"Fuck," he exhaled against my lips, and I could feel the heat of his flesh pulse along the walls of my pussy. "You feel so good, Evie. You feel so fucking good."

His voice was filled with rapturous worship of me and my cunt. A ripple of power nudged up and down my spine and settled in the muscles of my tunnel. I quivered and gripped him as the last of the pain receded.

"This feels good." I exhaled and tilted my hips, drawing myself up his length to the top, where I teased him by almost pulling completely off.

And then I slid back down, fast. I made a noise of surprise as my cunt relaxed and grew to accommodate his massive cock. It almost shocked me how fast I took to it and how easy it was after a few passes with a nice, hard dick.

I groaned and repeated it, almost pulling off him until he released a growl of frustration, sat up, grabbed me by my hips, and slammed me down onto him.

"Stop fucking around, Evie," he rasped and thrust up inside, swift, brutal strokes that felt so goddamned good I thought I might cry. "Stop fucking around and fuck me good. Fuck me hard. Let me feel that tight little cunt of yours."

I cried out, and my pussy fluttered at his invasion, as if it was hungry for him, desperate to draw him in deeper. He pounded me from below, and my breasts bounced in his face as I sat on his lap. He nuzzled them and fucked me. I held onto his muscled arms, and then his shoulders as I balanced myself while we finally found our rhythm and found each other at last.

"Come for me," he growled when I cried out again, and my pussy clenched in pleasure. "I can feel your tight cunt. Let it go, Evie. Come on my dick for me. Squeeze me tight."

It happened so fast, I called his name, "Kingston!," a single word as the orgasm slammed into me and broke me into a million shards of memory. Every one of them contained a piece of Kingston Taylor and the girl I used to be. Every little moment that had brought us here, to me losing my virginity at his brutal hands but finding myself on the end of his loving cock.

I wanted to be with Kingston, and I knew I would be. From here on out, we were going to be together no matter what life threw at us. Even in the midst of my destruction and the realization that I was being assaulted while I was passed out. That I'd been betrayed by my own stepfather. Even in all that, I was happy. I was joyous. For I'd found the place I had always meant to be.

In Kingston Taylor's arms, riding his dick, loving him hard, and fucking him harder.

"Evie," he grunted and slammed into me harder, fast and deep. "Come. Now."

And I did. I continued to float on waves of pleasure as Kingston exploded deep inside. I could feel his hot load hit my womb, I could feel his cock surge and pulse with its power, and I could feel my own greedy cunt milking him harder as he spent the last of himself in me.

"Oh god, I love this," I exhaled dreamily and rested my head on his shoulder. "I could do this forever. Let's never leave this room, never deal with everything that happened."

"I would if I could," he said, holding me close as his cock softened and our bodies cooled. "I can't though. I need to protect you forever. I need to see them go down in flames."

I loved that he wanted to keep me safe now, and I loved that he was so free with his words.

As we lay together in each other's arms, spent and in love with a fire I'd never known, I realized we had to take those words and put them into action.

As much as it was going to hurt me, I had to tear my family apart in order to escape the horror of what had happened.

I had no idea what that would entail, and at that moment in time, I had no idea of the storm about to come.

31

"So this is where you've been hiding!" Archer yelled as he and Valen burst through the door to the bedroom.

Valen paused and sniffed the air, raised an eyebrow and said, "You two have been fucking."

"You fucked the Tribute?" Archer asked in horror, gasping as if Kingston had committed a cardinal sin. It was mostly for show. I suspected there was more of an undercurrent of envy in there.

Kingston's slow, easy smile answered for him.

And the way I shrugged my shoulders and surely looked as guilty as I could be was the confirmation he needed.

"You fucked the Tribute!" Archer said and dove onto the bed next to us. "Does this mean she's fair game now?"

"No, fuck off," Kingston said, and curled his arm around me protectively.

"Come on, we always share," Valen said and climbed onto the bed on the other side of us. "This isn't the time to get greedy."

"Hey, I don't make the rules this time around. It's ultimately up to Evie," Kingston said, but I could feel him bristle at the thought of sharing me with anyone else. I loved that about him, but I was about to surprise him with a revelation. Something I'd been thinking about nonstop.

"I say yes," I replied and tucked my face against Kingston's chest, too embarrassed to face the Kings after my grand admission. "I wouldn't mind being shared."

"All at once or one at a time?" Kingston asked. He held me close, and I could feel the thud-thud of his heart pounding fiercely in his chest. It was as if love for me had bloomed inside of him and was filling him up, making him feel more solid than before. Now that he was mine, really mine, he was corporeal, our relationship come to life. It no longer existed in the shadows, contained in wisps of imagination or longing between the two of us.

"Does it matter?" I asked and rolled away to look from one face to the next. "You know how much I love you, Kingston. You know how much you've meant to me for years now. You'll always be my number one."

"I know," he replied, and his face softened. "I also know what kind of woman you're going to be. Your appetites are already uniquely voracious, and that will just grow as you mature."

"Are you saying I'll get hornier the older I get?" I laughed.

"Maybe," he chuckled.

"So, yes?" Archer asked, reaching for me. He cupped my face in his hands and looked at me with wonder. "Yes? The Tribute is ours?"

"Yes, I am yours," I said.

Valen reached around Kingston to run his hand down my arm. "Sounds like something I could get into."

"Not until later, though," I said as the horrific revelations of Reg and Mr. Taylor's depravity suddenly hit me. The drinks from earlier had worn off, and looking at everything with sober eyes was extremely painful. "Kingston and I realized something tonight."

I proceeded to let them know what had happened, but I glossed over the part about Kingston forcing himself on me. How could I categorize the maelstrom we'd both been through in mere words? I couldn't think of any way without making Kingston sound rapey or creepy. And he was neither to me.

Kingston chimed in and told them about what he'd seen. He described the images with a little more detail, and my stomach squeezed tight when I thought about what they'd done to me. I was on the verge of throwing up when he stopped.

"So *that's* why you were convinced she was a whore," Archer said, pondering everything we'd just told him. "It makes sense on your end, dude, but you still have a lot of making up to do."

"You owe her more than an apology," Valen said. "You'd better crawl on your knees and beg her for forgiveness and hope she gives it."

"I *do* give it," I said with a smile and twisted to see Valen. It was strange to have the three of them surrounding me on a bed, and yet at the same time, it felt perfectly natural and extremely comforting. Nothing could touch me now, not when I was in the middle of my protective Kings. "I forgave him the moment I realized what had happened. When I found out what he'd seen."

"How do we get back at them?" Archer asked. "How are we going to fucking destroy the bastards who did this to you?"

They'd caught up to us now after wading through the information overload. They'd reached the vengeance part of the night. Now that we were all on the same page, I let Kingston take over.

"First of all, Evie has to get out of her house. She's not safe there, and I can't let her take the risk of sticking around," he said. "And obviously, I can't stay with my old man. I'll fucking kill him if I have to see him. The problem is that we don't have the money, and we don't have anywhere to go. Archer, Valen? Which one of you can take us in with the least amount of family drama?"

I could tell it killed him to admit he was powerless right now—my alpha king with no money and no resources to keep him safe. He hated having to ask for help, but at least we had that option. We were lucky to have Archer and Valen to support us when we needed it.

"Us? She could stay with me," Valen said. "I do have house staff, but as long as there are no wild parties, they won't bother my parents. I don't know about you, Kingston. Two house guests might make waves."

"Both of you can stay with me," Archer said in an irritated tone. He seemed put out, offended that Valen had made the offer first. "Nobody's around at my place anyway, you know that."

"Where would you rather stay?" Kingston asked. "Of course you can't stay with me, although that would be preferable in my opinion."

He scowled at both of the guys, jealousy getting the best of him.

"How about we go to Archer's tonight, since that's where we started out, and then go from there?" I asked, sitting up. The thumping bass from the party below was still loud and vibrating the entire mansion. I could hear kids in the distance yelling and screaming in laughter as the night ramped up and drinks flowed even faster.

"Sounds good," Kingston said. "You're the problem solver."

He leaned over and kissed my earlobe from behind, sending shivers up and down my spine. It wasn't even totally from the kiss; it was from his words. Hearing him speak about me with admiration and love was more than I ever dreamed of.

We climbed off the bed, and as I stood up, my dress fell apart on the top and my breasts bounced out.

"Oh shit, I forgot about this," I said, looking down.

When I looked back up, there were three sets of eyes staring at me with lustful hunger burning in them.

"Guys, up here." I laughed and snapped my fingers. I covered myself with my other arm. "I need some way to make it out of the party without showing everybody my breasts."

"Here," Kingston said and shrugged out of his jacket. "This should cover you up."

I slipped it on and it worked. It was huge on me, and the style was long to begin with, so it hung down to my knees.

"Perfect," I said, holding my arms out and looking down. "Now I just need a floppy hat and I'll look like Paddington Bear."

They laughed and bent over backwards, reassuring me that I was too hot to be a literary character. When we finally left the blue room, they gathered close to me as if to shield me from the prying eyes of party guests. I had my own muscular army of bodyguards, and I liked it. I could get used to it.

I was ignored by pretty much everyone as we left, but the three Kings were like legit royalty. People crowded them as they pushed through the chaos of the party, every one of them begging for a few moments of their attention.

And yet, every one of the Kings brushed them off, ignored them outright, or made empty promises that they'd text them soon.

All because of me.

The power that surged through my veins was as addictive as the orgasms I'd had earlier. I loved being the center of the group, the axis of the most popular triad at Covington.

It hit different now that I knew they wanted me and that Kingston loved me.

"Text your driver," Kingston told Archer as we left the front entrance and walked down the steps leading to the wide, curving driveway.

"He's already on his way," Archer said, and just like that, Archer's Range Rover came to a halt, waiting for us.

"How'd you do that?" I asked, impressed. "That's next level communication, and a little freaky if you ask me."

Archer made wiggling motions with his fingers and said, "It's magic, my love."

And then he started laughing and admitted, "Naw, the driver was instructed to wait for us, so he was watching the front door. Nothing magical. Just well-paid, happy staff."

We climbed into the back seat and fell into silence on the way back to Archer's. The one good thing about the wealthy neighborhood in a town like Oakville was that it wasn't very big. It took us less than five minutes to get to Archer's mansion.

The more time I spent around here, the more confusing the layout got, though. Apparently, the wealthy didn't like straight streets or grid patterns. They preferred winding, curved boulevards with no signage and very few lights.

I was beyond exhausted by the time we settled back at Archer's place. And I was too emotionally spent to do anything other than bask in the warmth and safety of their affections. I was ready for bed, but not sex, and they all understood.

It was funny to me how quickly the script had flipped. I'd gone from being the target of their aggression to the object of their desire. I didn't know how it had happened, but there was something natural about it. A chemistry thing, how we all fit together, physically and mentally.

I slipped into one of Archer's tee shirts and a pair of his boxers while my mind tried to process the events of the day. The four of us climbed into Archer's king-sized bed and somehow settled into each other's bodies, finding spaces for all our legs and arms. My mind wouldn't settle down as I tried to get the image of Reg and Mr. Taylor out of my head. What they'd done to me... I didn't know how I finally slipped into sleep, but somehow I did.

I woke sometime just before dawn with Kingston behind me, his breath on my neck, and Archer in front of me, his leg strewn up on mine and his hands around mine as he slept.

Valen wasn't in the bed, but he was sleeping soundly sprawled in a chair next to it. He'd been too wound up to sleep, so he'd said, so he must have eventually gotten up, but even he had finally succumbed.

There was something very reassuring about waking up with them at night, something mythological, and the shreds of some ancient story floated through my head.

It hadn't just been about conquering and humiliating the enemy in that ancient civilization I'd read about. But they'd been all about the pack. Groups of men married to the same central woman. A warrior princess with the power, intelligence, and beauty to command the hearts of several men.

I felt like that, surrounded by my three. I was their warrior princess, but they didn't know it yet.

Sometimes, I didn't know it either. But this, on the first day I was living with the truth of my life, I was stronger than I was the day before. And when I faced down the men who had violated me, I would be stronger still.

* * *

Archer drove this time, but we took the same black Range Rover from the night before. Kingston sat in the front passenger seat, and Valen sat in the back with me.

I was all nerves—jangled, fried, taut nerves

stretched over the fiery surface of anxiety. We had eaten breakfast in Archer's sunroom overlooking his backyard, a spread put out by his chef, but I regretted it. The fruit and yoghurt I'd eaten seemed to be sloshing around with the coffee, creating a sickening slew of bad vibes and pent up negative energy.

I wasn't even sure if I was terrified or enraged. Maybe a little of each.

"It's okay," Valen said, rubbing my back with his big, gentle hand. "You're going to go in, get your stuff, and let us handle the rest. You can call your mom later."

I closed my eyes and steadied my breathing. I used the same techniques to calm my fear that I used to calm my dark anger when I had to. I focused on the way the breath felt going into my lungs, and how it felt being expelled. I focused on Valen's steady presence, the weight of his touch grounding me to the present. And I listened to Archer and Kingston talk in the front seat, going over the details of how they were going to take care of me.

We knew my mom and Natalie weren't home yet, so it would just be Reg if he was in the house. The best case scenario would be if Reg had fucked off to play golf for the day, but with my odd luck, that was unlikely.

So it was like a recovery operation. Archer and Kingston would keep Reg in check downstairs while I went upstairs with Valen. I would pack up and decide what I wanted to take with me, and we would carry it out to the car together.

Once I was safely out of the house, I didn't care what they did to Reg. Yes, he was married to my mom and was the father to my little bratty sister, but he was a rapist who had drugged me for, well, who knows how long?

I secretly hoped they'd hurt him really bad. I couldn't express it; guilt held me back from giving it a voice. That part of myself that was still obeying our culture, the part that tells girls they should value being polite and pretty above speaking up and doing what they want. The part that gets most of us into trouble in the first place, when we go against our gut instincts and choose to appease a man instead of standing up for ourselves.

I had been too kind to Reg for far too long. He'd always given me an uncomfortable feeling, and he'd always unsettled me. But me, being a good girl, hadn't said anything because I didn't want to rock the boat. I didn't want to upset Mom, ruin Nat's life, or face Reg's anger.

I was over it. I wasn't going to start kicking ass right away, but I was tired of obeying everyone and worrying about staying in my place.

We pulled up in front of our house, and it looked different to me, even though I'd only been gone a short time. I'd never been part of the family in a way that let me feel loved, so this place had never truly been a home. Yet now that I saw it through these eyes, the ones that knew the truth, I could see how pathetic it all seemed.

Reg was obsessive about appearing better off than we actually were. He was insanely meticulous with the lawn care and landscaping, pretending we had a gardener when in fact it was all of us out there busting our asses to make it nice.

He had all the toys that made him feel like a big

man. A motorcycle, a muscle car, a truck, and a travel trailer, guns, as well as a dirt bike and quad. But all of it was on payments, and all of those payments meant we were stretched thin every month. Even with Mom's job paying pretty well, we never had more than the absolute minimum.

"You gonna be okay, Evie?" Kingston asked from the front seat. "If you need us to do this for you, just let me know and we can pick up your things."

I took a long, steadying breath and released it just as slowly. "No, I can do this. Let's go."

We got out and walked up. Reg's car was there, but that didn't necessarily mean anything. He sometimes got rides from his golf buddies.

I was fumbling around with my key in the front door lock when we heard the rumbling of an engine and a white sports car came cruising around the corner onto our street. It was one of those sad dad restoration cars, twenty years old, allowing them to relive their teen years.

"Oh shit, my old man," Kingston said, and I hurried up with the key.

I got it in and felt the lock click when the car stopped in front of our house and the engine shut down.

I turned back to find Reg and Kingston's dad, Rick, climbing out, and both of them looked pissed off.

My stomach lurched, and I thought I was going to throw up.

32

"What's going on here, son?" Rick asked as they approached.

"We're working on a chemistry project together," Valen said, stepping in front of me. The three of them had me surrounded and were watching the men closely. The lie didn't work, though, and the two men knew something was up.

"I asked my son," Kingston's dad sneered and locked his eyes on Kingston as he approached. I'd never thought of Mr. Taylor as a particularly threatening man. He was a hard worker and rarely drank. He sometimes hung out at our place when Reg had the game on or was on the barbecue.

I'd caught him watching me a now and then, but no more than any other average older dude checking out a young girl.

Or so I thought.

Now that I knew what they'd done to me, Mr. Taylor took on a new form. An ugly persona with a threatening aura. A menacing presence that made my skin crawl and my hair stand on end on my arms, as if there were insects crawling beneath the surface of my flesh.

I panicked and pushed the door open and stepped inside. Valen and Archer followed, and Kingston after them. He turned to slam our front door shut, for whatever good that would do, but his father stuck his foot through and it caught his leather work boot.

"Well, shit, son," Mr. Taylor said, coming into my house. "What's going on in here? Why are you all acting so sketchy?"

Mr. Taylor wasn't as tall as Kingston, he wasn't as gorgeous as Kingston, and although he'd once been muscular, I was told, now he was soft and one of those skinny fat guys. He wasn't a big person, but his softness game him an average boring dad bod.

I'd never seen him act like this, though.

"What the hell are these fucking kids up to?" Reg bellowed and burst through the door. "Where the hell were you last night, Everly? We were just out looking for you. Your mom would be worried sick if I told her."

"You didn't tell her?" I asked, and for a moment, it felt like everything could go back to normal. As if Reg not telling Mom that I'd been out all night would fix this fracture that had appeared in the middle of my life and I could go back to the way it had been.

I would do anything to go back to how it had been, just because navigating this new world of mine was so scary.

"No, why would I?" he asked with a tight smile. "We've got secrets to keep from her, don't we, baby doll?"

And as soon as he said baby doll, it was like a dam broke inside of me, and years of emotional garbage, everything I'd been pushing down and trying to ignore, all came spilling out.

Every night I'd fallen asleep after Reg's special drink, only to wake up aching the next morning with no memory of the sleep I had. Every odd look, every time he'd cornered me, every time he'd belittled me or threatened my security in front of my Mom.

Every time he'd touched me in a way that made me want to jump out of my own body and run far from here. Every time he'd winked at me in a knowing manner, making it clear that even if I did realize his accidental brushes against my breasts or his hand dragging across my ass could be proven as deliberate, there was nobody to tell, anyway.

All of them converged in one massive wave of agonizing destruction, and there was no going back from it. There was no recovery mode.

"Did you rape me?" I asked him point blank. I surprised myself by not screaming. My voice was completely controlled, and I felt like I was completely in control.

He didn't even flinch, but the moment my words tumbled into the open, the air left the room and you could have heard a pin drop, as they say. Reg didn't reply. He just looked over at Mr. Taylor and raised his eyebrows.

Mr. Taylor opened his mouth to say something, but nothing came out, so he closed it again. His eyes darted from Reg to Kingston to me and back again. He licked his lips, his slick, fat tongue poking out of his mouth, and I gagged.

The thought of that tongue on my body, anywhere near my body, let alone tasting me...

"She asked you a question," Kingston said and loomed over Reg. "You'd better fucking answer it."

"And you'd better fucking act with some respect," Mr. Taylor said and stepped towards Kingston. "You don't know who you're talking to, son. Reg here is one of our direct connections to some pretty big money. We're finally getting our fair share of the Dirty Kingdom jackpot."

"It's okay," Reg said, putting his hand out to block Mr. Taylor. "I'll talk to her."

"So fucking talk," Valen said, stepping closer to me. "Fucking tell her what she wants to hear."

"I'll tell her alone," Reg said, his eyes unwavering and unmoving from my face. "Let me talk to you, Everly. I have a lot to tell you, but I don't want these guys to hear it all. If you choose to tell them afterward, that's up to you."

"You'll talk to her now," Archer snarled and stepped in front of him to block the view between us. "There's nothing you need to say to her that can't be said in front of us."

"No, I need to say it in private. I want to respect her modesty," Reg said and then added, "if there's any left."

Kingston stepped forward and clenched his fist, drew it back, and made to hit Reg. I reached out and grabbed his bicep, clinging to it as I said, "Stop!"

He did. His fist abruptly halted in midair, and he turned to me. "Are you sure? You heard what he said."

"I did," I replied. "And it's okay. I can handle this. I want to hear what he has to say."

I released his arm, and he dropped it to his side but didn't relax his fist. Archer and Valen were both poised in similar ways, with clenched fists and clenched jaws, staring at Reg like they could murder him for me.

I, however, remained calm. The same control I'd felt before had settled inside of me. I was calm. Eerily calm. No longer were emotions whirling around like fall leaves on the wind. No more was confusion reigning supreme. I felt as I could see everything coming at me as if in slow motion. I could predict what was going to happen before it did.

"Okay, let's talk," Reg said, and motioned for me to follow him to the dining room. I did, walking slowly to match his careful pace. For once in my life, I wasn't afraid of him. He didn't intimidate me. I was in control now. I had the power.

He gestured for me to sit in my mom's usual chair, and he sat in his. Behind him, above his gun cabinet, the wall was covered with family photos. There were so many with Reg and Nat cuddling, or her on his lap, or him kissing her on the cheek, maybe just slightly too close to her mouth to be appropriate. I'd never noticed them before. When you live with something long enough, it becomes background noise. Mere decoration. Or maybe you become blind to it deliberately to avoid confrontation.

Maybe you just give up after a while and choose to stop living. Stop existing.

I was beyond that state of mind. I was choosing life again, and I was choosing my love for Kingston. I didn't know yet if I loved Archer and Valen with the fierce determination and heat I had for Kingston, but they were two bright lights in the constellation of my freedom. They were part of the reason I felt this way now, stronger and more determined than ever. It took three of them to pull me out and lead me to myself.

"So?" I asked and raised my eyebrow. "What do you have to tell me?"

He leaned forward, his elbow almost touching my arm as he tented his fingers together in front of his face. "I'm sorry," he said. "I have to tell you that first of all."

"Sorry for what?" I asked, just to watch him squirm.

"For, you know," he replied. "I assume you've seen the photos."

"I haven't, but I know what they contain," I said. "I know what you did to me... What you've done to me."

His breath hitched in his chest and he said, "I'm so sorry, Everly. It wasn't my idea, I was forced."

"Who fucking forced you?" I asked with disdain bubbling to the surface of my calm exterior. "It sounds like you wanted to do it all on your own. For you and your buddy, Mr. Taylor."

"It's the Dirty Kingdom," he said. "All of this, it's all connected. Why else do you think they changed the school boundaries? They've been watching you for years. For fucking *years*!"

That shook me to the core. My calmness quaked for a moment, and I said, "Because of Kingston. They needed him to play football and to fight."

"They could have offered him a scholarship."

"They could have offered me a scholarship, too. It doesn't make sense."

"You never would have taken it," he replied. "You know that. They asked me about you, and I told them you would never take a free ride to Covington."

That was true. I did know I would have turned them

down. I would have spat on their offer and slammed it back into their faces.

"That is true," I said slowly, deliberately. "But you still had no right to rape me."

"It wasn't rape," he said and rolled his eyes just enough for me to catch. He stopped himself before he went fully, but I'd seen it.

"If it wasn't rape, what was it?" I asked. I was stunned at my ability to stay calm despite the rage rising in the back of my head like a tide of red, like blood flooding the world around me, drowning everything under its wave.

"It was just a little fooling around," he said and leaned back. "It's not like I fucked you. I never fucked you. I know you have to be a virgin to be Tribute."

I stood up at that, at his contempt leaking through into his fake apology. He was being performative in his repentance, and I wasn't going to accept it.

I walked towards him, and he smiled at me as if expecting a warm embrace. Or maybe a quick hand job before I told my guys that everything was okay. That Reg didn't really rape me.

But I didn't embrace him. I didn't take his cock in my hand and jerk him off. I was dead inside when I moved, unfeeling but single-minded. Burning logic drove my limbs and controlled my actions. I was more alive than I had ever been, and I was more in control than I'd ever allowed.

And in one swift move that caught him completely off guard, I gave into the darkness. I let myself slide into the shadows and embrace the side of me I'd always shunned.

"What's going on?" he asked when I stepped around him. "Are you done?"

I wasn't done. I was just getting started.

I flicked the latch on his gun cabinet, and the door swung loose. I reached inside to the handgun I loved, the little, sleek black Glock with low recoil.

Reg didn't know it. In fact, nobody knew it. But when he was gone, I would take this gun from his cabinet, and I would go into the woods behind our house. Far into the woods, twenty minutes' walk into the wild part, where there were no houses and nothing but logging roads and quad trails.

And I would shoot it. I enjoyed the feel of it in my hand. I loved the way my muscles quivered when it jolted backwards in my hand and I worked to steady it.

He had boxes and boxes of ammo, and he never noticed five or ten bullets here or there. Nobody did.

I was a boring girl, a sad girl, a girl with no future. The kind of girl who had to be drugged in order to be compliant, the kind of girl who was only necessary for her tits and her cunt.

So I'd flown under the radar right under his nose and right in his house.

I gave thanks for Reg's laziness and arrogance because the Glock was always put away loaded and never had the safety on.

In all, it took seconds before I had it pointed at the back of his head. I inhaled, pulled back the slide, released it, and exhaled.

He turned at the click, as I'd planned, jumped up, and yelled, "What the fuck, Ever—"

And I pulled the trigger.

The gun exploded, and the bullet entered his chest,

just below his collarbone. Bone and blood burst out of the hole in the back. Being shot at such close range was messy and loud, I found out. Not like shooting at a target alone in the woods.

That's when my adrenaline kicked in, and I shot him again. And again. I emptied the gun in him. Five rounds; it hadn't been full. I started to cry as soon as he slumped down towards me, sliding along my body as he fell. Blood streaked down the front of me, and Reg's body landed with a dull thud at my feet. I dropped the gun with a clatter and my hands began to shake.

"What happened, Evie?" Kingston bellowed as he ran. He made it through the dining-room door and skidded to a halt. "What'd you do?"

"I killed him," I said and shuddered, fighting against the tears that threatened to erupt. "I fucking killed him for raping me. He was going to keep doing it. He was going to do it to Nat."

Kingston crossed over to me as Archer and Valen came racing into the dining room, stopping when they spotted Reg's body. Blood was pooling on the hardwood floor under him, and his face was waxen and ashy.

Kingston pulled me into his arms and pressed my face against his chest as if he could shield me from the horror of Reg's bloodied corpse.

He couldn't. I'd done it, I saw it happen. It would forever be replayed in my head over and over.

And even though I cried because of the release I needed, I didn't feel bad about it at all.

Kingston led me out, and Valen and Archer stayed huddled around me. When we reached the foyer with Mr. Taylor, he was on his phone screaming at 9-1-1

"Somebody's been shot!" he yelled and looked me

up and down. "I don't know who! Just get the fuck over here now!"

I was covered in blood. It streaked my jeans and sweater up and down with gore, and I probably looked like a fucking mess. I felt like a fucking mess.

"Reg," Kingston said. "Everly shot Reg because he fucking deserved it. You deserve it, too, you fucking bastard."

"The cops are on their way," Kingston's dad said. "They're coming along with the ambulance. You'd better stick around."

"She's not sitting here next to her rapist," Archer said and pushed him out of the way with a hard shove. "You're lucky you're not laying on the ground next to your friend."

I broke away from Kingston's grasp and whirled to slap his dad across the face. Mr. Taylor grew red and angry. He reached for my hand, managed to grab me by my forearm, and twisted. I gasped in pain and rolled my torso to keep up. It felt like he was trying to break it.

Archer punched him in the back of the head, and Mr. Taylor grunted in pain but still gripped me tight.

"You'll never get away with this, you little bitch," he hissed between his cruel lips. "This goes right to the top. You're going to jail, you little cunt."

"I'll just show the cops the pics I found," Kingston said with confidence. "You're the one going to jail, Dad."

"Who do you think wanted the photos? Who do you think paid to come in and lick her sweet little virgin slit?" he asked with a mocking grin. "Tell them all and see what happens."

I cried out in pain as he twisted harder, and he began to laugh. A horrible sound, like metal dragging along concrete, but filled with loathing for me and my Kingston.

I tried to pull away when Valen punched him too, this time on the side of his head. His temple. His grip loosened slightly, and I said, "Do it again!"

All three boys swung at the same time. Kingston made contact with his father's face, Archer with the back of his head, and Valen with his temple. Mr. Taylor released me, and I jumped back as he slowly sagged to the floor, his eyes rolling back in his head.

"Let's go," I said, the calm logic taking over again. I rubbed my arm with my other hand. "We have to get out of here."

"But the cops—" Valen started to say.

"Aren't gonna do shit but take her to jail!" Archer cut him off.

"We have to go. We can figure it all out later," I said as the first siren hit my ears. It had only been a few minutes from the time I followed Reg to the dining room to this exact moment. Oh, how a lifetime could change in the course of a few breaths.

"We'll go back to my place," Archer said and took my hand. I felt the heat of where he'd struck Mr. Taylor in his knuckles.

Mr. Taylor wasn't moving on the floor of the entranceway. I hadn't had time to grab my things. I wasn't ready to leave the house like this, and I worried that Nat would hate me for killing her dad.

But ultimately, I had to get out of there. We had to go.

"Okay," I said, and turned to the door. "That's the only way out right now. Let's go."

The four of us rushed out of my house, vastly

different from the people we'd been earlier that day. Each one of us had been changed, and each one of us had been exposed to the darkness, both inside ourselves and in the world around us.

Oakville was no longer a safe, sleepy little town, and I was no longer a boring girl who could fly under the radar and slip unnoticed through everybody's lives.

All eyes would be on me now: the Tribute, the murderer, and the lover of three men.

Some people would hate me, some would envy me, and the right ones would love me back.

I stopped to take one more look at the house I'd once considered a mansion, the place that had never been my home. Valen gently tugged at my blood-smeared sweat and said, "We need to hurry, buttercup."

I looked at him with a smile, slipped my hand into his, and said, "Lead the way."

Archer got behind the wheel, Kingston in the passenger seat, and me with Valen in the back seat. As the black Range Rover sped down my street heading towards town, the sirens got louder and pierced my very soul with their klaxon call.

I looked back out the window and saw lights flashing towards our house.

We turned the corner and were out of sight by the time they got there, and I sunk down into the seat to let it all wash over me. The darkness was bigger than before, but it comforted me now. It was no longer a thing to be feared, and I would not lose myself in it. I would embrace it and become the person I was meant to be.

"What are you thinking?" Valen asked me as I curled up in his arms.

"I'm thinking about fucking each and every one of you," I said and smiled against his chest. I closed my eyes and let the sensations of the moment float me away from the trauma of my life. "And after that, I'm thinking we have to burn Dirty Kingdom to the mother fucking ground."

THE END

Continue in Dirty King, book 2.

ALSO BY AMELIA WINTERS

Covington High Series

- Dirty Kingdom, book 1
- Dirty King, book 2
- Dirty Queen, book 3
- Dirty Court, book 4

The Family Series (Covington Continuation)

- Dirty Reign, book 1

The Savage Dark

- Lords of Darkness

ABOUT THE AUTHOR

Sign up for my newsletter to keep in touch. Find out about beta or ARC opportunities, get sneak peeks at new books, and have access to giveaways!

http://eepurl.com/hBcvpr

Scan the QR Code to find my newsletter!

facebook.com/Author-Amelia-Winters-110161967967643

instagram.com/author.amelia.winters

Milton Keynes UK
Ingram Content Group UK Ltd.
UKHW021320071223
433964UK00027B/1519